P9-ELQ-980

THE HERO'S GUIDE TO
Saving your Kingdom

THE HERO'S GUIDE TO Saving YOUR Kingdom

Written by

CHRISTOPHER HEALY

With drawings by

TODD HARRIS

WALDEN POND PRESS
An Imprint of HarperCollins*Publishers*

Walden Pond Press is an imprint of HarperCollins Publishers.
Walden Pond Press and the skipping stone logo are trademarks and registered trademarks of
Walden Media, LLC.

The Hero's Guide to Saving Your Kingdom
Text copyright © 2012 by Christopher Healy
Illustrations copyright © 2012 by Todd Harris
All rights reserved. Printed in the United States of America.
No part of this book may be used or reproduced in any manner whatsoever without written
permission except in the case of brief quotations embodied in critical articles and reviews. For
information address HarperCollins Children's Books, a division of HarperCollins Publishers,
10 East 53rd Street, New York, NY 10022.
www.harpercollinschildrens.com

Library of Congress Cataloging-in-Publication Data is available.
ISBN 978-0-06-211743-4

Typography by Amy Ryan
12 13 14 15 16   CG/RRDH   10 9 8 7 6 5 4 3 2

First Edition

For Dashiell and Bryn, my heroes

⇥ TABLE OF CONTENTS ⇤

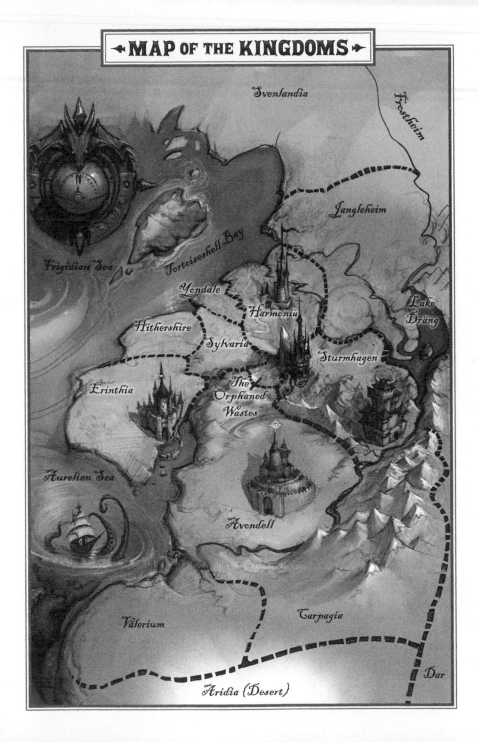

THINGS YOU DON'T KNOW ABOUT PRINCE CHARMING

Prince Charming is afraid of old ladies. Didn't know that, did you?

Don't worry. There's a lot you don't know about Prince Charming: Prince Charming has no idea how to use a sword; Prince Charming has no patience for dwarfs; Prince Charming has an irrational hatred of capes.

Some of you may not even realize that there's more than one Prince Charming. And that none of them are actually *named* Charming. No one is. *Charming* isn't a name; it's an adjective.

But don't blame yourself for your lack of Prince Charming–based knowledge; blame the lazy bards. You see, back in the day, bards and minstrels were the world's only real source of news. It was they who bestowed fame upon people. They were the ones who sculpted any hero's (or villain's) reputation. Whenever something big happened—a damsel was rescued, a dragon was slain, a curse was broken—the royal bards would write a song about it, and their wandering minstrels would perform that tune from land to land, spreading the story across multiple kingdoms. But the bards weren't keen on details. They didn't think it was important to include the *names* of the heroes who did all that damsel rescuing, dragon slaying, and curse breaking. They just called all those guys "Prince Charming."

It didn't even matter to the bards whether the person in question was a truly daring hero (like Prince Liam, who battled his way past a bone-crushing, fire-blasting magical monster in order to free a princess from an enchanted sleeping spell) or some guy who merely happened to be in the right place at the right time (like Prince Duncan, who also woke a princess from a sleeping spell, but only because some dwarfs told him to). No,

Fig 1.
Standard
BARD

those bards gave a man the same generic name whether he nearly died (like Prince Gustav, who was thrown from a ninety-foot tower when he tried to rescue Rapunzel) or simply impressed a girl with his dancing skill (like Prince Frederic, who wowed Cinderella at a royal ball).

If there was anything that Liam, Duncan, Gustav, and Frederic all had in common, it was that none of them were very happy about being a Prince Charming. Their mutual hatred of that name was a big part of what brought them together. Not that teaming up was necessarily the best idea for these guys.

If we were to peek ahead to, say, Chapter 20, we would see our heroes in a small mountain town called Flargstagg, sitting in just about the worst tavern in all of creation: the Stumpy Boarhound. The Stumpy Boarhound is the kind of dank and miserable place where pirates and assassins play cards while plotting their next despicable crimes (which often involve robbing the tavern itself). It's not the type of place where you would expect to find even one Prince Charming, let alone four. And yet, in Chapter 20, there they all are: Liam, bruised and soot-stained, with fish bones in his hair; Gustav, in charred and dented armor, massaging his bald, bright red scalp; Frederic, covered with enough dirt to make you think he'd just crawled out of a grave; and Duncan, with a big bump on his forehead, and wearing . . . is that a nightshirt? Oh, and there are about fifty armed thugs surrounding their table, all of whom seem eager to smash the princes into paste.

Of course, by Chapter 20, you can't fault the princes for looking like wrecks. They're lucky to be alive after their run-ins with the witch, the giant, the bandits, the—well, you'll see. Basically, the fact that they're about to get into a major brawl is none too surprising, considering the kind of week these princes have just had. But we're getting ahead of ourselves.

Before we reach that turning-point night at the Stumpy Boarhound, we need to head back to the peaceful kingdom of Harmonia, where the whole adventure—or *mess*, depending on whom you ask—began. We have to go back to when Prince Frederic managed to lose Cinderella.

1

PRINCE CHARMING MISPLACES HIS BRIDE

Frederic wasn't always helpless. There was a time when he aspired to become a hero. But it seemed it wasn't meant to be.

From the moment he was born—and immediately placed into the delicate swishiness of a pure silk bassinet—Prince Frederic led a life of comfort. As heir to the throne of the very wealthy nation of Harmonia, he grew up with an army of servants standing ready to pamper him in every way imaginable. While learning to crawl, he was fitted with lamb's-wool knee pads to keep his baby-soft skin from getting scuffed. When he wanted to play hide-and-seek, butlers and valets would hide in the most obvious places—behind a feather, under a napkin—so that the boy wouldn't have to work too hard to find them. Pretty much anything young Frederic could have wanted or needed was handed to him on a silver platter. Literally.

The only thing Frederic had to do in return was live the life of a proper gentleman. He was allowed to attend as many poetry readings, ballroom dances, and twelve-course luncheons as he wanted. But he was forbidden to take part in any activity that could be considered remotely risky or dangerous. Appearances were very important to Frederic's father, King Wilberforce, who vowed that no one in his family would ever again suffer the cruel mockery that had been heaped upon his great-grandfather, King Charles the Chicken-Pocked. "Not a scar, not a bruise, not a blemish" was the motto of King Wilberforce. And he went to extreme measures to keep his son away from anything that might give him so much as a scratch. He even had Frederic's pencils pre-dulled.

For most of his early years, Frederic was perfectly happy to skip out on pastimes like tree climbing (twisted ankles!), hiking (poison ivy!), or embroidery (pointy needles!). King

Fig. 2
Prince
FREDERIC

Wilberforce's warnings about the hazards of such endeavors sank in good and deep.

But at the tender age of seven, Frederic was inspired to try something daring. He was in his private classroom, being taught to write his name with fancy curlicue letters, when a commotion down the hall caused his tutor to cut the lesson short. Frederic followed his tutor down to the palace gates, where many of the servants had gathered to gawk at a visiting knight.

The old warrior, who was battered and exhausted from a recent bout with a dragon, had staggered up to the palace seeking food and shelter. The king invited the weary visitor inside. This was the first knight Frederic had ever seen in real life (and frankly, even the ones he'd read about in books weren't very exciting—his favorite bedtime story was *Sir Bertram the Dainty and the Quest for the Enchanted Salad Fork*). During the knight's short stay, a fascinated Frederic followed him everywhere, listening to his tales of ogre battles, goblin wars, and bandit chases. There was a look in the man's eyes that Frederic had never seen before. Frederic could sense the knight's thirst for thrills, his yearning for action. The knight was a man who thrived on adventure the way Frederic thrived on tea cakes.

That evening, after the knight departed, Frederic

asked his father if he could take sword-fighting lessons. The king dismissed his request with a smile: "Swords are sharp, my boy. And I need a son with both ears attached."

Young Frederic was undaunted. The next day, he asked his father if he could take a shot at wrestling instead. King Wilberforce shook his head. "You're what they call petite, Frederic. You'd have your spine snapped in an instant."

The day after that, Frederic requested a spot on the jousting team. "That's more dangerous than the other two combined," the king moaned disapprovingly. "You'll be skewered like a cocktail weenie."

"Archery?" Frederic asked.

"Eyes: poked out," the king insisted.

"Martial arts?"

"Bones: broken."

"Mountaineering?"

"Eyes broken. Bones poked out."

By the end of the week, King Wilberforce couldn't take it anymore. He needed to put a stop to Frederic's thrill-seeking dreams. He decided to set his son up for a fall.

"Father, can I try spelunking?" Frederic asked eagerly.

"Cave exploration? You'll fall into a bottomless pit," the king chided. Then he changed his tone. "But you can try animal training if you'd like."

"Really?" Frederic was stunned and thrilled. "You mean with *wild* animals? Not hamsters or goldfish?"

The king nodded.

"You don't think I'll be eaten alive?" Frederic asked.

"Oh, I fear that you will, but if you're so determined to put your life at risk, perhaps I shouldn't stand in your way," his father said, weaving his deception.

The next day, with his heart racing, Frederic was led down a winding basement corridor to a storeroom in which all the old coats of arms, spare scepters, and crates of outgrown baby clothes had been shoved up against the walls to make room for an enormous cage. Inside that cage: a pacing, panting tiger. The animal let out a low growl as soon as it saw the young prince.

"Wow, I didn't know we'd start with something so big," Frederic said, considerably less eager than he had been a minute earlier.

"Are you ready for this, Your Highness?" the animal's trainer asked. Frederic barely had time to nod before the trainer slid back the bolt and let the cage door fall open. The trainer uttered a quick word to the tiger, and the big cat burst out into the room, rushing straight at Frederic.

Frederic screamed and ran. The giant tiger, easily three times his size, dashed after the boy. Frederic darted among the crates of tarnished goblets and out-of-tune lutes, looking for someplace to hide. "Why aren't you stopping it?" he shouted at the trainer.

"I *can't* stop it," the trainer replied. "It's a *wild* animal. Your father told you this would be dangerous."

Frederic ducked under a heavy wooden table, but the tiger swatted it away as if it were nothing more than a piece of dandelion fluff. Frederic scrambled across the floor in an attempt to get away from the beast, but was soon backed up against a stack of rolled tapestries. There was nowhere left for him to go. With tears running down his face, Frederic shrieked as he saw the tiger's open mouth coming at him.

When the tiger snatched him up into its maw, Frederic was too terrified to realize that the animal had no teeth. The big cat calmly carried the limp, weeping boy back to its cage and set him down gently on the floor—which is what it had been carefully trained to do. For this was no ordinary tiger: This was El Stripo, the talented and cooperative star of the Flimsham Brothers Circus. The Flimshams were famous for their visually horrifying—but impressively safe—act in which El Stripo's trainer would stuff the tiger's mouth with up to five infants from the audience and then instruct the animal to spit them back to their mothers. The babies almost always landed in the correct laps.

It took Frederic a few seconds to realize he hadn't been eaten. At which point his father appeared. Frederic ran into the king's arms, burying his wet face in his father's royal robes.

"Do you see now?" the king asked. "Do you see why I say you can't do these things?" Behind Frederic's back, he flashed El Stripo's trainer a thumbs-up.

King Wilberforce's plan had worked. The prince was so deeply frightened by his experience with the tiger, so chilled to the core, that he never asked to try anything daring again. *Father was right,* he thought; *I am not cut out for such bold escapades.*

Fear ruled Frederic from that moment on. He even found a few Sir Bertram the Dainty stories to be a little too scary.

Instead Frederic focused his energies on taking etiquette lessons, putting together stylish outfits, and becoming exactly the kind of prince his father wanted him to be. And he became pretty darn good at it. In fact, he began to love it. He was proud of his excellent posture, his artful flower arranging, and his flawless foxtrot.

More than a decade passed before the thought of adventure found its way back into Frederic's mind. It happened on the night of the big palace ball, at which it was hoped that Frederic would find a bride (he never left the palace, so this type of event was the only way for him to meet girls). Among the dozens of elegant women at the ball that night, there was one girl who caught Frederic's attention immediately—and it wasn't just because she was beautiful and elegantly dressed. No, she had something else: a daredevil gleam in her eyes. He'd seen that look only once before—in that old knight all those years ago.

Frederic and the mystery girl had the time of their lives dancing together. But at midnight she ran off without a word.

"Father, I have to find that girl," insisted Frederic, newly inspired and feeling a bit more like his seven-year-old self again.

"Son, you've never been outside the palace gates," the king replied in a foreboding tone. "What if there are *tigers* out there?"

Frederic shrank away. That tiger episode had really done a number on him.

But Frederic didn't give up entirely.

He instructed his trusted valet, Reginald, to find the mystery woman for him. It turned out that Ella (that was her name) wasn't a noblewoman at all; just a sooty cleaning girl. But her story—the way she mixed it up with a fairy and used magical means to escape her wicked stepfamily—intrigued Frederic (even if he hoped he'd never have to meet any of her relatives).

When he told his father he wanted to marry Ella, the king sputtered in surprise. "I thought I'd fixed you, but apparently I didn't," the king scowled. "You don't get it at all, do you? An ill-bred wife would destroy your image more than any scar or broken limb ever would."

Up until that point, Frederic had always believed that the king enforced strict rules because he feared for his son's safety. But now he saw that wasn't necessarily the case. So, for the first time, Frederic stood up to his father.

"You do not rule me," he stated firmly. "Well, technically you do, being as you're the king. But you do not rule my heart. My heart wants Ella. And if you don't bring her here to be with me, I will go to her. I don't care how dangerous it is out there. I would ride a tiger to get to her if I had to."

In truth, Frederic was utterly intimidated by the thought of venturing out into the real world. If his father refused to meet his demands, he had no idea if he would be able to follow through on his threat. Luckily for him, the king was shocked enough to give in.

And so, Ella came to live at the palace. She and Frederic were officially engaged to marry, and the tale of the magical way in which the couple met became the talk of the kingdom. Within days, the minstrels had a new hit on their hands, and the tale was told and retold across many realms. But while the popular version of the story ended with a happily-ever-after for Prince Charming and Cinderella, things didn't go as smoothly for the real Frederic and Ella.

Ironically, it was Ella's bold and venturesome spirit—the very thing that Frederic found so attractive about her— that came between them. Ella's dreadful stepmother had treated her like a prisoner in her own home and forced her to spend nearly every waking hour performing onerous tasks, like scrubbing grout or chipping congealed mayonnaise from between fork tines. While Ella suffered through all this, she dreamed of a more exhilarating life. She fantasized about riding camels across deserts to search ancient temples for magic lamps, or scaling cloud-covered peaks to play games of chance with the rulers of hidden mountain kingdoms. She honestly believed that *anything* could happen in her future.

When Ella met Frederic at the ball, it was the climax

of a day filled with magic and intrigue, and she assumed it was the beginning of a nonstop, thrill-a-minute existence for her. But life with Frederic was not quite what she'd expected.

Frederic tended to sleep in. Sometimes until lunch. And he'd often spend over an hour grooming himself to his father's specifications. By the time Ella finally saw him each day, she would be more than ready for some sort of excitement. But Frederic usually suggested a more subdued activity, like picnicking, listening to music, or quietly admiring some art.

Don't get me wrong: Ella enjoyed all those things—for the first few days. But by the fourteenth picnic, she began to fear that those same few activities were all she was ever going to do at the palace. Her unchanging routine made her feel uncomfortably like a prisoner again. So one morning, she decided she would speak frankly with Frederic about what she needed.

That morning, as usual, Frederic slept late. When he eventually got up, he spent fifteen minutes (pretty quick for him) browsing a closet filled with ultra-fancy suits, before finally deciding on a crisp white outfit trimmed with gold braiding and tasseled shoulder pads. The five minutes after that were dedicated to straightening his short, light-brown hair. Unfortunately, a few stubborn strands refused to stay in place, and so the prince did what he did whenever he got frustrated:

"Reginald!"

Within seconds, a tall, slender man with a thin, pointy mustache popped into the prince's bedroom. "Yes, milord?" he asked in a voice stiff enough to match his rigid posture.

"Good morning, Reginald," Frederic said. "Can you fix my hair?"

"Certainly, milord," Reginald said, as he grabbed a silver brush and began using it to tidy the prince's bed head.

"Thank you, Reginald," Frederic said. "I'm off to see Ella, and I want to look my best."

"Of course, milord."

"I think I'm going to have Cook surprise her with breakfast in bed."

Reginald paused. "I'm reasonably sure, milord, that the young lady has already eaten breakfast."

"Drat," muttered the prince. "So it's happened again. How long ago did she wake up?"

"About three hours ago," Reginald replied.

"Three hours! But I asked you to wake me when Ella got up."

"I'm sorry, milord," Reginald said sympathetically.

"You know I'd love to help you. But we're under strict orders from the king: Your beauty sleep is not to be disturbed."

Frederic burst from his seat, waving away Reginald's brush. "My father *ordered* you not to wake me? He's still trying to keep me and Ella apart."

He rushed to the door of his bedroom, then quickly back to the mirror for one last check of the hair, and then out and down the hall to look for his fiancée.

Ella wasn't in her room, so Frederic headed to the gardens. He paused briefly to sniff a rosebush, when he heard the sound of approaching hoofbeats. He looked over his shoulder to see that a large white horse was bearing down on him, tearing through the garden at a fast gallop, leaping over one hedgerow after another. The prince tried to run, but the golden tassels of his jacket caught on the shrub's thorns.

Frederic tugged frantically at his stuck sleeve as the horse's rider pulled up on the reins and brought the steed to a halt. From the saddle, Ella looked down at him and laughed. She wore a distinctly unfancy blue dress, and her tied-back hair was disheveled from the ride. Her strong, athletic build and warm, healthy glow were a stark contrast

to Frederic's slender frame and sun-deprived complexion. "I hope you haven't been stuck there all morning," she said, only half joking.

"No, this just happened," Frederic said, relieved. "I don't suppose you could possibly hop down and lend me a hand?"

Ella slid off the saddle, patted her horse's nose, and crouched down to help free the prince's jacket from the thorns. "I told you those tassels would get you into trouble someday," she said.

Fig. 3
Lady
ELLA

"But they're what all the most fashionable noblemen are wearing these days," Frederic said brightly.

He brushed himself off and struck a chest-out, hands-on-hips pose to show off his outfit. He hammed it up to get a laugh out of Ella. It worked.

"Very nice," Ella said with a chuckle. "I'd love to see you up on a horse sometime," she hinted, petting her mare's pink nose.

"Yes, I'm sure I'd look positively heroic up there," Frederic said. "It's a shame I'm allergic to horsehair." He wasn't allergic; he was afraid of falling off.

"A terrible shame," Ella sighed.

"I didn't realize you knew how to ride," Frederic said. "Considering the way your stepmother kept you under lock and key, I wouldn't have thought you had much time for equestrian lessons."

"I didn't," Ella said. "Charles, your head groom, has been teaching me these past few weeks. I usually practice in the mornings, while you . . . um, while you sleep."

Frederic changed the subject: "So, have you heard the song that Pennyfeather wrote about you? That bard of ours certainly has a way with a quill. The song is very popular, I hear. Supposedly, the minstrels are singing it as far as Sylvaria and Sturmhagen. Before you know it, you'll be more famous than me. Or even more famous than Pennyfeather. Though I don't really like the fact that he called you *Cinder*ella. Makes you sound dirty and unkempt."

"I don't mind," said Ella. "I *was* dirty and unkempt for years. I was always covered in soot and cinders from cleaning the fireplace, so at least I see where he got the name from."

"Speaking of names," said Frederic, "have you noticed that the song refers to me as 'Prince Charming'? My real name's not in there at all. People are going to think I'm the same prince from that Sleeping Beauty song or the Rapunzel one. Here, listen and tell me what you think." He called out to a passing servant, "Excuse me, my good man. Could you please fetch Pennyfeather the Mellifluous for us? Tell him that the prince and Lady Ella would like a command performance of 'The Tale of Cinderella.'"

"I'm sorry, milord," the servant replied. "Mr. Pennyfeather is unavailable. He hasn't been seen for days, actually. It's the talk of the palace; we assumed you would have heard by now. No one knows where the royal bard is."

"Well, that explains why I haven't been getting my lullaby these past few nights," Frederic said thoughtfully.

"Frederic, maybe something awful has happened to Pennyfeather," Ella said, sounding a bit too excited by the prospect. "We should check into it. Come on, let's go. We need to figure out the last person to see him. Let's start by asking at the gate—"

"Oh, I'm sure it's nothing so dramatic," Frederic said quickly. The only thing he had a harder time imagining than a crime occurring within the royal palace was himself investigating such a crime. "He's probably just off at a bard convention somewhere, one of those gatherings where they vote on the precise number of feathers a minstrel should have in his cap—that sort of thing. But don't worry, just because Pennyfeather himself isn't here doesn't mean we can't have music. I'll just send for—"

"Never mind the song, Frederic," Ella said, taking a deep breath. "Remember how we were just talking about my sheltered childhood?"

Frederic nodded.

"Now that I'm free, I want to have new experiences. I want to find out what I'm capable of. So, if we're not going to look into Pennyfeather's disappearance, what can we do today?" she asked. "What kind of adventure *can* we have?"

"Adventure, right." Frederic pondered his options briefly. "It is a lovely day. Nice and sunny. I'm thinking picnic."

Ella slumped. "Frederic, I need to do something different."

Frederic stared at her like a lost baby rabbit.

"I hear there's a troupe of traveling acrobats in town," Ella suggested. "Maybe we could get them in here to teach us some tumbling."

"Oh, but I've got that problem with my ankle." He had no problem with his ankle.

"How about a treasure hunt?" Ella proposed excitedly.

"Some of the kitchen staff were gossiping about a bag of stolen gold that one of your father's old valets hid in the tunnels below the castle. We could try to find it."

"Oh, but I can't go below ground level. You know what dampness does to my sinuses." Dampness did nothing to his sinuses.

"Can we go boating on the lake?"

"I can't swim." This was true.

Ella huffed. "Frederic, what *can* we do? I'm sorry if this sounds rude, but I'm bored."

"We could have a different *kind* of picnic," Frederic offered hopefully. "We could do breakfast food for lunch. Croissants, poached eggs. How's that for shaking things up?"

Ella walked back to her horse and hopped up into the saddle. "Go ahead and order your picnic, Frederic," she said flatly. "I'm going to ride a bit more while you wait."

"Okay," Frederic said, and waved to her. "I'll stay right here."

"I'm sure you will. You're very good at that," Ella replied. And she rode off.

An hour or so later, Frederic sat out on the palace lawn (well, on a carefully unfolded blanket, actually—he didn't want to get grass stains on his white pants), waiting for his lunch and his fiancée to arrive. A servant arrived and set down a tray of breakfast delicacies in front of Frederic. "Milord," the man said, as he bowed and backed away. "There's a message there for you."

Frederic saw a folded piece of paper nestled between a bowl of grapefruit slices and a plate of chocolate-chip waffles. He picked up the note, with a sudden sinking feeling about what it might say.

❖ ❖ ❖ ❖ ❖ ❖ ❖ ❖ ❖ ❖ ❖

Sweet, good-hearted Frederic,

I'm terribly sorry to do this to you, and I hope that someday you will understand why I had to leave. You seem very comfortable in your life here at the palace. I can't make you into someone who wants to climb mountains, paddle rushing rivers, and explore ancient ruins. You don't want to do those things, and that's fine. It's just not your cup of tea. Your cup of tea is, well, a cup of tea.

But I need something more.

When you mentioned that song about Rapunzel, it got me thinking. The prince in that story tried to rescue Rapunzel, but Rapunzel ended up rescuing HIM.

Now, THAT girl is an inspiration. So, I'm heading off to find her. I think Rapunzel and I will hit it off. I think she'll make a great partner for hunting down Pennyfeather. And even if we end up finding him at a boring old convention like you say, who knows what kind of adventures will be in store for us along the way?

Frederic, you are a lovely man and I have nothing but good wishes for you. For what it's worth, that night at the ball really was the most romantic night of my life.

All the best,
Ella

Frederic dropped the letter onto his empty plate. *So,* he thought, *the ball was the most romantic night of her life, huh? Well, that's not saying much coming from a girl whose typical nights consisted of scraping dead spiders out of cracks in the floorboards. And look how she signed it. "All the best"? That's how you sign a thank-you note to your dog walker.* Frederic had completely lost his appetite.

"Reginald!"

"Am I really that boring?"

Frederic was back in his room, sitting slumped on the

edge of his cashmere-covered bed, while Reginald, rigid as ever, stood next to him, awkwardly patting the prince's head.

"There, there, milord," the valet answered. "I don't think the Countess of Bellsworth would call you boring. Do you remember how elated she was when you taught her how to cha-cha? You have many, many admirers, sir."

"Yes," Frederic said sorrowfully. "But Ella is apparently not among them."

"It seems that Lady Ella simply seeks a different kind of life than that which you can provide for her here at the palace," Reginald said.

"Poached eggs! How stupid can I be?" Frederic smacked himself on the forehead.

"There will be other women, milord."

"I don't want any other women. I want *Ella*. Reginald, what do you think I should do? And be honest with me; don't just tell me what you think my father would want you to say."

Reginald considered this request. He'd been caring for Frederic since the prince was a child. And he'd never been more proud of Frederic than when he saw the young man stand up to his overbearing father. Frederic could use someone as feisty and fearless as Ella in his life.

"Don't let her get away," Reginald said, dropping his overly stiff posture and speaking in an unusually casual tone.

"Wow," Frederic gasped. "Did you just get two inches shorter?"

"Never mind me," Reginald said. "Did you hear what I told you? Get a move on! Go after Ella."

"But how?" Frederic asked, still bewildered to hear his longtime valet speaking like a regular person.

"We'll put you on a horse. Charles can show you the basics. You don't need to be the world's best rider; you just need to be able to get around. Stick to the roads and you'll be fine."

"But—"

"I know you're scared, Frederic. But here's my advice: Get over it. Ella wants someone as adventurous as she is. A real hero."

"Then I've got no hope." Frederic sulked. "I'm a fantastic dresser. My penmanship is top-notch. I'm really good at being a prince, but I'm pretty lousy at being a hero."

Reginald looked him in the eye. "There's a bit of courage in you somewhere. Find it. Go catch up with Ella, wherever she is. And just see what happens. She might be impressed enough that you've left the palace."

"There's no way my father will allow me to do this."

"We won't tell him."

"He'll notice I'm gone eventually. And when he does, he'll send his men to retrieve me."

"Whichever way you go, I'll send them in the opposite direction."

"I'm still not sure I should. It's really dangerous out there."

"That's your father talking," Reginald said. "Look, if you go on this journey, you're not just doing it for Ella, you're also doing it for that little boy who once wanted to try everything."

"You mean my cousin Laurence, who broke his leg trying to fly with those wax wings?"

Reginald looked at him soberly. "Frederic, you don't really remember your mother, but I do. And I know what she'd want you to do."

Frederic stood up. "Okay, I'll go."

"That's the spirit," said Reginald.

Frederic marched out of his room. A second later, he marched back in.

"I should probably change into something more appropriate for the outdoors," he said.

Reginald put his arm around him. "You don't own anything more appropriate for the outdoors," he said with a smile. "Come, let's get you down to the stables."

The next morning, after several hours of secret, intensive riding lessons, Prince Frederic trotted out through the palace gates on horseback, with Reginald and Charles the groom waving him good-bye. His eyes were tightly closed, his arms wrapped around the horse's neck. Then something dawned on him.

"Wait," he called back to Reginald. "I don't know where I'm going."

"Ella's note said she was going to find that Rapunzel girl," Reginald said. "Those bards are never very good about telling you exactly where their stories take place. But based on the clunky rhymes, I'm pretty sure 'The Song of Rapunzel' is the work of Lyrical Leif, the bard from Sturmhagen. Humph. With a name like Lyrical Leif, you'd think the guy could come up with better lines than, 'Her hair was real long, not short like a prawn.' Anyway, I'd try Sturmhagen. Head south."

"But Sturmhagen? Isn't it supposed to be full of monsters?" Frederic said, his eyes growing wider by the second.

"Ride fast," Charles the groom called out. "With any luck, you'll catch up to Lady Ella before you reach the border."

"I can't ride *fast*," Frederic said. "I'm trying hard to make sure I ride *forward*."

"Then so far you're succeeding," Reginald yelled. "Stay strong!"

Frederic gripped his horse tighter, wondering what in the world he'd gotten himself into. Within twenty-four hours, he would be sniffling through a rainstorm, wishing he'd never left home. In a little over a week, he'd be quivering in the shadow of a raging giant. Another week after that, he would end up at the Stumpy Boarhound. But for now, he was on his way to Sturmhagen.

2

PRINCE CHARMING
DEFENDS SOME VEGETABLES

Sturmhagen wasn't a big tourist destination, mainly because of all the monsters. The kingdom's thick and shadowy pine forests were crawling with all sorts of horrid creatures. And yet, that fact never seemed to bother the people who lived there. For most Sturmhageners, the occasional troll attack or goblin raid was just another nuisance to be dealt with, on par with a mouse in the pantry or a ferret in the sock drawer. These are *tough folks* we're talking about. Take the royal family, for instance: King Olaf, at age sixty, was seven feet tall and capable of uprooting trees with his bare hands. His wife, Queen Berthilda, was only two inches shorter, and once famously punched out a swindler who tried to sell her some bogus "magic beans."

Prince Gustav, who stood six-foot-five and had shoulders broad enough to get stuck in most doorways, was nonetheless the smallest member of his family. Growing up as the "tiny" one among sixteen older brothers, Gustav felt a desperate need to appear bigger and more imposing. This usually involved puffing out his chest and speaking very loudly: Picture a six-year-old boy standing on top of the dining room table, posing like a statue of a war hero, and shouting, "The mighty Gustav demands his milk cup be refilled!" This didn't make him look impressive—it made him look strange. His older siblings mocked him mercilessly.

Fig. 4
Prince
GUSTAV

The more people laughed at him, the more distraught Gustav became. He stuffed balls of yarn into his sleeves to make his muscles look larger (and sadly, lumpier). He tied bricks to the bottom of his boots to make himself taller (and clomped around like a sumo wrestler in a full-body cast). He even grew his hair long, just so he would have more of *something*. Unsurprisingly, his brothers continued to tease him.

In his later teen years, Gustav became a frustrated, angry loner. For as much of the day as possible, he avoided contact with other people (which was not necessarily a bad thing for the other people). He would roam on horseback through the pine forests of Sturmhagen, hoping to find some creature he could fight—and thereby prove his strength and heroism. One day he stumbled upon something incredible.

There was a tall tower standing all by itself in a forest clearing. Oddly, it had no doors and no stairs. But it did have a girl stuck up in a room at the very top—a girl with eighty feet of hair. She lowered her shimmery blond locks down to Gustav, and he used them as a rope and climbed up to her. Once inside the small tower room, Gustav learned that the girl's name was Rapunzel and that she was the captive of an evil witch.

Fig. 5
TOWER

Now, Gustav was not exactly a ladies' man; in fact, this may have been the first time he'd ever made eye contact with a girl. But he was struck by

Rapunzel. She was so different from the girls he'd seen around the castle, especially his brutish cousins, who liked to hold him down and smack him with their thick, whiplike pigtails. Rapunzel was all soft, pillowy curves and delicate, graceful movements. She smiled at him warmly, held his hand, and spoke to him kindly. *So this is why people like girls,* Gustav thought.

Overtaken by feelings that were entirely new to him, Gustav opened up. He complained about his brothers, and, to his surprise, Rapunzel listened. Gustav was in heaven. He yammered on for hours, until Rapunzel realized the sun was going down. The witch would be returning soon, she said, and she begged Gustav to go for help.

Gustav climbed back down Rapunzel's hair, hopped on his horse, and took off in the direction of the royal castle. But he stopped just a mile or so away from the witch's tower. There was no way he was going to round up his brothers to come and help him. They would take all the credit and probably even steal Rapunzel's attention away from him. No, this was going to be *his* rescue, *his* heroic deed.

Under the darkening sky, he

Fig. 6
Lady
RAPUNZEL

turned around and rode back to the tower. Rapunzel let down her hair for him but was confused to see Gustav reenter her prison room alone.

"Where are the others?" she asked.

"I need no others," Gustav said with total confidence. "I will rescue you myself."

"Did you get a ladder?" she asked hopefully.

"No," he said, suddenly sounding less sure of himself.

"How are we going to get out then?"

Gustav had no plan, so he said nothing. He just peeked around in the corners of the room, pretending he was looking for something.

Moments later, a scratchy voice called from outside, "Rapunzel, let down your hair."

"It's Zaubera," Rapunzel whispered. "Quick, you must hide."

"I hide from no one," Gustav said. "Let her up. When she steps into the room, I will kill the witch."

"But—"

"Just do it," Gustav insisted.

Rapunzel let down her hair.

When Lyrical Leif later chronicled the event in his song about Rapunzel, Prince Charming's "battle" with the witch went on for three lengthy verses. In reality, it was over in less than three seconds. As soon as the witch stepped over the windowsill, Gustav leapt at her. The evil old woman caught him and, with superhuman strength, hurled him from the tower. Done and done.

Gustav's landing was particularly nasty. He came down face-first into a painfully prickly briar patch. So painful, in fact, that the thorns scratched his eyes and blinded him. He spent the next several days stumbling through the forest, feeling his way from tree to tree. It was pitiful. After nearly a week, he collapsed from hunger.

Rapunzel, in the meantime, managed to get free (though how she pulled off that feat was a mystery to everyone but her and the witch). She searched the woods for Gustav, and eventually found him sightless and starving. Rapunzel cradled him in her arms and wept. And here's the really amazing part: As soon as her tears hit Gustav's eyes, his vision was restored.

Once the story got out—and boy, did the minstrels get a lot of requests for this one—Gustav's brothers treated him worse than ever. He couldn't show his face in the castle without hearing mocking calls like, "Look out, Prince Charming, I think I see a scary shrub! Don't worry, we'll call Cousin Helga to come save you!"

Gustav considered this the lowest point of his life. He'd

become famous for being a failure. He'd never been much of a people person to begin with, and this only made things worse.

One day, after being jeered by a group of shepherds (according to Gustav, the sheep were laughing, too), the big prince retreated into the forest, climbed a tall tree, and sat among its highest branches, hoping to avoid human contact. Rapunzel found him anyway.

"Come down," she called. "Come back home with me."

"Go away," Gustav said. "Can't you see I'm in a tree?"

"I see how the words of others hurt you," Rapunzel said. "But you'll hear no harsh words from me."

"Oh, that's right—you're Little Miss Perfect," Gustav grumbled from up above. "It's all your fault, you know. It's because of you that everyone thinks I'm a joke."

"I'm sorry you feel that way," Rapunzel said, craning her neck to see him. "You know I only meant to help. When I saw you in that condition—"

"I would've been fine."

"You were half-dead."

"More like *half-alive*. See, that's your problem, Mega-Braid. You're always trying to fix something that doesn't need fixing."

"Fixing people is my gift."

Gustav snorted. "Well, I'm returning it. Go re-gift it to someone else."

Rapunzel was silent for a moment, then said, "I should. It's selfish of me to keep this gift to myself. The world is full of people in need; I'm wasting my talents here, trying to give you reasons to like yourself."

"What?" Gustav jumped down, breaking several branches on his way to the ground. "Why don't you use your power on yourself, Miracle Girl? You've obviously got something wrong with your brain. 'Cause I like myself just fine. I *love* myself. What's not to love? I'm a better fighter than anyone, a better hunter, a better horseman—"

"If you truly like yourself as you are, why do you feel the need to prove yourself better than everyone else?"

"Leave," Gustav barked. "You said it: Go help someone else. I don't need anybody."

Rapunzel gathered her hair and began to walk away.

"You're right," she said as she left. "Helping others is what I was meant to do. I don't understand you, Gustav. But maybe you do understand *me*, after all."

He never told anyone that Rapunzel had left. But her departure only made Gustav more determined than ever to show the world he was a hero worthy of respect. He spent his days riding around the countryside, looking for someone to rescue.

Months later, on the outskirts of Sturmhagen, Rosilda Stiffenkrauss and her family were busily plucking beets from the ground, when the nearby trees parted with a rumble and a hulking troll stepped out of the forest, sniffing the air with its tremendous nose. If you've never seen one before, trolls are about nine feet tall, covered with shaggy, swamp-colored hair, and may or may not have horns (this troll had one crooked horn jutting out from the left side of its head). Many people, upon seeing a troll for the first time, think they are being attacked by a big, ferocious pile of spinach. Rosilda Stiffenkrauss, however, had lived in Sturmhagen her entire life and knew a troll when she saw one.

Fig. 7
TROLL

"Oh, for pete's sake," she sighed. "Here comes another one. Come on, kids; everybody inside until it goes away."

The big, greenish man-thing grunted and lumbered toward the farming family with a hungry smile on its hideous face. Rosilda quickly ushered her eleven children inside their small wood-frame house, where they all watched from the windows as the monster sat down amid their crops and started tossing handfuls of freshly picked beets into its mouth. Rosilda was furious.

"Stinking up the yard is one thing," she spat, "but there's no way I'm letting that beast devour our produce."

The thickset, red-faced farmer woman wiped her hands on her apron, threw open the door, and marched back outside. "Get your grimy hands off our beets!" she yelled. Her wild and frizzy carrot-orange hair bounced with every angry word. "We spent the whole morning pulling those things up, and I'll be darned if I'm going to let you gobble them all!"

Rosilda picked a shovel up off the ground and raised it over her head, threatening to clobber the vegetable thief, who was nearly twice her size. Her children crowded in the doorway and cheered her on. "Mom-my, Mom-my!"

The troll looked up at her in shock, as bright red beet juice ran down its chin. "Uh," the thing grunted. "Shovel Lady hit?"

"You're darn right I hit," Rosilda growled back. "Unless

you drop those veggies and head back into the woods you came from."

The troll looked from the woman's scowling face to the long, rusty shovel she waved menacingly overhead. It dropped the handful of beets it had been about to eat.

"Shovel Lady no hit Troll," it mumbled as it stood up. "Troll make no trouble. Troll go."

Enter Prince Gustav. Clad in clanking, fur-trimmed armor and wielding a large, shining battle-ax, he charged at the troll on horseback.

"Not so fast, beast!" Gustav shouted as he approached, his long blond hair flowing behind him. Without stopping his horse, he leapt from the saddle, turning himself into a human missile, and knocked the troll flat onto its back. The prince and the troll rolled through the garden in one clanking, grunting mass, smashing down freshly sprouted beet plants, until the creature finally got back to its feet and tossed Gustav off. The prince crashed through the wooden planks of the farmer's fence but nimbly picked himself back up, ready to charge the monster again. That was when Gustav spotted the bright red beet juice around the troll's mouth.

"Child eater!" he screamed. All the children were, of course, perfectly fine—and had actually filed back out into the yard to watch the fight—but Gustav was too focused

on the monster to notice. The prince swung his ax. The troll caught the weapon in its large, clawed hands, yanked it away from Gustav, and tossed it off into a corner of the farmyard, where it shattered several barrels of pickled beets with a crunch and a splat.

"Starf it all," Gustav cursed (which prompted some of the older children to cover the ears of the younger ones).

Now unarmed, the prince stood face-to-face with the troll. The monster was nearly three feet taller than him, but Gustav showed no hint of fear. Gustav didn't really do "fear." Annoyance, consternation, occasionally embarrassment: Those were emotions Gustav was familiar with. But not fear.

"Why Angry Man do that?" the troll asked. Gustav charged at the creature, but it grabbed him in mid-run and lifted him into the air. The troll spun the prince upside down and rammed him headfirst into the ground with a pile-driver-like maneuver. Dazed, Gustav tried to crawl away, but the troll, still holding him by the feet, swung him to the left, smashing him through a stack of wooden crates. The monster then swung him back to the right, wrapping him around a fence post. Gustav swung his fist at the troll, but his punch didn't even land. The creature hoisted him overhead and was ready to chuck him up onto the farmhouse roof, when Rosilda stepped up behind the troll and smacked it in the back of the head with her shovel.

"Ow!" The troll dropped Gustav in the dirt and rubbed the sore spot on its skull. "Shovel Lady said Shovel Lady would not hit Troll."

"That was before you started beating up on that poor man," Rosilda snapped. "Now get out of here."

"But Angry Man hit Troll first."

"I don't care. You get out." She raised the shovel again.

"No more, no more. Troll go." And the huge creature shuffled off toward the forest. The children burst into cheers and danced around the garden.

Rosilda held her hand out to Gustav, who still lay on the ground. He angrily waved the woman's hand away and stood up by himself. "I had it under control," he scolded. "You shouldn't have put yourself in harm's way."

"You know, the troll was about to leave when you jumped on him," Rosilda said. "Everything was fine. And now look—you've wrecked our garden."

Gustav surveyed the yard. There were broken fences, smashed barrels, squashed beets, and row after row of flattened plants. "You care about a few vegetables? The monster ate your children!" he shouted.

"It did no such thing," the woman scoffed.

"It had blood on its mouth."

"Beet juice."

"Are you sure?" Gustav asked, looking around at the giddy, dancing children. "It must have eaten at least one kid. Have you counted them?"

"Now look here, my knight in shining armor," Rosilda said as she handed Gustav the beet-stained ax he'd lost. "I know how many wee ones I've got, and none of them are in the belly of a troll. Perhaps if you'd taken a second to stop and think before you—"

Rosilda paused and stepped closer to Gustav. "Wait a minute," she said with a grin. "I know who you are. You're the prince from that Rapunzel story."

At that point, the children swarmed around Gustav, oohing and ahhing. He said nothing.

"Yeah, I'm sure it's you," Rosilda said. "Prince Charming himself."

"My name is Gustav."

"I've been to the royal castle, you know," she said. "I've *seen* you there."

Gustav looked stern. "No, you're thinking of my brother. He's Charming. I'm Prince Gustav. Gustav the Mighty."

At that, a small boy and a small girl each started

climbing up one of Gustav's arms.

"Okay, Your Highness," Rosilda said. "Why don't you open up your royal wallet and pay us for the damage you've done to our farm?"

"I carry no gold with me," Gustav said, with a child sitting on each shoulder pulling at his hair. "But I'll tell the royal treasurer to send you some money."

He tried to walk away before the woman pried any further into his least favorite topic, but was slowed down by two more children, one sitting on each of his feet, hugging his heavy, fur-lined boots.

"Tell me one thing, Your Highness," Rosilda called to him. "Why didn't you get a ladder?"

That question *again*? It was more than Gustav could bear. He shook off the children, who all dropped, giggling, into the dirt. "Pah!" was all he offered in response.

"When you get back to your castle, why don't you tell that Lyrical Leif that he needs to write some new material?" Rosilda said with a smirk. "It's been months now, and I'm gettin' tired of hearing about how that sweet girl saved your life."

"For your information, that weaselly song-spitter hasn't shown his face around Castle Sturmhagen in weeks," Gustav snarled. "And I say, good riddance!"

He abruptly turned his back on Rosilda and hopped onto his dark brown warhorse. He planned to speed off and kick up a cloud of dust at this annoying woman, but before he could spur the horse on, a newcomer approached the farm. This fellow was also on horseback, riding a light tan mare. He was hunched awkwardly in the saddle and moving very slowly. The rider stopped and looked up when he reached the farmyard gate. Gustav, Rosilda, and the children all stared at the stranger's very odd attire: a dusty white suit, decked with gold trim and tassels.

"Hello," the man said with a weary smile. "This might sound a bit strange, but are any of you familiar with the tale of Rapunzel? She's a girl with really long hair, and—"

The delighted children bounced around and pointed at Gustav. "Oh," said the stranger. "You know the story?"

Rosilda chuckled. "He *is* the story. That's Prince Charming, right there."

The stranger's eyes widened, and he sat upright. "Really? You're joking. No? Oh, that's wonderful. You don't know how terrible this last week has been. I came all the way from Harmonia. I've been riding all over, not getting nearly enough sleep, stopping at every village and farm I could find. I'm practically starving—you wouldn't believe the things that pass for scones in some of these places. I have had to sleep at inns where they obviously don't change sheets between guests; I have washed my face in the same water that fish *do things* in. I'm sorry; I'm rambling. The point is: I've gone through all of this in hopes of finding someone who could point me in Rapunzel's direction. And now I've run into *you*. You, of all people. And it's even more amazing than you think, because *I'm* Prince Charming, too!"

Gustav narrowed his eyes. "You're a crazy man."

"No, I'm sorry, I'm just a little excited. You see, my name is Frederic. But I'm also a Prince Charming. I'm from the Cinderella story." He flashed a broad smile and offered his hand to Gustav. Gustav didn't take it; he had no idea what this lunatic was talking about, and he certainly didn't trust him. The children, on the other hand, applauded wildly at the mention of Cinderella's name. Frederic gave them a quick salute.

"Okay, let me start over," Frederic said to Gustav. "I'm looking for my fiancée, Ella—that's her real name. She left Harmonia about a week ago. All I know is that she was going to Sturmhagen to find Rapunzel. So, if you could be so kind as to lead me to Rapunzel . . ."

"Follow me," Gustav said, and started his horse off into the field.

"Oh, fantastic. So how far away is she?"

"I'm not taking you to Rapunzel," Gustav said. "I want to speak to you out of earshot of this rabble." And with that, he was off.

"Oh," said Frederic. "Um, good-bye, children!" He waved to the farmer and her family, and then accidentally walked his horse in a circle three times before getting the animal to follow Gustav down the road.

"Humph," Rosilda grumbled. "And these are the guys everybody wants to marry? I don't get it."

The two men trotted along the meadow-lined dirt road in silence for a while, until Frederic finally spoke. "Soooo . . . You mentioned something back there about *not* taking me to Rapunzel."

"That's right," said Gustav. "I'm not taking you to Rapunzel."

"And why is that?"

Feeling they were far enough from the farm, Gustav brought his horse to a stop. "Look," he said seriously, "are you really the prince from that other story?"

"Yes," said Frederic as he struggled to line his horse up beside Gustav's. "Are you really Rapunzel's prince?"

Gustav huffed. "I'm not *her* prince, but yes, I am the

one from that dumb song. I can't take you to Rapunzel, because she ran off somewhere."

"Oh." Frederic looked crestfallen. "So we have something else in common."

"I didn't want that farmer woman and her little imps to hear that Rapunzel was gone," Gustav said. He glared at Frederic. "And if *you* tell anyone, Fancy Man, you'll regret it."

"I won't," Frederic replied. "But if it's such a big secret, I'm curious as to why you decided to tell me at all."

Gustav honestly wasn't sure why he'd chosen to confide in this ridiculous stranger. Maybe he figured that if there was anyone in the world who could possibly understand him, it would be another of the poor fools cursed to be Prince Charming. But could this guy really even be a prince? He looked like a deranged doorman. *My brothers would eat this guy for lunch,* Gustav thought. *But then again, if my brothers would hate him, maybe he's not so bad.*

"What happened to your woman?" Gustav asked.

"Ella left because she thought I was boring," Frederic said. "But you don't look boring at all. So I'm guessing that wasn't *your* problem."

"Boring? Ha! No, it's far worse than that. Rapunzel is off *helping* people," Gustav spat. (He simply could not entertain the possibility that his behavior had something to do with Rapunzel's departure.)

"I don't understand," Frederic said. "Helping people is bad?"

"You know the story, right?"

Frederic nodded.

"So you know about the bit with the briar patch?"

"Was it really her tears that restored your sight?" Frederic asked.

"Who knows?" Gustav mumbled. "But *she's* convinced she saved me. And once that song started going around, it got worse. She was the brave heroine with magical tears. And what was I? I was the jerk who got beaten by an old lady and rescued by a girl. Anyway, she believes she can heal people, so she went off to spread goodness around the world or some nonsense like that. And I'm left here with a reputation to fix. . . ."

"I'm really sorry to hear—"

"Hold your words," Gustav cut him off. It suddenly hit him that this bizarre man in the silly suit might be offering exactly what he needed—the opportunity for a heroic deed. "This Cinderella person you're looking for—she's in some kind of danger? She needs help?"

"Well, not that I know of," Frederic replied.

"She's in danger," Gustav stated matter-of-factly. He saw Frederic flinch at the word "danger"; it should be easy enough to convince him that his girlfriend needed rescuing.

"Sturmhagen is no place for amateur adventurers," he went on. "There are monsters at every turn."

"Tigers?" Frederic asked in a barely audible whisper.

"Sure, why not? We've got everything else," Gustav answered. "You know, I saved that farm family from a troll right before you showed up."

"Are you serious?" Frederic asked, biting his thumbnail.

"Deadly serious," Gustav said. "Was the girl armed?"

Frederic shook his head.

Gustav tried to stifle his excitement.

"I never step foot outside without my ax," he said, motioning to the huge weapon that was now strapped to his back. Frederic got a glimpse of the big blade—still dripping with red—and nearly fell off his horse.

"No one's safe in these woods without a weapon," Gustav said. "What was she wearing?"

"A blue dress, I think."

"A dress?" Gustav scoffed. "Look at me. *This* is how you prepare for Sturmhagen." Gleaming armor plates covered his shoulders. Strapped to his upper arms, wrists, and legs were more metal guards, all lined with heavy fur trim. His torso was draped with a fur-lined tunic. Underneath that, more armor. And his tall iron boots looked strong enough to kick their way through a solid wall.

"I don't even think I could walk in all that," Frederic said.

"If that girl's been out here by herself for a week already, we'd better move fast. Her life is probably being threatened as we speak."

"Oh, my," Frederic said. "Well, um, will you, um, will you—"

"Yes, I will save your woman," Gustav declared. "Come! We're off!"

And with that, Gustav galloped down the road toward the dark, dense forest.

"Please don't go so fast!" Frederic called as he followed in a sloppy zigzag. "This saddle really chafes!"

3

PRINCE CHARMING CLAIMS
HE IS NOT AFRAID OF OLD LADIES

Over the years, Frederic had met his fair share of other princes. None of them were anything like this prince of Sturmhagen. Gustav was so gruff. He had no patience, no manners, and ridiculously poor communication skills. Frederic could only presume the man's flamenco dancing was just as awkward. He wasn't at all surprised that Gustav hadn't been able to hold on to his relationship with Rapunzel. But considering his own fiancée had run off, who was he to judge?

As the two princes rode across the countryside in search of Ella, Frederic began to grow frustrated with Gustav. For one thing, the big man always insisted they camp outside. Anytime Frederic suggested they look for an inn,

Gustav would respond with, "Bah!" Or sometimes, "Pah!" Or even, "Pffft!"

Every night, Gustav would contentedly sprawl out on bare grass, and then mock Frederic for attempting to curl up on a trio of spread-out handkerchiefs.

"Cleanliness, Gustav," Frederic would say defensively. "I'm doing what I can in the name of cleanliness." *Dirt*, of course, ranked fourth on King Wilberforce's list of "Enemies of the Nobleman," just below *nose hair*, but above *hiccups*.

As the days rolled by, Frederic also began to doubt Gustav's skills as a tracker. He watched Gustav sniff the air, cup his hand to his ear to "listen to the wind," and occasionally dismount from his horse to nibble the edge of a leaf. He couldn't imagine how any of that would help them locate Ella.

And in reality, none of it would. Gustav had no idea what he was doing.

Eventually, Gustav took them off-road, into the thickest stretches of Sturmhagen's pine forests, where the trees were so tall they blocked almost all sunlight. Every flutter of a bird or skitter of a mouse made Frederic flinch and drop his reins. The path was nearly nonexistent, and he and Gustav had to squeeze their horses between trees to get by. More than once, Gustav pushed aside a large branch and let it snap back into Frederic's face.

Hours later, they finally spotted shafts of daylight ahead. "Aha," Gustav said. He stopped his horse and hopped down. "Now I know where we are."

"Now?" Frederic asked. "You mean we've been lost all this time?"

"Look there," Gustav said, pointing out into a small clearing beyond the trees, where they could see a solitary stone structure. "Zaubera's tower."

"Zaubera? Is that the witch?"

"No, she's some *other* old lady who has a tower in the woods," Gustav quipped sarcastically as he rolled his eyes.

"*This* is where you led me?" Frederic asked in disbelief. "To one of the most dangerous places in Sturmhagen? *And* the one place Ella is guaranteed *not* to be? This is the tower Rapunzel *escaped* from. Why in the world would Ella come *here* to look for her?"

Gustav ignored his protests. "Let's check it out," he said, and stepped out into the clearing.

Frederic grabbed the bigger man's arm and yanked him back into the trees. "What if the witch is there?" Frederic asked.

"Witch, are you there?" Gustav called out. He paused

for a second, listening for a response. "She's not there. Let's go." He stepped into the clearing, and Frederic pulled him back once more.

"Wait," Frederic said. "This witch—Zaubera—she's pretty powerful, right?"

"She's an old lady," Gustav tossed off. "I'm not afraid of old ladies. Are you?"

"Ones who can pick me up and throw me, yes."

"Look," Gustav said. "Here's all you need to know about Zaubera."

Zaubera was possibly the most powerful witch in the world. She hadn't always been, though. There was a time when she wasn't even evil. Zaubera was just a farmer woman living by herself in the small town of Jorgsborg. She was a dabbler in the magical arts, just as every member of her family had been for generations. But she never used her talents to do anything more than grow the tastiest turnips the world had ever seen. Still, the magic freaked out her neighbors. Despite her many attempts to befriend her fellow Jorgsborgians, Zaubera was always ignored—or worse, mocked. One particular group of local children used to stand at the edge of her property and call her names like "worm lips" and "hedgehog hair." Discouraged, Zaubera gave up and retreated to her cottage to live the life of a hermit.

Then came the fateful day when one of the local hunters managed to capture one of Sturmhagen's giant, fire-breathing beavers. The man brought the creature back to town to show off his catch—big mistake. The beaver broke loose and went on a rampage, setting nearly every home in Jorgsborg ablaze. As the fire raged out of control around her, Zaubera projected a magical force field around her farm, keeping herself and her home safe from the flames. But she noticed a trio of children trapped by the flames, the same children who insulted her daily. Zaubera dropped the shield around her home and protected the children instead. She lost everything she'd worked for, but, she thought, at least the townspeople would finally appreciate her.

Suddenly, a hero arrived. The armored Sir Lindgren galloped into town on his white stallion and quickly slew the beaver. He then rode up to Zaubera and told her to release the children. Confused, she dropped her shield. Sir Lindgren scooped up the kids and rode away.

As the town began to rebuild and people returned to their homes, the townsfolk didn't thank Zaubera. In fact, they shunned her more than ever. And then she caught wind of a new bard song, "The Ballad of the Knight and the Beaver," in which the hero knight not only slays the beast but rescues three children from the clutches of a wicked witch. It was at that point that something in Zaubera snapped.

Fine, she thought. *If they want a villain, that's what I'll give them.* She got her gnarled hands on some ancient spell books and taught herself some dark magic. Then she wreaked havoc on the town. She used fireballs to blast down every cottage that had been rebuilt. She tore up gardens with sorcerous winds. She shot bolts of mystical lightning at the very children whose lives she'd saved earlier, sending them running, screaming and crying. Everyone fled. And no one ever returned to Jorgsborg.

Zaubera had gotten a taste of what it felt like to be truly feared. And she wanted more. The whole world should be trembling in fear of her, she thought. She'd heard about other witches that had become notorious for deeds that weren't even remotely impressive. Putting someone to sleep? So unoriginal. Trying to cook a couple of kids? That didn't even require magic! No, Zaubera deserved

Fig. 8
The Witch
ZAUBERA

to be more infamous than all of them. She needed word of her wickedness to spread across the kingdoms. And for that, she couldn't rely on a few sizzled kids. She'd need to go big. She'd need to get the notice of the bards.

On the day she caught a wandering peasant swiping some turnips from her newly replanted garden, she came up with the perfect plan. Instead of simply frying the man where he stood, Zaubera offered to let him go in exchange for his young daughter. The peasant was surprisingly quick to agree to this (he was not a very good dad), and that was how Zaubera ended up with Rapunzel. The witch locked the girl away in an impenetrable tower and then waited gleefully for some heroes to try to rescue the fair maiden. She knew they would come. Heroes just can't stay away when they hear about a person in danger; heroes crave the glory that gets heaped upon them when they pull off a rescue. Oh, how Zaubera hated heroes. And when some stupid heroes showed up to storm her tower, she planned to blast them into nothingness; the levels of pain and destruction she would cause would simply be too great for the bards to overlook.

But no one came. Rapunzel's father never sent anyone to try to get his daughter back. He never even told anyone she was gone. Like I said, he was a very bad father. He just sat home and enjoyed his stolen turnips.

Years went by, during which Zaubera was stuck with a prisoner she never really wanted. But the witch used the time wisely, learning every terrible magic spell she could—a spell to bind her enemies, a spell to grant her superhuman strength, even a thesaurus spell to help her think up new and creative ways to insult people. Before long, she was a master of dark magic. Then, one day, out of the blue, she got the rescue attempt she was hoping for. Sort of.

One of the lunkhead princes of Sturmhagen tried to attack her, and she made quick work of him. But the fool had come alone; there was no one to share the story of how Zaubera had destroyed the prince. No one except Rapunzel, that is. Desperate for fame, Zaubera set Rapunzel free to tell her tale. She never considered the possibility that the longhaired lass would save that near-dead lunkhead and become the hero of her own story.

After "The Song of Rapunzel" became popular—the song in which the bards made the witch sound incompetent by implying that Rapunzel *escaped* on her own—Zaubera was more determined than ever to prove her wickedness to the world. She also now had a vendetta against heroes *and* bards.

The witch spent weeks concocting her Supreme

Scheme for Infamy. Instead of kidnapping one prisoner this time, she was going to kidnap five. And she was going after captives that people would actually miss and *want back*, prisoners that the world's heroes would be climbing over one another for the chance to rescue: She was going to snatch the bards themselves.

And that's exactly what she had spent the past few weeks doing. She didn't worry about anybody getting wise to her plan before she was ready—there was no communication between kingdoms. And without bards, who was going to tell the people that the bards were missing?

Sturmhagen, Harmonia, Erinthia, Avondell, and Sylvaria: When the heroes of these five kingdoms hear that I've got their beloved lute-pluckers, they'll come running, the witch thought. *And when they arrive, they'll bear witness to the grandest display of evil power this world has ever seen. No one will ever ignore Zaubera again.*

Of course, Gustav didn't tell any of that to Frederic— Gustav didn't know any of that. What Gustav said to Frederic was: "She's an old lady. End of story."

Gustav strolled cockily out into the clearing, with Frederic quivering behind him. As it turned out, someone had heard Gustav's shout after all. A girl's head popped out of the tower's lone window, some sixty feet above the ground.

"Who's out there?" Ella shouted, as she looked down. She was stunned to see her fiancé. "Frederic, is that you? What are you doing here?"

"Ella!" Frederic squealed with delight. "Oh, my goodness. It's you! I, uh, I came to find you."

"You did?" Ella said. "Wow. You did. You're really here."

Okay, this is it, Frederic thought. *Time to show her what you've got.* "It's the all-new me, Ella. I've slept on dirt. I'm ready for adventure now."

Frederic couldn't see Gustav behind him, but he could *feel* his eyes rolling.

"How'd you get up there?" Frederic called.

"It's a long story," Ella said.

It's not really a long story. Here it is:

Ella rode into Sturmhagen (it took her two days to cover the distance Frederic traveled in a week) and visited a village where she hoped to gather some information about Rapunzel.

"Do any of you happen to know Rapunzel?" she asked a group of townsfolk strolling down the street, and then tried (unnecessarily) to jog their memories by singing a few bars. "Listen, dear hearts, to the tale I must share; the tale of a girl with very long hair. . . ."

Zaubera, out on the prowl, slunk by just at that moment, pondering a cleverly theatrical way to spread news of the bards' kidnappings. It might be a poetic touch, she thought, to snatch a passing minstrel and use him or her to *sing* about the crime.

And when Zaubera saw some loudmouth in a dress singing to a crowd on a street corner, she figured she'd found her minstrel. Only it was really Ella. As soon as the crowd dispersed, the witch sidled up to her.

"Get your facts straight, you chuckleheaded throat-warbler!" Zaubera spat. She then trapped Ella—who was utterly baffled—in a binding spell and took her back to the tower.

See, it wasn't that long.

"I'm so glad you're here," Ella said. "Please, go get help before the witch comes back."

"No, we're not leaving without you!" Frederic yelled.

"Who's that with you?" Ella asked.

"Oh, this is Rapunzel's prince. He helped me find you. And he can get you down. He's got experience with this."

He turned to Gustav and asked him quietly, "How do we get her down?"

Gustav walked to the base of the tower, looked to the window above, and yelled, "Cinderella, let down your hair!"

Ella looked perplexed. "But it only comes to my shoulders!"

Gustav walked back to Frederic and shrugged. "That's all I've got. I'm out of ideas."

Frederic was befuddled. "Well, there must be *some* way up there. I mean, *she* got up there." He called up to Ella, "How did you get up there?"

Ella glimpsed something out of the corner of her eye. "Run! She's coming!"

Frederic and Gustav darted under the cover of the nearby trees. They saw a tall, thin woman draped in red and gray rags emerge into the clearing. Her pale skin was creased and lined, and tufts of white hair shot from her head in random directions.

"Zaubera?" Frederic asked.

Gustav nodded. "Let's watch and see how she gets up there."

With a voice like broken bagpipes, the witch yelled up to Ella in the tower. "I could have sworn I heard you talking to someone, dearie. When I get up there, I had better find you alone." Then she turned toward the woods and called out, "Reese!"

Soon there was a loud rumble. Branches shook and leaves fell as a man taller than the tower itself muscled his way through the trees and stomped into the clearing. The giant reached Zaubera in one enormous step, then knelt and placed his hand on the ground, palm up, for the witch to climb onto. He easily lifted the old woman up to the tower window, and she stepped inside.

"Well," said Frederic. "We can't get in *that* way."

That was when Gustav went berserk. He whipped out his big, double-bladed ax and ran into the clearing with a long, thundering shout of "Stuuuuuuuurm-haaaaaay-gennnnnnn!" The giant, dumbfounded, simply stood and stared. So did Frederic.

Gustav slammed his ax into Reese's humongous shin. With a bellow of pain, the giant grabbed his injured right leg and began hopping up and down on his left foot. The ground trembled with every hop, causing Gustav to tumble over himself. He dropped his weapon as he fell, and the heavy ax blade plunked down into the loamy soil. From the trees, Frederic watched in horror as his companion crawled to retrieve the weapon, unaware that he was directly in the shadow of the giant's enormous right foot. Gustav was about to be squashed like a bug.

Think! Frederic told himself. *What would Sir Bertram the Dainty do?* The answer came to him. In *The Case of the Ill-Mannered Milkmaid,* Sir Bertram had to get the attention of a governess who was about to use the wrong kind of wineglass. Frederic could use the same tactic here. Eight years of yodeling lessons were about to pay off. Frederic cupped his hands to his mouth and let out a long: "Yodel-odel-odel-odel-ay-hee-hooooooo!"

It worked. Nothing annoyed Gustav more than yodeling. As soon as he heard the trilly alpine melody, he glanced angrily at Frederic—who was frantically gesturing upward. Gustav dove out of the way just as the giant's big bare foot smashed down—and landed directly on the lost battle-ax.

"Yow!" Reese bellowed, hopping in pain once again. Only this time, he couldn't keep his balance. The giant staggered backward and collapsed into the stone tower.

Fig. 9
Reese, the
GIANT

"Uh-oh," Reese moaned. The entire structure wobbled, and huge chunks of stone began to shower down.

"Oh, no," said Gustav as the tower collapsed into a pile of stone and clouds of dust. Another failure. And this time there would be a song about how he not only didn't rescue the girl, but actually *killed* her by accident.

"Ella!" Frederic screamed. *This is my fault,* he thought. *Ella is gone, all because I tried to be something I'm not. I should have listened to my father.*

But as the giant sat up and brushed away the loose bricks and stones that littered the clearing, he revealed an astonishing sight. Inside a shimmering green bubble of energy, the witch stood completely unharmed. And Ella was draped over her bony shoulder, alive and kicking hard.

"A magic shield," Gustav said. Frederic nearly fainted with relief.

"Reese, you big oaf! Look what you did!" Zaubera hissed.

Reese pointed a huge finger at the princes. "It was their fault."

The witch turned to see whom Reese was talking about, but Frederic had already hustled Gustav back into the trees. Hiding under a gorse bush, the two princes listened to Zaubera.

"Don't tell me you're blaming the bunnies, Reese," the witch said.

"No, ma'am," the giant said. "It was a couple of men. They were trying to get the girl."

Gustav popped up out of the bush. "Put Cinderella down, old lady!"

Fig. 10
Force
BUBBLE

Frederic leapt up onto Gustav's back and yanked him back down into the shrubbery.

"See?" Reese said, feeling vindicated. "Should I smash them?"

"Never mind those buffoons, Reese," Zaubera said as her thin, colorless lips curled into a smile. "Did you hear what they just called our prisoner here?" The witch grabbed a handful of Ella's hair and looked her in the eyes. "Well, look at this," Zaubera chuckled. "Forget the singing ransom-grams, Reese. I've got a genuine celebrity for a hostage. Cinderella. This is going to require a much more spectacular announcement. Ooh, this is going to be fun."

Ella glared back at her, unwilling to show the witch any fear.

"But what if the heroes follow us, ma'am?" Reese asked.

"Hero, singular," Zaubera replied. "One of them is a complete coward. And yes, the hero will follow us. That's what heroes do. We'll just be ready for him. When we catch him and his sidekick, you can grind their bones into bread. Now come."

"Yes, ma'am," the giant intoned in his booming voice. "But bread made from bones sounds awful, you know."

"I didn't hire you to be a meal planner, Reese," grated the witch. "Start walking."

"All right," the giant rumbled. "Have you ever tried it? Bone bread, I mean. I can't imagine it tastes good. And you'd still need flour, no?"

"Shut up, Reese."

"My foot hurts."

"Try wearing shoes, imbecile."

After a couple of minutes, their voices and Reese's thundering footsteps could no longer be heard. The princes crawled from under the gorse bush. Out of habit, Frederic tried to dust off his soiled and torn suit but quickly realized it was a lost cause.

"Okay, let's go," Gustav said.

"Go where?" Frederic asked.

"You want your woman back, right?" Gustav said. "We're following them."

"No," said Frederic. "We're not. I am not going anywhere with you. You nearly got Ella killed. You would have died yourself, if I hadn't done something."

"You yodeled," Gustav snarled with contempt.

"At least I did *something*," Frederic returned. "How could you not have noticed those horribly callused toes looming above you?"

Gustav brought his face very near Frederic's, close enough for Frederic to feel his breath. "Are you telling me I'm not a good enough hero for you?"

Frederic tried very hard not to blink.

"Are you saying that I can't do this?" Gustav hissed. "That I can't rescue someone? That you—Mr. Silky White Pants and Fancy Golden Dingle-Dangles—are better than me?" His forehead touched Frederic's.

"No," Frederic muttered. He was only slightly less afraid of Gustav than he was of the giant. "I'm not saying that at all. Of course I need your help."

Gustav inched back.

"You did find Ella, after all," Frederic went on. "I'm sorry I underestimated you there. But this isn't just about finding a missing person anymore; this is a rescue mission. And a dangerous one, considering there's a witch *and* a giant involved. So maybe the two of us aren't enough. Maybe we could use a little extra help. Another set of hands, maybe. That's all."

Gustav thought about this for a moment. "I suppose it wouldn't hurt to have another swordsman at my side," he said.

"Someone with a little more experience in rescuing people from witches and monsters, perhaps?" Frederic offered.

"Ha!" Gustav laughed. "Who are you going to get? That guy from 'Sleeping Beauty'?"

4

PRINCE CHARMING LOSES SOME FANS

Liam never doubted that he was a hero. If anything, he was a little too sure of it. You can't really blame him, though; people had been treating him like a demigod ever since he was a young child. The adulation began shortly after the birth of Princess Briar Rose, the daughter of the king and queen of Avondell. In a rare instance of international communication, they announced that they were looking for a suitable prince to whom she could be engaged. When the princess came of age, she would marry this prince, forever joining her kingdom with his.

As it so happened, the kingdom of Avondell sat upon a seemingly endless chain of gold mines. Whichever nation managed to hook up with Avondell would become super rich. Gareth, the king of Erinthia, which sat just across the border (and therefore just out of reach of Avondell's gold), wanted in on that. The treasure-hungry King Gareth suggested his then three-year-old son, Liam, as a worthy future husband for Princess Briar. Unfortunately, lots of other countries were itching for a shot at Avondell's gold as well, and the competition for Briar Rose's tiny hand was fierce. Little princes from around the world lined up to present themselves before the royal couple of Avondell—and each seemed to have a special skill. There was a tap-dancing toddler from Valerium and a baby from Svenlandia whose parents claimed he could "speak dolphin." A four-year-old from Jangleheim absolutely rocked on the flügelhorn. And a five-year-old prince from Sturmhagen (one of Gustav's brothers) demonstrated his ability to kick a chicken forty yards.

Afraid that little Liam wouldn't stand out in the crowd, his father resorted to trickery. Just as Liam toddled out in front of the king and queen of Avondell, two masked assassins burst into the throne room. They were actually actors hired by Gareth, and each wore a cinnamon stick—young Liam's favorite treat—tied around his boot. The two "assassins" positioned themselves between the preschool prince and the royal couple—and as soon as

Liam excitedly grabbed at the cinnamon sticks on their legs, the actors proved how good they were at their craft. As the boy pulled and tugged at the sweets, the actors threw themselves around and howled in pain. They spun, flipped, and smashed into each other. To the rulers of Avondell it looked as if the three-year-old was beating the grown men senseless. When the royal guards reached the scene of the "fight," little Liam was standing over two seemingly unconscious assassins, slurping happily on a cinnamon stick.

After that, there was no question as to which prince would be selected to wed Briar Rose. The king of Erinthia took his son home in triumph. The boy was treated to awards, parades, and festivals held in his honor. The two actors, by the way, were unable to prove their innocence and were locked away in an Avondellian dungeon for life, but King Gareth didn't worry about that: He was going to be rich (well, rich*er*—he *was* already a king).

Young Prince Liam thrived on all the attention, though he was unsure of exactly why he was getting it.

"Why does everybody love me so much?" he asked his father.

King Gareth didn't want to tell his son the truth—that, for the most part, the people of Erinthia were as greedy as their king was, and they cherished Liam because they knew he would someday make their nation unbelievably wealthy by marrying into the Avondell fortune. Instead he told his son, "Because you're a hero."

That was all Liam needed to hear. From that point on, he devoted himself to being a one-man army, on call to rescue anyone in need. And he was really good at it. He had strength, courage, agility, and natural skill with a sword. He even looked the part: tall and lean, with caramel-toned skin, bright green eyes, and lustrous, black hair that appeared permanently windswept.

Here's what a typical day for Liam might be like: Breakfast; foil a burglary; lunch; rescue lost children from ferocious wolves; serve as guest of honor at ribbon-cutting ceremony for new blacksmith shop; dinner; carry frail grandmother from burning building; healthy snack; bed.

Of course, Liam never realized it was all unnecessary, that he could have lolled about in a hammock all day, sipping juice from a coconut, and his people *still* would have idolized him—which

Fig. 11
Prince
LIAM

was fortunate, because Liam's reputation as a hero meant everything to him.

The one time Liam wasn't around to stop a crime—when the legendary Sword of Erinthia, a priceless heirloom, was stolen from its display case in the royal museum—he prepared himself for the worst. He assumed the unending stream of praise and admiration would quickly dry up, so he gathered the citizenry to apologize to them all publicly. He was shocked to see that people arrived carrying signs that read, WE HEART LIAM. Somebody had even carved a butter sculpture of him. Seriously, they didn't care about the heroics.

At least, they didn't until the Sleeping Beauty incident. If Liam hadn't come to the rescue there, the royal wedding would have been at risk. When an evil fairy put Princess Briar Rose—and all the people of Avondell—under a spell that would have kept them asleep for a hundred years, you'd better believe the people of Erinthia wanted Liam to head over there and save the day. Which he did, of course.

Liam tracked down the bad fairy, snuck up on her, and held her by the wings until she revealed that kissing Briar Rose would break the curse. Once he had the information he needed, Liam nobly released his foe. The fairy repaid this kindness by transforming herself into an enormous toothy demon and trying to bite Liam's head off. After a long-drawn-out battle featuring backflips, body slams, karate chops, and even a few good horse kicks, he won the day by running the fairy-beast through with his sword.

One quick peck on the lips later, Briar Rose and her entire kingdom were eyes-open and celebrating.

The weeks that followed were among the happiest of Liam's life. He was treated to parties and processions in both kingdoms, and a seemingly endless stream of awards and gifts. The only sore spot came when minstrels began spreading "The Tale of the Sleeping Beauty" far and wide. Liam had never been much of a fan of Erinthia's royal songsmith, Tyrese the Tuneful—the man seemed too obsessed with singing about bad guys ("The Ballad of the Bandit King," "The Giant Goes A-Smashing," "The Bandit King Rides Again," etc.) to bother writing songs about any of Liam's heroic exploits. And now that he finally had, he managed to leave Liam's name out of the story entirely. The prince was seriously irked but took solace in all the adoration he got from his hometown crowd.

After the hullabaloo finally died down, it occurred to Liam that he had never really spoken to Briar Rose other than to say, "Good morning. You can consider yourself rescued." He was curious to know more about her. So he did something extremely rare: He sent her a note. Even more shocking, he suggested they meet. In person. Two people from different kingdoms—who are engaged to be married—seeing and talking to each other. Crazy, I know.

Liam sent a message suggesting that he and Briar meet in the Avondellian royal gardens and spend some getting-to-know-you time together. He was surprised when the princess's reply came back reading, "What's to learn? I know your name. I know where you live. Just be there on the wedding day."

Liam decided to try again. His messenger returned to Avondell with a new note in which Liam eloquently and passionately explained why it was so important for him and Briar to truly know and understand each other before they got married. This time the response was slightly more positive: "Whatever."

And so they met. Back when Liam had first seen the sleeping Briar Rose, he thought she was, indeed, a beauty (which made the whole kissing part somewhat easier). With pale white cheeks and thick, auburn curls that surrounded her head like an enormous, poufy halo, the princess had appeared soft and sweet, almost angelic. But as Liam walked into the rose garden that day and saw Briar standing with her hands on her hips, her brows arched, and her lips twisted into a tight knot, he was taken aback. Something seemed much harsher about her. Liam tried to overlook it and approached her with a gentlemanly bow.

"Thanks for meeting with me," he said. "With the wedding only a few days away, I'm looking forward to getting to know the real you."

Catching him completely off guard, Briar put both hands against his chest and pushed him down onto a nearby bench. "Listen up, hero," she barked. "Don't think that just because you offed some witch, you can take charge here."

"She was a fairy, not a witch," he said, stunned by Briar's forcefulness. "And I'm not sure what you're upset about."

"I know you've got a pretty high opinion of yourself," Briar said. "But that's not going to fly with me. My parents raised me to be a proper princess. That means I get what I want, when I want it. In this marriage, you work for me."

Liam was flabbergasted. "I work for the people," he said. "I offer my services wherever I'm needed."

"The people! Ha!" Briar snorted, whipping her impressive mane of curly hair. "The *people* are here to shine my tiaras and cook my puddings. I had to spend my entire childhood in hiding because of that stupid witch—"

"Fairy."

"— and now that I'm finally in my rightful place, I'm going to start living like the princess I was meant to be. If I want entertainment, someone will dance for me. If I am thirsty, someone will give me their jug of water. If I want a cake, someone will use their last ounce of flour to bake me one. Watch this."

Briar reached down and messily yanked handfuls of rare orchids up out of their flower beds. She crumpled the priceless blooms between her fingers and threw the broken stems and petals down onto the cobblestone path. "You know who's going to travel to the farthest reaches of Kom-Pai and fight off venomous snakes in order to find new orchids for me?" she asked with a wicked grin. "The people."

Briar strolled up to Liam and flicked a loose flower petal into his face. "What's the matter, hubby? Speechless?"

"Don't call me hubby," Liam said, with a note of disgust. Even with all the monster battles he'd fought and death traps he'd escaped, this conversation was the single

Fig. 12
Princess
BRIAR
ROSE

most unnerving experience he'd ever had. "You know, I'm not sure I want to marry you," he said.

"Why not?"

"Because you're mean."

"Wah, wah," she fake-cried. "Get a backbone, hero."

"Please tell me this is some sort of joke."

"You wanted the real me, you got it. Briar Rose doesn't censor herself for anyone."

"Then there's no point to any of this," Liam said sadly. "I can never love someone like you."

"That's where you're wrong, puppy. It's common knowledge that I'm your true love."

"According to whom?" Liam exclaimed. "The evil fairy who tried to kill us all? *She's* the one who said 'true love's kiss' would break the spell. But she also turned into a monster and tried to eat me. We're supposed to take *her* word for it?"

"Blah, blah, blah, blah," Briar mocked, opening and closing her hand like a puppet's mouth. "You and I are still getting married. Our parents arranged this years ago. And you're a real catch: You're well liked, you come from a respected family, and you're not too hard on the eyes. You're just the kind of guy I want sitting on a throne next to me to make people feel safe and unthreatened before I turn their lives into nightmares."

"I'll never go along with this," Liam insisted.

"It's not like you have much of a choice in the matter. Face it, you're stuck with me, Prince Charming." Briar poked a finger into his chest with every syllable of *Prince-Charm-ing*, then sat down on a bench across from Liam and kicked her feet up onto a birdbath, knocking away a frightened wren as she did. "Now go peel me some kumquats."

Liam walked away without a word, got on his horse, and headed back to Erinthia, where he gave word that he would be addressing the people that afternoon.

The citizens of Erinthia gathered by the thousands outside the royal palace, all eyes on the gold-trimmed marble balcony overhead, from which their prince would soon be addressing them. Applause broke out as a set of stained-glass doors opened wide and Liam strode out to greet the crowd. He wore a billowy blue tunic with black pants tucked into brown leather boots; there was a sword at his side, and a wine-colored cape fluttering behind him in the breeze. Before he spoke, Liam took a moment to gaze on the wildly enthusiastic audience below. *Who needs a wife,* he thought, *when I've got all these devoted fans?*

Liam's mother and father, Queen Gertrude and King Gareth, stepped out onto the balcony behind him. They were followed by Liam's twelve-year-old sister, Princess Lila, who ran up and gave Liam a quick smooch on the cheek before retreating to the back of the balcony. Lila, who wore her chestnut hair in loose, dangly ringlets and liked to roll up the sleeves on the elegant gowns her parents forced her to wear, might have been young, but she was Liam's closest confidante—and the only person in Erinthia who appreciated Liam for his actual good deeds. Yet even she didn't know why Liam had scheduled this appearance.

The king tapped Liam on the shoulder. "We are all eager to hear your big announcement," Gareth said, hoping that Liam had decided to honeymoon in Valerium as he and the queen had suggested. The lobster rolls were so good there this time of year. "I wanted to have Tyrese here to record it all, but no one seems to know where he is at the moment."

"Don't worry about the bard, Father," Liam said. "I'll make this quick."

He faced the crowd.

"People of Erinthia," the prince said. The din of voices below hushed. "Thank you for coming out today. And thank you for all the kindness you have shown me and my family." He gestured to his parents, and the crowd erupted into applause again. As soon as the noise died down, Liam continued.

"I've got some important news about the royal wedding."

"Will there be cheesecake?" someone shouted.

"No, I'm sorry. No cheesecake. Actually—"

"Will you be taking your vows in a hot-air balloon?" another voice called out.

"No, of course not. Why would someone do that? So, about the wedding—"

"Will there be little sausages on toothpicks and a choice of dipping sauces?" yet another person yelled.

"No."

"What about cheesecake?"

"I already said there'd be no cheesecake. Look, people, please let me—"

"Will you ride up the aisle on a unicorn?"

"There's not going to be any wedding!" the prince blurted out. The entire crowd gasped in near unison, as did the king and queen. "I'm sorry. But that's what I've called you all here to tell you. The wedding is off. Princess Briar Rose and I have discussed the matter, and we've decided that we're better off just as friends." No matter how much he disliked Briar, he didn't want to bad-mouth her to his people.

As the citizenry murmured with agitation, the king skittered forward, next to his son, and addressed the crowd. "Ha-ha. Oh, that Liam. Your prince is just joshing with us all."

"No, Father, I'm not," said Liam. "I'm serious."

"I told you'd he'd eventually ruin everything," Queen Gertrude griped bitterly. "He was always too much of a Goody Two-shoes."

"Listen," said Liam. "Briar and I just aren't right for each other."

"But you love her!" the king shouted, his thick mustache fluttering as he spoke.

"No, I don't," Liam said plainly.

"You kissed her and broke the spell," the queen insisted. "True love's kiss!"

"I don't think that's how it worked," Liam said with a sigh. "I think anybody's kiss would have woken her. Besides, how could I love somebody I'd never met before?"

"Because that's just the way things work!" the king thundered. "You are marrying Briar Rose. It has been written!"

"By you," Liam said, beginning to get as angry as his

parents. "You decided everything when I was three years old. Did anybody ask *me* who I wanted to marry?"

"You don't get a choice," Gertrude snapped.

"Look: Father, Mother," Liam whispered. "Have you spent any time with her? She's not a nice person."

"Do you think I care about that?" Gareth growled. "Her family is rich beyond imagination!"

Liam was startled by his father's greedy admission. He leaned over the balcony railing and yelled out, "Sorry, people. No wedding!"

Before he knew it, the crowd was booing as loudly as they'd been cheering only a minute earlier. Shouts of "Our hero!" were replaced by jeers of "Traitor!" Liam had never known the people of Erinthia to be unhappy with him. It was like having a tank full of beloved pet goldfish suddenly turn into angry piranhas. He was confused and a bit frightened.

"You should be ashamed of yourself!" one woman cried.

"Some prince you are!" yelled one man.

"I wanted cheesecake!" wailed another.

Liam called down, "People, trust me. I am still the same hero you've always known, am I not?"

"No!" someone called out, and threw a shoe at the

prince. Soon other objects—canes, rocks, sandwiches—started hurtling up toward the balcony.

"Unbelievable," Liam muttered. "It's a riot."

A tomato smashed into King Gareth's face, leaving a splatter of red pulp in his wiry mustache. Gertrude struggled to wipe the mess from her husband's ample facial hair. "Don't hit *us*!" she scolded the angry crowd. "We *want* him to get married!"

Gertrude caught a stale dinner roll that came flying at her, and hurled it back down into the mob.

"Quick, come inside!" It was Liam's sister. She grabbed him by the hand and pulled him inside the palace.

"Lila, do you know what's going on?" he asked as the princess shut the ornate glass doors behind them. "I could always tell that our parents were excited about Avondell's riches, but I still assumed . . ."

"Apparently the money is the *only* thing Mom and Dad care about," she said. "I guess the same goes for all those people out there, too. I know they've been looking forward to a royal wedding for ages now, but . . . yikes."

"I expected disappointment," said Liam. "But for them to turn on me like this—"

"Look, as soon as things calm down, I'll speak to everyone and try to smooth this out," Lila said.

"Lila, please don't take this the wrong way," Liam said. "But you're twelve."

"I know," Lila said slyly. "Which means I can hit my awkward phase at any moment. But right now, I've still got the 'cute kid' thing going for me. It's great for winning people over. Believe me, it's the only reason I still wear my hair in these annoying ringlets that Mom likes. Anyway, look, I'll remind those people out there of all the amazing things you've done over the years. You've always been my hero. I'll make sure you're theirs again, too."

Liam had never felt closer to his sister than in that moment.

Fig. 13
Princess
LILA

"You might have a lot of work cut out for you," Liam said. "And what about Mom and Dad? I really think they're going to force me to marry Briar Rose against my will."

"I'll take care of them, too," Lila said. "Don't ask me how yet, because I'm not sure. I guess I've got to convince them that it would be worse to lose their son than to lose oodles and oodles of gold. It may take a while. In the meantime, you should take a vacation."

"Vacation? Where?"

"Outside the kingdom. Everybody in Erinthia seems pretty steamed at you right now. So, go someplace where the people only know you from the 'Sleeping Beauty' story."

"Ha! *That* story. No one outside of Erinthia even realizes I'm the hero in that story—it doesn't mention my name!"

"That's exactly what I mean," Lila said. "You can just be Prince Charming for a while. Everybody *loves* Prince Charming. Go bask in that glory for a while."

"What glory? Prince Charming isn't a hero," Liam groused. "The only thing anybody thinks Prince Charming ever did is kiss a girl and wake her up. I deserve credit for a lot more than that."

"Better to be loved for something lame than to be hated for no good reason, right?" Lila said.

Liam contemplated his sister's advice. Lila was just a kid, but she was crafty. She'd gotten herself into—and out of—all sorts of scrapes in the past. And there was definitely a logic to her plan. Liam's thought process was interrupted by a sudden bang as a roasted turkey crashed through the door, sending shards of glass and loose stuffing across the embroidered carpet.

"Someone out there has a very strong arm," Liam said.

His sister pushed him toward a stairwell that led down to the palace cellars, and the two shared a quick embrace. "People will love you again, don't worry," she said. "Now, sneak out through the cook's delivery entrance. I need to go rescue our greedy parents."

She left Liam on the top step and rushed back toward the balcony.

"Thank you, sis," Liam called. As he started down the stairs, he heard the princess yelling at the crowd of rioters outside: "All right, who threw the bird?"

Liam quietly sneaked through the cellars and into the royal stables. Since nearly everyone in the kingdom was out front by the balcony, there were no grooms or stable boys around to see him hop up onto his black stallion and take off through the palace yard's back gates.

5

PRINCE CHARMING IS THE
WORST PERSON IN THE WORLD

Liam headed toward the kingdom of Sylvaria. It was far enough away that the people there wouldn't recognize him, and it was unpopular enough (thanks to its notably eccentric ruling family) that no one was likely to go there looking for him. Unfortunately, in order to get to Sylvaria, he had to pass through Avondell, where he was greeted with taunts, jeers, and an overripe cantaloupe that splattered open on the side of his head. He assumed Briar Rose was somehow responsible for everybody hating him. And he was right. You see, Sleeping Beauty was, as Liam put it, mean. She was accustomed to getting her way— even more so than most royal children. And for that, you can blame her upbringing.

Shortly after Briar Rose was born, her parents held a party and invited a bunch of fairies (at the time, people judged how successful a party was by the number of fairies that showed up). But the royal couple forgot to invite one very evil—and very easily insulted—fairy. As payback for being snubbed, that evil fairy threatened to put a curse on the baby. The fairy couldn't curse Briar, however, if she couldn't find her. So the king and queen kept their daughter hidden away in a magically protected safe house with a personal staff that catered to her every whim. To say that Briar was spoiled would be putting it mildly. In order to make sure the girl never wanted to leave the safe house, her servants did anything she wanted. *Anything.*

When Briar Rose said she wanted to ride an elephant, for instance, members of her staff trekked across mountainous miles of wilderness to seek one out. And when they failed to locate an elephant, one poor butler was forced to paint himself gray, overeat for a month, glue a long stocking to his nose, and let the girl climb on his back. Briar wasn't stupid; she knew the man wasn't an elephant. But the notion that she could make people do such humiliating things was far more entertaining to her than riding a real elephant would have been.

Since people generally tripped over themselves to please

her, you can imagine Briar's shock and consternation when Liam became the first person to ever say no to her. She was infuriated by her fiancé's abrupt cancellation of their wedding and decided to get revenge by informing her people of how the "rude and ruthless" Prince Liam had heartlessly dumped her.

With Avondell's bard—Reynaldo, Duke of Rhyme— missing in action for weeks, the kingdom's minstrels were restless and eager for new material. So Briar Rose called them all together and gave them a juicy new story to spread. According to Briar's version of events, Liam had stormed into her palace ranting like a lunatic about the horrible taste he'd had on his lips ever since he'd kissed her. He informed her that he could never live in Avondell, since all Avondellians smelled of old potatoes. Then he spit in her milk glass, tore her portrait off the wall, and stomped on her servants' toes on his way out.

"That's great stuff, Your Highness," said one minstrel. "But not exactly a song. More like just a rant."

"So don't sing it, rant it," Briar said. "The people want news; this is what you're going to give them."

And that's just what happened. Once that story was out, the citizens of Avondell had no intention of giving Liam a chance to explain himself. Instead they just hurled insults—and food—as he rode by.

"You'd all still be asleep if it weren't for me," Liam griped as a handful of grapes bounced off his face.

"You're despicable," a woman yelled at him.

"Villain," hissed another.

"If you people had any idea what your princess was really like . . . ," Liam mumbled under his breath.

"You monster!" a disgruntled schoolteacher joined in. "Get out of our kingdom!"

"Believe me, I'm trying," Liam said. He spurred his horse to move on faster but didn't get past the mob quickly enough to avoid a hail of couscous that was flung in his direction. This was not going to blow over quickly, he realized. Liam had never felt more alone in his life. And to be completely honest, he was bummed about Briar Rose. It was an arranged marriage, so he'd never had any illusions that she would be the perfect girl for him. But he'd at least hoped he'd be able to tolerate her presence.

Liam had a bit of a romantic streak. He'd always envisioned himself sweeping some lovely maiden off her

FiG. 14
EMBARRASSMENT

feet someday. But in his dreams, his future bride was someone, well, more like himself—a bold and breathtaking woman who would join him in his thrilling exploits. She was smart and resourceful, like that Rapunzel he'd heard about, or bold and daring, like Cinderella. She sure as heck wasn't Briar Rose. But those fantasies appeared to be just as dead and gone as his days of being hero-worshipped. Liam didn't know what to do with himself. So he trotted on, hoping to get as far from "his" people as he could.

Once he reached Sylvaria, he breathed a sigh of relief— not just because he was away from hecklers, but also because the place was just so darn cute. Raccoons and chipmunks scampered among the bright and lively greenery; vibrant wildflowers sprouted up everywhere; blue jays and mockingbirds twittered from the limbs of friendly looking oaks and elms. Sylvaria was the kind of place that made you feel comfy and safe. But looks can be deceiving.

Liam hadn't gotten far into Sylvaria when he came across a trio of dwarfs cutting wood by the side of the road. They wore heavy beards and even heavier backpacks. They paid no attention to Liam as he rode up to them; they simply continued hacking at logs with their miniature hatchets.

Now, I'm going to assume you've never actually met any

Sylvarian dwarfs. They're not like other dwarfs. The dwarfs of Sylvaria are notoriously cranky. If you think about your own grouchiest moment—like, say, the angry reaction you have after stubbing your toe, shouting out in pain, and having somebody tell you, "Oh, be quiet; that didn't hurt"— that's how Sylvarian dwarfs behave when they're happy.

They're also quite persnickety. It doesn't take much to get them riled up. For example, they insist on the spelling "dwarves" instead of "dwarfs." If "wolf" becomes "wolves" and "half" becomes "halves," they argue, why doesn't "dwarf" become "dwarves"? The Sylvarian dwarfs once started a war with the Avondellian elves simply because the elves were bragging about the fact that they got to pluralize with a *V*. Prince Liam had never met any Sylvarian dwarfs either, nor was he familiar with their reputation, which is why he decided to ask this trio for directions.

"Excuse me, sirs. Could

Fig. 15
Sylvarian
DWARF

you tell me if there's an inn nearby?"

"Are you talking to us?" the first dwarf asked, barely glancing up at Liam from under his jaunty, ear-flapped cap.

"Yes," said Liam. "I'm unfamiliar with the area, and I need to find a place to rest."

"Oh, and I suppose you mistook us for a bunch of maps with legs," said the first dwarf.

"Can't you see we're busy here?" barked the second.

"Yes," said Liam. "I was just hoping you could tell me if there was an inn nearby."

"There must be an echo around here," said one of the dwarfs, and the three continued their woodwork.

"I repeated the question because I didn't get an answer," Liam snipped. He'd been in a rather foul mood to begin with, and dealing with these grouches only frustrated him further.

"You've got goop on your head," the second dwarf said.

"It's cantaloupe," Liam replied.

"Thought so," said the third dwarf. "I hate melon."

"I'm not a fan myself," Liam said. "Now, about that inn . . ."

"Oh, I'm sorry," the first dwarf sneered sarcastically, as he and the others stopped chopping. "I forgot that we're all supposed to drop what we're doing whenever a smug stranger comes up to us with a question. Who are you supposed to be, anyway?"

"For your information, I happen to be Prince—" Liam stopped himself. His anger with the dwarfs had peaked, and he was about to give them a royal shouting-down when he remembered his sister's advice about keeping a low profile. If Briar Rose's lies about him had spread into Sylvaria, the worst thing Liam could do was to tell these dwarfs his real name.

"Charming," he said through clenched teeth. "I'm Prince Charming." It pained him to say those words.

The dwarfs looked at one another, then back to Liam. "No, you're not," they said in unison.

"Honestly, I am. Maybe you've heard the story. . . ."

"Oh, we know the story," said the first dwarf. "And you're not the guy from the story."

"Really, I am," Liam said. "I kissed a cursed princess and woke her from a sleeping spell."

"Yeah, like I said, we know the story. Prince Charming did that, all right," said the first dwarf. "But that's not you."

"Why are you so insistent that I'm not Prince Charming?"

"Because we've met Prince Charming, and you're not him," the first dwarf replied. "Now get out of here and stop pretending to be someone you're not." He and his companions raised their axes in a threatening manner.

That clinches it, Liam thought. *Briar Rose has definitely gotten to these guys.* She hadn't, though. Not this time. Like I said, the dwarfs are just really cranky. But Liam left anyway.

A mile or so down the road, he found a nice quiet spot and stopped. He dismounted his horse and sat under a big oak tree to think. He used the bottom of his cape to wipe the cantaloupe mush from his hair. *How have I managed to sink this low, this fast?* he wondered. Despondent and exhausted, he fell asleep.

He was awakened some time later by a tentative voice. "Excuse me, sir?"

Still half-asleep, he squinted through his drowsy haze at two figures standing before him. One was wearing an ornate but ragged white suit that made him look like the leader of a zombie marching band. The second was twice the size of the first and appeared to be half Viking, half bear. "Hey, you!" barked the bigger of the two. "Wake up!"

Liam's eyes popped open, and he leapt to his feet, his hand going directly to the hilt of his sword. "Stay back!" he warned.

The big, armored man was unimpressed. "Do we really need this guy?" he said to his companion. "Look at him. He's wearing a cape."

The smaller man spoke up. "Sorry to startle you. We mean no harm. Are you Prince Charming, by any chance?"

"What?" The question took Liam by surprise. He kept his hand on his sword, ready to unsheathe it.

"Sleeping Beauty's Prince Charming: Is it you?"

Liam was unsure of how to answer. "Why do you ask?"

"Because we've been looking all over for you. We've come to ask for your help."

"My help?" Liam asked.

"Yes," the dirty-suited man said, while his companion glared menacingly. "We need your assistance rescuing a young maiden from a witch. You've, um, you've done that kind of thing before, right?"

"It was a *fairy*," Liam griped. "Ugh, the world would be better off without those stupid bards and their poor fact-checking."

"Aha!" the man said with a smile. "So you *are* Prince Charming."

Liam relaxed a bit. "Yes. But I hate that name."

"So do we," the stranger rushed to say. The big man grunted in agreement.

"What do you mean?" Liam asked.

"I'm a Prince Charming, too," the smaller stranger said. He pointed to his companion. "So is he. Although perhaps not so charming right now. If you'll allow us to explain . . ."

And Frederic and Gustav filled Liam in on everything that had happened to them thus far. Liam was stunned and intrigued by their tale.

"But how in the world did you find me here?" Liam asked.

"Well, we started asking around to see if anyone knew where 'Sleeping Beauty' was supposed to have taken place," Frederic explained. "One old man said Frostheim, which turned out to be *completely* wrong, so we wasted a lot of time going there. But eventually we ran into a traveling candelabra salesman who told us he was positive there was a Prince Charming in Sylvaria, so we headed here. We worked our way across pretty much the entire kingdom with no luck until we ran into a group of exceptionally rude dwarfs. When we asked them if they knew where Prince Charming was, one of them said, 'I'll tell you where he's *not*. He's definitely *not* down the road over there, because the guy who just went down the road over there is definitely *not* Prince Charming.'

"It struck us as an odd response, so we decided to look for the person they were talking about. And lo, it was you."

"Yeah, I don't know what's up with those dwarfs," Liam said. He was beginning to feel his old energy coming back. The knowledge that his heroics were being praised in far-off kingdoms invigorated him. "So where you two come from, the song about me is pretty popular?"

"About *you*?" Gustav smirked. "It's all about the girl."

"True," Liam admitted. "How does that manage to happen anyway? *I* vanquish the villain, *I* save everybody, and somehow it becomes *her* story."

"We all got the same treatment," Frederic said. "What can I say, the people love princesses. Something about the fancy dresses, I think."

"I know," Liam said. "But 'The Tale of the Sleeping Beauty'? That doesn't even sound exciting." He widened his eyes and wiggled his fingers in mock excitement. "What's that? A girl falls *asleep* in this story? Ooh, tell me more! Tell me more!"

The other men laughed, and Liam smiled. He'd never thought he'd meet other people who might understand what it was like to be a Prince Charming.

"So will you come back to Sturmhagen with us and help us rescue Ella from the witch?" Frederic asked.

Liam pretended to think about it for a few seconds, but really, there was never any doubt in his mind. A few minutes earlier, he had considered calling it quits, retiring to the mountains and trying to make a living as a goatherd. Or maybe by selling little acorn-head figurines by the side of the road. But neither of those options was very appealing. And then, as if by fate, along came two fellow princes, heroes like him (even if they seemed a tad unusual). And they offered him an epic quest, a mission to rescue a kidnapped maiden—*that* was something he could sink his teeth into. Plus, it would go a long way toward restoring his reputation as a good guy. "You came to the right prince," he said.

All three men saddled up. "There's one thing I don't understand," Liam added as they started off. "How did that candelabra salesman you met know I'd be here?"

"All I can tell you is that he said there was a Prince Charming in Sylvaria," said Frederic. "And he was right."

"It's a bit mysterious," Liam said. "Gustav, do you have any thoughts?"

"You smell like melon," said Gustav.

"Thank you," said Liam. "That was very constructive."

6

PRINCE CHARMING HAS NO SENSE OF DIRECTION

As the three princes made their way through the lively forests of Sylvaria, Liam treated the others to a thorough account of exactly how he defeated the evil fairy ("She swung to the left, I dodged to the right. She swiped high, I ducked low"). Frederic listened intently, awed by every detail. Liam was quickly becoming Frederic's new idol—and Gustav didn't like it.

"Killing fairies is no great feat," Gustav said. "I probably step on four or five of them every time I hop off my horse. But I suppose that's the biggest threat you get in a tea-and-crumpets land like Erinthia. Just wait until we get to Sturmhagen. Then you'll know what real danger is like. Giants, ogres, dog-men. The *beavers* in Sturmhagen can smack you unconscious."

"I'm not exactly looking forward to going back there," Frederic said. He motioned toward the pleasant scenery that surrounded them. "This, on the other hand, is the kind of forest I could get used to."

"You don't like Sturmhagen because a fancy-man like you can't handle a little action now and then," Gustav said.

"No argument there," Frederic agreed. "But honestly, wouldn't you rather live someplace where you could have a picnic without worrying that a troll is going to steal your petits fours?"

"You're joking, right?" Gustav replied.

"Look around, Gustav," Frederic continued. "Wouldn't you prefer these fuzzy little squirrels to ogres and goblins? I mean, I'm terrified of the very idea of ogres. The squirrels only make me mildly nervous."

Gustav shook his head. "Stop talking."

"Don't be fooled by the beauty of this place," said Liam. "This forest may hold more dangers than you might think. The woods of Erinthia can look just as serene, but one time, a few years back, I was ambushed there by bloodthirsty bandits. There were seven of them, and by all rights, I never should have made it out alive. But I noticed that the leader of these thugs had a strange twitch in his right eye—"

"Stop talking," Gustav said.

"But I haven't gotten to the best part," Liam said.

"*Stop talking*, Cape-Man!" Gustav barked. "There's someone in the bushes!"

At that moment, a man burst out from behind some nearby shrubbery. The three princes were all startled, as was the newcomer, who yelped and did a dancey little jump when he saw them. But as soon as he realized that the three men on horseback didn't seem to be criminals or monsters, he calmed down and flashed them a smile. The stranger was a slight, shortish man. He wore a velvety blue tunic with puffed cap sleeves and a frilly white ruff around his neck. The tunic was belted at the waist, so that the bottom of the garment flared out like a skirt. He had a short, green half cape on his shoulders, and a feathered green cap partly covered his wavy black hair. On his legs, he wore striped tights. Vertically striped tights. Green and blue vertically striped tights.

"Oh, hello," the man said. "I'm so happy to run into you fellows. You see, I was out for a nice walk in the woods and—heh-heh—I must have taken a wrong turn somewhere, because I got a little lost."

"How do we know you're not a bandit?" Frederic asked.

Gustav snorted. "No bandit would be caught dead dressed like that."

"Oh, you don't recognize me? You're obviously not from around here, then," the man said. "I'm Duncan, prince of this kingdom. At least I think it's this kingdom. Are we still in Sylvaria? Anyway, it's nice to meet you all."

Now, I know what you're thinking: Really? Snow White's prince just happened to wander through an enormous, miles-deep forest and bump right into the other three princes? That sounds unlikely.

But you see, unlikely things had been happening to Duncan for his entire life. When he was five, he went sledding down a large hill, veered off course, and just happened to land

Fig. 16
Prince
DUNCAN

in a giant chest of gold coins that had been lost hundreds of years earlier. When he was eleven, he got up in the middle of the night for a glass of water, accidentally tripped down a flight of steps, and just happened to bowl over a thief who was in the process of stealing the crown jewels. And then one day, while out on his daily stroll, he just happened to stumble upon a beautiful princess who'd been put under a sleeping spell. A lifetime of astonishing coincidences like these had led Duncan to believe that he possessed some sort of mystical "good luck power." He didn't, of course. Coincidences can happen to anyone, and luck is a completely random phenomenon. But Duncan truly believed *his* luck was magical.

The other thing you need to understand about Duncan—and you might have already guessed this—is that he was odd. All the princes had their issues—Frederic was easily intimidated, Liam's ego could stand to be reined in a bit, and Gustav could use some impulse control—but Duncan was flat-out strange. We all know somebody who's a bit eccentric—the girl who talks to herself, maybe, or the boy who eats the erasers off his pencils like they're gumdrops. They could be wonderful people, but thanks to their quirky behavior, they don't have the easiest time making friends. This was true of Duncan as well.

If Duncan *were* to become your friend, he would bring a lot of positive energy to your day, he'd certainly make you laugh, and he'd prove himself to be perhaps the most loyal pal you would ever have. Nobody ever got close enough to Duncan to learn this, though. His questionable fashion choices and weird habits (such as trying to play his teeth like a piano) had a way of turning people off.

One time, when Duncan was eight years old, he entered an art contest with a scribbly drawing of two stick figures kissing potatoes. Before a winner could be chosen, a freak wind blew over a candle in the royal art studio. The ensuing fire burned up every contest entry except Duncan's. And so his sketch, "Spud Love," was awarded the top prize by default. Now, Duncan realized that the other contestants might have been upset about the way things turned out, and he thought he could make them all feel better by including them in a new art project. Not a terrible idea. But Duncan—overly excitable and endlessly enthusiastic Duncan—had a knack for saying things in exactly the wrong way. He marched out of the award ceremony, holding his potato sketch over his head, and singing, "Huzzah! I am King Crayon! Follow me for more fantastic flights of artistic fancy!" Nobody followed him. Nobody invited him to any birthday parties after that, either. And with him being a prince and all, that's pretty bad.

It certainly didn't help matters that Duncan's family was just as "different" as he was. Duncan's parents, the king and queen of Sylvaria, were one of the least popular couples in their own kingdom. Their tendency to serve nothing but asparagus and kidney beans ensured that no one accepted their dinner invitations. Their court jester even quit, because the king always interrupted his acts— like spinning plates or juggling eggs—with shouts of "Ooh! Let me try that!" (and the king's attempts inevitably resulted in a throne room littered with broken dishes and splattered yolks). Duncan's sisters, Mavis and Marvella, spent most of their time painting each other's toes—not *toenails*, but toes. No exaggeration, they were a weird family.

By his early teen years, Duncan resigned himself to loneliness. Friends were something other people had, not him. He led a solitary existence for a very long time. Until the day he found Snow White in the woods. There she was, a beautiful woman lying in a glass coffin, surrounded by weeping dwarfs. Duncan startled the mourners when he appeared.

"Yikes! It's a dead girl," he blurted. "Did she eat some of those polka-dot berries my dad always warns me about?"

At first the dwarfs cursed at him for interrupting their grieving, but just as Duncan was about to go, one of them, struck with an idea, called out to him, "Wait, you're a human. We could use you."

"That's right, I *am* a human," Duncan responded with a cheery smile. "You guys are so smart." He was trying to compliment the dwarfs, in hopes of befriending them, but his innocent comment ended up sounding sarcastic.

"Gee, thanks, jerkface," the dwarf sneered. The dwarf *was* trying to be sarcastic, but Duncan didn't pick up on that.

"You're welcome," he said. "But my name is *Duncan*."

"Quit yapping, human," the dwarf barked. "Are you going to help us or not?"

"Help how?" Duncan asked. "Do you need help lifting the coffin? Because I'm not very strong. If you need some funeral music, however, I do have my flute with me."

"She's not dead, dunderhead," the dwarf said. "She's under a witch's spell."

"Then why'd you put her in a coffin?" Duncan asked. "That's pretty final, don't you think?"

One of the dwarfs raised his fist, ready to give Duncan a solid punch, but a few of the others held him back.

"The spell can be broken," said one of the more civil dwarfs.

"Okay," said Duncan. "That sounds promising. So, how do we do it?"

"Kiss her," commanded a dwarf. "We've heard about these slumber spells. They can be broken by a kiss."

"So why haven't any of you kissed her?" Duncan asked.

The dwarfs wrinkled their noses in disgust, spat, and made "yick!" noises. "No way," said one. "She's like our sister. It would be gross."

"Anyway, it wouldn't work," said the dwarf who appeared to be the leader. "It's common knowledge—not that you have any—that an evil spell can only be broken by *true love's* kiss."

"Well, *I* can't be her true love; she and I have never even met," Duncan said.

"Technicalities," the dwarf replied.

"Are you afraid? What's the matter, never kissed a girl before?" another dwarf taunted.

"Ha-ha! Oh, no, no, no. That's not it at all. How ridiculous," Duncan fake-laughed. "It's just that kissing a girl while she's asleep feels, you know, a little wrong. But hey, it's to save a life, right? And she *is* kind of cute."

"Do it!" shouted several dwarfs together.

Duncan leaned over the apple-cheeked girl, put his lips to hers, and watched her eyes flutter open. "That was awesome," he giggled.

Duncan lucked out once again: Snow White fell in love

with him. As it turned out, the two had a lot in common. They were both short. They both liked bird-watching, lanyards, and lengthy flute solos. They got married right away.

Snow White was a princess, and she was marrying a prince, so you'd imagine the royal wedding was a huge, mega-popular event, right? But barely anybody showed up. On one side of the chapel, the only guests were Duncan's parents, his sisters, and the few royal courtiers they forced to attend. On the other side were Snow White's wrinkly old father and seven stone-faced dwarfs. That's because Snow White was odd, too. And kind of a loner. Most of her life had been spent in the forest, talking to animals rather than people. She was no more popular than Duncan. Or at least that was the case until the minstrels made her a legend with the latest song from Wallace Fitzwallace, royal bard of Sylvaria.

Shortly after the wedding, "The Tale of Snow White" started making the rounds, and people from all over Sylvaria stopped by the castle, hoping to see the famous princess and her Prince Charming. Of course, as soon as they realized that the Prince Charming in question was

Fig.17
113　Snow
WHITE

Duncan, they voiced their disappointment: "You? This must be a prank. Do you realize that the word 'charming' is supposed to mean that people *like* you?"

Life had been hard enough for Duncan before, when nobody spoke to him; now that he was Prince Charming, people spoke to him about why they didn't want to speak to him.

Soon Prince Duncan and Snow White moved out of the royal castle (and away from mocking, gawking visitors) to a secluded manor in the countryside. There, Duncan let his quirkiness flow freely. He organized his toothpick collection alphabetically (they were all filed under *T*); he practiced sitting upside-down; he loudly yelled out the name of every animal that ran through their yard (not the type of animal it was, but the actual *name* he thought it should have, like "Chester," "Skippy," or "J. P. McWiggins"). Defying all odds, Snow White found him entertaining. Duncan was the first human she enjoyed spending time with.

Fig. 18
CHESTER

Even Snow White had her limits, though. She was the kind of solitary soul for

Fig. 18
SKIPPY

whom sharing a house with another person would always be something of a chore. And sharing a house with a high-energy chatterbox like Duncan often felt like living with an entire troupe of circus performers. As time went by, Snow felt cramped and crowded. Eventually, her patience wore out.

One morning, she went out into the garden by herself for some peace and solitude. Duncan followed her outside, as he always did. "I bet I can find more worms than you," he said.

Fig. 18

J. P. McWIGGINS

On a different day, Snow White might have accepted the challenge, grabbed a spoon, and started digging. But her nerves were on edge.

"No!" she exploded, and her outburst surprised both of them. "Sorry, I don't know where that came from. I think I just need a little quiet time."

"Sure thing," Duncan said. He folded his hands, looked out into the surrounding forest, rocked on his heels, and whistled.

"Um, darling?"

"Sorry." He stopped whistling, and remained silent for all of thirty seconds before shouting, "Captain Spaulding!"

Snow White was so startled she nearly fell over. "What? Who?" she gasped.

Duncan could sense the testiness in her voice, and he found it very unnerving. "That raccoon over there," he said sheepishly. "I named it Captain Spaulding."

"Look, Duncan," Snow said, taking a deep breath. "I hope you don't take this the wrong way, but the main reason I liked the dwarfs was because they barely talk to anyone."

"Okay, I get it," he said nervously. "No talking for a while. I can handle that. I'll just get my flute."

"No," Snow said. "Go do something else. Without me."

"Without you?"

"Yes. You can do things without me, you know. Go take a walk somewhere. Find some other princes to play with. Believe me, it'll do you good."

"I see," Duncan said. This was the first time Snow had ever reacted negatively toward him. It brought back all sorts of uncomfortable old emotions. He was suddenly feeling like a seven-year-old boy again, standing alone outside that clubhouse door that said NO PRINCES ALLOWED. Snow White was the only person who had ever really liked him, and he feared he was losing favor with her now, too. He was overreacting, of course, but a sensible reaction would have been greatly out of character for Duncan.

"Okay then, I'm off for a walk in the woods," he called out to her as he left, hoping that some time away from him would make her realize how much she missed his company. "I'm sure I'll have tons of fun all by myself. "

Pretending to be carefree and not at all anxious, he blew Snow a kiss and strolled out of the garden, whistling. Within twenty minutes he was hopelessly lost. Two days later, after countless miles of wandering through the woods and eating nothing but berries (but not the polka-dot ones), he happened upon Frederic, Liam, and Gustav. *My magical luck brought these men to me,* he thought happily. *Just when I was at my lowest, loneliest moment: three new friends.*

Duncan filled everyone in on his story.

"So, *you're* the Prince Charming from Sylvaria," Liam said, finally understanding that the candelabra salesman had sent Frederic and Gustav to look for Duncan, and not him.

"Sadly, yes," Duncan replied. "Most people aren't too happy about that."

"Well, here's a coincidence you're not going to believe," Frederic said.

"Try me," Duncan replied. "I believe almost everything."

Frederic, Liam, and Gustav explained to Duncan who

they were and how they came to be together. Well, Frederic and Liam did most of the talking—Gustav basically grunted and mumbled things like "We don't have time for this." Duncan became more and more animated as he listened. By the time the other princes had finished their story, he was shimmying in place.

"Do you need to, um . . . *go?*" Liam asked.

"Ha! No," Duncan burst out. "This is the most fabulous thing ever! Here we are, the four Princes Charming. All together in one place."

"Prince Charmings," said Gustav.

"No, *Princes Charming*," Duncan cheerfully corrected. "'Prince' is the noun; that's what gets pluralized. 'Charming' is an adjective; you can't add an *S* to it like that."

"It sounds stupid," Gustav said.

"Anyway, my answer is YES!" Duncan beamed.

"What was the question?" Liam asked.

"I'm coming with you," Duncan said. "To rescue Cinderella. That sounds like a *fantastic* thing to do."

"No, you're not," Gustav said bluntly.

"Yes, I'm coming," Duncan insisted.

"Are you sure?" Liam asked. "I mean, we weren't actually going to ask—"

"Absolutely," Duncan declared with a huge smile.

"This was meant to be. I'm coming with you."

"Oh, for crying out loud," Gustav moaned. "Another one with a cape? And an itty-bitty cape at that!"

"I think it's rather snazzy," said Frederic.

"Why, thank you," said Duncan. "I wanted something that I could swish over my shoulder for dramatic entrances—and yet not get caught in doors."

"All right, fine," said Liam. "We can always use another sword. Are you any good with a blade?"

"Ha!" laughed Duncan.

Liam furrowed his brow. "Is that 'Ha,' as in, 'How silly of you to ask; everyone knows I'm the best swordsman in the land'?" he asked hopefully.

"No, that was 'Ha,' as in, 'I've never even held a sword,'" Duncan answered. "But I will provide all the flute music we need. Leroy!"

The other three stared at Duncan, perplexed.

"Who's Leroy?" Frederic asked.

"Oh," Duncan said. "There's a bunny over there between those trees. He looked like a Leroy to me."

Awkward silence.

"Well, we should probably get moving," Liam said. He held his hand out to Duncan. "Hop on. You can ride with me."

"One moment, please," Duncan said. "Snow might be worrying about me, since I did, you know, vanish a few days ago. I need to get a message to her."

"Good luck with that," Gustav smirked. "You don't know where you are, remember?"

"Too true. I have no idea how to get home from here," Duncan replied. He opened up a small bag that hung at his belt and felt around inside it. "I just need a . . . ah, here we go." He pulled out a quill pen, a small piece of paper, and a tiny bottle of ink.

"You carry a desk set around with you?" Frederic asked, impressed.

"Not usually," said Duncan. "But I had this pen and ink in my bag from a few days ago when I was taking inventory of our chipmunks, and luckily, it's still in there."

Leaning his paper against the hindquarters of Liam's horse, Duncan jotted down a short note:

Dearest Snow,
You were right! Met other princes in the woods. Going with them to rescue Cinderella. See you when we get back.

Toodles, D.

"How are you going to get it to her?" Liam asked.

"I don't know," Duncan replied. He rolled the paper up and tied it tight with a blade of long grass. He tossed his little scroll on the ground and shrugged. "As I was saying before, I have magical luck. I'm just assuming this note will get to Snow somehow."

"Tell me again why we're letting this guy come with us," Gustav said.

Suddenly a robin darted out of the branches of a nearby tree, snatched the scroll up in its clawed feet, and flapped out of sight. Duncan beamed. After a few seconds, Liam said, "Well, that doesn't mean the note is going to get to Snow White, wherever she is."

"No," said Duncan, still smiling. "But you have to admit, it was pretty neat. Shall we go?" He climbed up to sit behind Liam on his horse. He sat backward at first; then Liam helped him turn around.

"Last chance to bail out," Liam said, a bit hopefully. "And no hard feelings if you do."

"Where else am I going to go?" Duncan said. "I was lost in the woods."

"Fair enough," Liam said. And the quartet set off.

"Well, I for one am happy to have you along, Duncan," Frederic chimed in. "I liked that trick with the robin."

"Pah! He's not magic, you know," Gustav said to Frederic. "All he did was give some bird a new little stick for its nest. So what? Even *you* are a better prince than he is."

Frederic's eyes widened. "Gustav, was that a compliment?"

"At least you don't wear a cape."

"So, Duncan," Liam asked, changing the subject. "You and Snow White got married, eh?"

"Oh, yes. We're happily in love," Duncan replied, not wanting his new buddies to learn that he and Snow had had any sort of tiff.

"So, you believe that myth about sleeping spells?" Liam asked. "That it needs to be a kiss from someone's true love in order to break the curse?"

"Of course not," Duncan scoffed. "Snow was a total stranger to me when I first kissed her. No, I think anybody's kiss would have worked."

"Thank you!" Liam shouted triumphantly. "That's what I've been saying all along, but nobody believes me. Will you please tell that to the stupid people of my kingdom?"

"Sure," Duncan said. "But you'll need to point out which are the stupid ones. I'd hate to get that wrong. Hey, who wants to hear me whistle the alphabet backward?"

The princes continued to chitchat as they went on through the forest, with Duncan trying to gauge how the other princes felt about him. He'd never been very good at determining whether someone was entertained or annoyed by him. But he was pretty sure he saw both Frederic and Liam smile a few times. He was going to have to work a little harder on Gustav.

As they rode along, Duncan didn't worry at all that they were heading off to do battle with a villainous witch and her giant bodyguard. He was sure that whatever happened, it would all end just fine. Because he believed he was magic. Which he wasn't.

He did, however, have an almost supernatural way of distracting people. While he blathered on about the best uses for thimbles and his favorite shape of noodle, none of the princes noticed the MISSING poster tacked to a roadside tree, the poster that bore a sketch of a man wearing a big, floppy feathered cap and holding a mandolin.

7

PRINCE CHARMING HAS NO IDEA WHAT'S GOING ON

While the four princes were setting off on their rescue mission, the damsel they planned to rescue had long since rescued herself. Here's how it went down: After the collapse of the witch's prison tower, Ella was carried across Sturmhagen in the burlap shirt pocket of Reese, the giant. Concerned for both herself and Frederic—what in the world had *he* been doing there?—she knew she had to plot an escape as soon as possible. Throughout the very bumpy (and itchy) trip, she slowly worked at pulling loose a thread that ran across the bottom of the huge pocket, thankful, for once, that her stepmother had forced her to do all of the family's sewing and mending. As she furiously unraveled the stitching, she listened to Zaubera, the witch, berate her humongous henchman.

"You clumsy oaf," Zaubera yelled from her seat on Reese's fat palm. "You klutzy doofus. You uncoordinated lummox." She'd cast the thesaurus spell on herself.

For the most part, the giant remained silent and took the abuse. But every now and again, he'd murmur, with surprisingly proper speech, "I don't appreciate the way you're speaking to me." To which Zaubera would respond, "Do you think I care? You bunglesome clodpole."

Ella wasn't fast enough to create a human-size hole in the giant's pocket before they reached Zaubera's home (giants can get pretty much anywhere quickly; they take big steps). But she had taken note of Reese's frustration with his unmannered mistress and planned to use it to her advantage.

When the giant plucked her from his shirt, Ella got a glimpse of her new surroundings. She was in the mountains, outside a tremendous fortress constructed entirely of stark black stone. Grotesque, carved granite gargoyles jutted out from every ledge and rain gutter, and the walls were crisscrossed with eerie purplish ivy. But the structure's most prominent feature was its two-hundred-foot-tall observatory tower. Topped off by a pointed, bloodred roof, the tower looked like a colossal

spear stabbing into the heavens.

Zaubera snapped her fingers, and her stronghold's huge wooden double doors swung open. The witch prodded Ella inside and directed her up ten flights of stairs (only halfway up the sky-high tower). There, Ella was locked inside a cramped room furnished with nothing more than a splintery wooden cot and threadbare blanket.

A few moments later, through her cell's lone window, Ella saw the witch emerge from the fortress. Floating behind her was a massive bubble, inside of which Ella could see a jumble of people piled upon one another. She couldn't tell who they were or even how many of them were in there; all she could really make out was a tangle of arms and legs, lots of shiny, shimmery fabric, and several oversize floppy hats.

"Stay alert, Reese," Zaubera warned. "Those two nimrods will eventually show up here for another rescue attempt. I know their types. The skinny one will have wanted to rush out for help, but the big hero will push him straight to us. I don't expect him to give us any real trouble, but just as a precaution, I figure it's best to split up the La-La Lads here, put them each in his own separate prison. At least until I'm ready for the finale."

"Sounds sensible, ma'am," Reese said.

"I don't need to remind you that you've got the most important hostage right here, Reese," Zaubera warned. "I'm going to come back here with some assistance for you."

"Oh, that's not necessary, ma'am," Reese said.

Zaubera narrowed her eyes. "Do you fear me, Reese?"

The giant's huge Adam's apple bobbed up and down. "Yes," he said.

"That was the right answer, Reese," Zaubera said. Then she curled her fingers and launched a crackling ball of energy into the giant's already injured shin. Reese's howl of pain echoed through miles of forest.

"Don't foul things up," she said as Reese crouched down to massage his scalded leg. And she left.

Ella looked at the giant. An enormous tear appeared to be welling up in the corner of his eye.

Zaubera left, with her bubble of glittery prisoners bobbing behind her as she walked. As soon as the witch was out of earshot, Ella leaned out the window and spoke to the giant at his eye level. "Why do you let her treat you like that?"

Reese flinched in surprise, causing the earth to rumble. Ella gripped the windowsill.

"Sorry about that," the giant said after the tremor

subsided. "The prisoners don't usually talk to me. Especially the famous ones."

"Famous? Oh, please, just think of me as your average, garden-variety hostage," said Ella, realizing that her captor was a bit starstruck. "But you didn't answer my question. The witch, she's terrible to you. Why don't you just—I don't know—squish her?"

"Oh, I couldn't do that, ma'am," Reese said. "That would be awfully impolite. My mother didn't raise me that way. She always told me never to hurt a lady."

"But it's okay to kidnap young women?"

"Mum never said anything specifically about kidnapping. But look, I never did hurt you now, did I?"

"No, I suppose not. As far as kidnappers go, you've been a perfect gentleman."

"Why, thank you. My mum would be proud to hear it."

"Tell me something, sir," Ella said.

"Oh, please, ma'am," the giant interrupted. "Call me Reese."

"Thank you. Tell me, Reese: Your mother sounds like a very well-mannered woman. What would she think of that witch you work for?"

"That's an interesting question." Reese scratched his head, sending huge white flakes of dandruff fluttering down like a freak snowstorm. "I think she'd certainly have some problems with her. Mostly the name-calling. Mum isn't a fan of that sort of thing."

"So how did you get hooked up with someone as rude as your boss?" Ella asked.

"Mum had been after me for quite a while to get a job, so when I saw the ad, I thought I'd go for it."

"Witches put out ads for henchmen?"

Reese nodded. "You just have to know where to look."

"Fascinating," Ella said. "So what do you do for the witch?"

Reese looked worried. "Well, it's all part of a big secret plot. So, I apologize, but I don't think I should say. At least not until I check with the witch."

"That's okay, Reese," Ella said, trying to sound as gracious as possible. "I am your prisoner, after all, stuck here with no place to go. I suppose you can tell me whenever you want."

"You bring up a good point, ma'am," the giant said. "Who are you going to tell, right? I suppose it wouldn't hurt to share a few of the details with you."

Ella smiled.

"Well, the witch has been snatching up those singing folks—the bards," Reese said.

Pennyfeather! Ella tried to mask the thrill she felt.

"She's got five of them," Reese continued. "She needed somebody to keep an eye on the prisoners while she prepares for her big finale. She calls the whole thing her Supreme Scheme for Infamy."

"So she hired you to help," Ella guessed.

"Not originally, no. Her first helper was this ogre named Grimsby, but she turned him into a smoking pile of bacon after he let one of the prisoners escape. Took the witch days to get the little singing guy back again."

"I see. That's when she hired you."

"No. After Grimsby was a pair of dog-men. But they were too easily distracted by squirrels. So . . . bacon."

"And then you?"

Fig. 19 Rejected
HENCHMEN

Reese nodded.

"So where is she putting the bards now?" Ella asked.

"In some of her other towers, I suppose," Reese said with a shrug. "She's got towers all over the place."

"Aha, so you wouldn't know exactly where those towers are, then?"

"Afraid not, ma'am. The witch'll probably hire some other guards for those fellows, anyway. I've got to stay here and watch you."

"And you're doing a spectacular job, by the way," Ella said with a curtsy.

"Why, thank you, ma'am." The giant crossed his arms and flashed Ella a big, gap-toothed smile (it's hard for giants to find a toothbrush big enough for good dental hygiene).

"So, Reese, what's this big finale I keep hearing about?"

"Ah, yes. The Grand Finale of Doom," Reese said. "The name is a bit highfalutin, but the witch insists it's going to be a massacre with *pizzazz*—her word, not mine." Ella flinched at the word "massacre." *The witch is going to kill the bards,* she thought. *With no bards, the minstrels will have no new material. What will they sing about? Where will the people get new stories? How will anyone know anything?* It was almost too unbearable an idea to contemplate.

The giant went on. "The whole thing's taking an awful lot of preparation. I was shown a diagram of what's supposed to happen, but I couldn't really understand it. It had lightning bolts and flying skulls, you name it. In one section of the sketch, it looked like the witch was shooting bears at people out of cannons. Personally, I think it's a bit much. 'Why not just drop a rock on them?' I asked. But the old lady tells me I'm not thinking big enough. 'Where's your sense of drama?' she says."

"This is very informative, Reese."

"Thank you, ma'am. I do my best to be helpful."

Aside from the bit about murdering the bards, the conversation was quite pleasant. It was so politely engaging, in fact, that it reminded her of chatting with Frederic. And the thought of Frederic put another idea in her mind— one that would aid in her escape. "But Reese, I think you could be of service in a more important way."

"What can I do for you, ma'am? You are my captive, after all, and I will do whatever I can to make your stay comfortable."

"Have you ever been inside this tower, Reese?"

"Oh, no, ma'am. I've never really seen the inside of the fortress at all. I can poke my head in through those big double doors down there, but I get stuck at the shoulders.

And considering what happened to that last tower, I don't want to chance it."

"Do you have any idea how damp and moldy it is in here?"

"Is it now?" the giant asked, sounding somewhat embarrassed. "That's terribly inhospitable. I'll have to make sure that gets cleaned up when the witch returns."

"Thank you, but I'm not sure it can wait. I'm terribly allergic to molds, you see." She tried to sound weak and woozy in the way Frederic did whenever he got a paper cut. "It's so bad in here, I'm starting to get a bit dizzy. I'm afraid I might fall and hurt myself."

"Oh, we don't want that to happen," Reese said. "You should sit down for a spell."

"There's no furniture in here. If I sit, I'll be even closer to the moist, moldy floor. No, I have to try to stand. Even though I'll probably pass out." Ella made her voice faint and quivery. "And I don't want to collapse and cause any harm to myself, because then it would be as if *you* hurt me by keeping me in here. And you're a gentleman who would never hurt a lady. Oh, I'm having such difficulty breathing."

"But what can I do, ma'am?" Reese asked, distressed by the situation.

"I'm sure some fresh air would help. Please just take me outside for a few moments."

"Oh, I can't, ma'am. The witch said—"

"The witch? The same woman who called you all those horrible names? What she says is more important than your own honor?"

"I'm sorry, ma'am. I can't."

"Look, Reese, I'm not asking you to set me free. I just need some air. You can put me back in your pocket."

"Oh," said Reese, surprised by the suggestion. "That's rather accommodating of you. Well, I suppose it is the polite thing to do." He held his open palm by the window of Ella's cell. "Go ahead, jump on."

Ella hopped through the window onto the giant's hand, and he placed her gently into the same pocket where, hours earlier, she had begun creating an escape hole.

"There you go, ma'am," Reese said. "I hope that helps."

"It's much better already, thank you," Ella replied as she immediately began tugging at the loose thread.

"I can't believe she put you in a cell that was so unwelcoming," Reese said. "I told her she ought to cast a dehumidifying spell in there."

Ella faked a big, loud yawn as she worked. "Oh, all that mold left me in such a weakened state. I'd better take a nap."

"Good thinking, ma'am," Reese said. "You rest up now. I won't bother you."

The giant sat down with his back against the tower and began humming softly. Twenty minutes later, Ella had unraveled enough thread to create a human-size hole in Reese's pocket. She quickly slipped through it, stealthily slid down the giant's big round belly, and ran off into the nearby woods, feeling exhilarated by her escape, though also a bit sad at the thought that the witch would probably turn Reese into a heaping mound of smoking bacon when she realized her most important prisoner was missing.

Reese, too, was worrying about smoking bacon mounds when he eventually peeked into his pocket and found it empty—which was why he broke the top off a nearby pine tree, carved it into a vaguely female shape, stuck some straw on it for hair, wrapped a little sheet around it for a dress, and placed it inside Ella's cell, hoping Zaubera wouldn't notice.

Ella, meanwhile, was racing through the thick, monster-filled forests of an unfamiliar country. She gave no thought to the potential dangers. There were five prison towers to find. And five people to rescue. Her heart beat rapidly, not out of fear, but with excitement.

8

PRINCE CHARMING IS AFRAID OF THE DARK

Not even Duncan's sunny disposition was enough to ward off the epic storm that broke over central Sylvaria. As torrents of heavy rain pelted them from above, the four princes galloped through the forest on unhappy horses. A new boom of thunder shook the earth every few seconds, and wild winds whipped loose tree limbs across the riders' path. In the sudden and pervasive darkness, the once cheery woodlands took on a more threatening tone.

"Up ahead!" yelled Liam, who was leading the way. "A house, just beyond those trees!"

The horses skidded to a muddy stop in front of a small cottage. It was the kind of place where you'd expect to find a little old gingham-clad grandmother stirring a pot of porridge or gruel or some other pastelike food. Frederic pointed out a small stable behind the building, and the princes led their mounts into it. The men hopped down onto the hay-strewn ground but could barely see one another in the darkness. Soon, however, there was a rustle of movement and a flash of light.

"Look what I found," Duncan said proudly, holding a lantern.

"Lucky, huh?" Frederic smiled.

"Wait, what's your game, Mini-Cape?" Gustav barked accusatorily at Duncan. "Why aren't you wet?" While the other three men were dripping, Duncan was—aside from damp leggings—noticeably dry.

"The wind blew Liam's cape over my head," Duncan offered apologetically.

Gustav grumbled something very unprincely about capes.

"Duncan, bring your lantern," he ordered. "Let's go to the main house."

The door of the cottage was open, so the princes stepped inside. The soft lantern light revealed the one-room house to be utterly empty—nothing to see but bare floorboards and the occasional dead fly.

"Plenty of space for somersaults," Duncan said.

"No beds," Frederic added glumly. "So much for finally getting a good night's sleep."

"No fireplace either," said Liam. "It's going to take a while for us to dry out."

"Wimps," Gustav muttered.

"It won't be the most comfortable place to hole up for the night, but it's better than being out in the storm," Liam said.

With a clank and a thud, Gustav plopped himself onto the floor. Liam wrung out his cape before doing the same. With a "Good night, fellow princes," Duncan blew out the lantern's flame, throwing the room into pitch blackness.

Frederic curled himself into a tight ball. "Well, it's not like this will be the first unpleasant night I've had since being on the road with you, Gustav," he said.

"That's right. We've slept in worse places," Gustav replied. "And you haven't heard me complain once, have you?"

"You complained when I wiped the gooseberries off your face," Frederic said.

"That was an invasion of my personal space," Gustav retorted.

"I'm sorry, but there was a huge glop of berries stuck to your cheek. Was I supposed to leave it there?" Frederic said. "It was like that scene from *Sir Bertram the Dainty and the Disheveled Duke* where the duke had spinach stuck between his teeth and—"

"I *love* Sir Bertram!" Duncan gushed. "Did you read the one where he had to find those lost lobster bibs before all the dinner guests reached their second course?"

"*The Mystery of the Mystical Gravy Boat*," Frederic gleefully confirmed. "That's one of my favorites."

Frederic and Duncan continued to jabber on excitedly about Sir Bertram. Neither of them had ever met another person who shared his wild enthusiasm for the dandy adventurer.

"This is going to be a long night," Gustav groaned.

"I thought you never complained," Liam said.

"Shut up, Baron von Cape," Gustav said. "Or I'll make you sleep between the two yippity-yappers."

Eventually, exhaustion won out and all four princes fell asleep.

Liam was in the middle of a dream in which the people of Erinthia were holding a "We Want You Back" carnival— women were throwing flowers to him, dancers were reenacting his battle with the evil fairy, his parents were leading the crowd in a cheer, and Briar Rose was nowhere to be seen—when he was awakened by a sudden, bright light.

"Douse that flame, Duncan, we're trying to sleep," he mumbled, his eyes still half-closed.

"I don't know who Duncan is," said the hulking, deep-voiced man holding the lit lantern. "But if he's also trespassin' in my house, I'll pound 'im the same way I'm gonna pound you."

A lean, wiry man with a beaklike nose and a thin, wispy mustache raised a second lantern. "Well, whaddaya know, Horace," the smaller stranger said in a nasal voice. "Looks like we got visitors."

The other princes began to stir.

Fig. 20
HORACE and NEVILLE

"Hold back," Liam cautioned as he stood up. "We mean no harm. If you'll let us explain—"

"Starf it all," Gustav snarled, and leapt at the beefy Horace.

"Gustav, no!" Liam shouted. "*We* are the trespassers here. We need to hear these fellows out." But Gustav was already pummeling Horace.

"A little help here, Neville?" the massive Horace requested of his companion, as he blocked Gustav's flurry of punches.

Neville, the hawk-nosed man, called over his shoulder: "Boys! Get in here!"

Suddenly eight more men—all dressed in the black garb of thieves—rushed into the room. "Bandits," Liam hissed as he reached for his sword.

"Scoop 'em up," Neville ordered, and stepped back to let his band of brigands do the dirty work. Frederic—for whom waking up was always a challenge—only managed to blearily say, "Five more minutes, Reginald," before two of the attackers had a rope around him.

Duncan jumped to his feet and began quivering with nervous excitement. "Oh, my goodness! Is this a fight?" he cried. "I've never seen a real fight before! Is this a fight?"

Two of the bandits threw a large sack over his head and yanked him down. "No, this is *not* a fight," one of them chuckled.

Meanwhile, with sword in hand, Liam was facing off against four bandits at once. The first charged him, swinging a wooden club. Liam deflected it with his blade as he kicked a second bandit into the wall. The third attacker dove at the prince's legs, but Liam jumped just in time to avoid him. As he landed boots-first on the back of the diving bandit, Liam banged the handle of his sword over the head of the man with the club, sending him to the ground as well. The fourth bandit, afraid to get too close, hurled a dagger at Liam. But the prince swung his sword and batted the knife back at the man who'd thrown it. The handle of the dagger slammed into the bandit's forehead and knocked him out.

Panting, Liam looked around the room. Frederic was quivering on the floor with his hands and feet tied together. Duncan appeared to be inside a large bag. But where was . . .

Gustav came flying through the air—tossed like a javelin by the hulking Horace. Gustav's big, armored body slammed into Liam and bowled him over. In a ball of arms and legs, the two princes looked up to see bandits surround them on all sides.

"We can take them," Gustav said, right before Horace slammed the two princes' heads together. Everything went black.

9

PRINCE CHARMING IS A WANTED MAN

It wasn't that Lila hated being a princess, but she seriously disliked the kind of princess her parents wanted her to be. King Gareth and Queen Gertrude spent years trying to groom their daughter into a Proper Young Lady, the kind of girl they could one day marry off to an excessively wealthy prince in exchange for fat sacks of gold and gems. (They had a bit of a one-track mind, those two.) But Lila had little to no interest in galas or banquets, brooches or waltzes. Whenever she didn't show up for a scheduled posture lesson, you could probably find her lying atop the high bookshelves of the royal library, where she'd climb to find a quiet place to read a book on dragon anatomy or a history of famous escape artists. On any given day, you might catch her picking the lock on her classroom window and shimmying down a trellis, in order to avoid a quiz on corsage placement. Lila's disobedience infuriated her parents, and when they had finally reached the peak of their frustration with her—after the girl skipped a ballroom dance in favor of creek walking (and at the same time, gown ruining)—they officially grounded her until marriage.

Fig. 21
LILA

It was only through the intervention of her brother, Liam, that Lila was let off the hook. Liam spoke to the king and queen on his sister's behalf, reminding them that Lila was still very young and telling them that they had to give her time to explore her many interests. Lila was different from other princesses; she was a girl who enjoyed reading alchemy textbooks, dissecting grasshoppers, and designing elaborate imp traps. "Wouldn't it be more interesting to see what kind of person Lila grows up to be," Liam asked, "than to force her into a mold that obviously doesn't fit her?"

This was long before the Wedding Cancellation Fiasco, when Liam's parents still gave a lot of weight to anything he said. They didn't completely let up on Lila's lessons, but they called off her punishment, and even let her take up some hobbies of her own choosing, like chemistry, clock making, and tree house construction.

But often, Gareth and Gertrude just forgot about Lila. Once they decided not to be constantly annoyed by her, the princess was easy to overlook. The king and queen, like almost everyone else in Erinthia, spent the majority of their time focused on Liam.

Lila was thinking about her brother—and how much she felt she owed him—as she approached the doors to Briar Rose's throne room in Avondell. The crowds back home in Erinthia simply weren't calming down. In fact, as rumors about the vicious manner in which Liam had supposedly broken off the engagement started trickling across the border, the Erinthian people started hating Liam even more. Citizens were burning capes in protest.

The only person who could set the record straight, Lila thought, was Briar Rose. So she traveled to Avondell to request her aid.

Lila had ridden alone. She assumed her parents wouldn't be keen on any plan to help Liam escape his forced wedding, so she told her mother she was going to her room to conduct an experiment that would compare the intestinal linings of several different reptiles ("I'll have plenty to eat in there, so don't expect me for dinner! Or breakfast!"). That was sure to make her parents steer clear for a few days at least.

"Would it please the young lady to make her intentions known?" asked one of a pair of stiff-backed guards.

"Yes, sure, I'm here to see Briar Rose," Lila said as she straightened the collar of her canary-yellow gown and brushed a loose ringlet of hair from in front of her eyes.

"*Princess* Briar Rose?" the guard corrected.

"Oh, yes, sorry. Princess Briar Rose," Lila said. The guard didn't move a muscle. Nor did he say anything more. He just looked at her, waiting.

"The most royal and . . . impressive Princess Briar Rose?" Lila tried. "Her Gracious Majesty Princess Briar Rose? Of the great and powerful kingdom of Avondell. She who is also known as the Sleeping Beauty of legend.

And who I hear has really nice hair?" The guard still stared at her expectantly. Lila sighed, beginning to feel like she'd failed before she even got to lay eyes on Briar. "I'm sorry, I don't know what else you're waiting for me to say."

The second guard pointed at Lila. She pointed at herself in response and raised her eyebrows questioningly. The guard nodded. Lila shrugged and shook her head; she had no idea what the man was getting at. "Announce *yourself*," he whispered.

"Oh," Lila said, standing taller. "I am Lila, princess of Erinthia and current Cross-Duchy Science Fair champ. And sister of Prince Liam of Erinthia." The first guard scowled at the mention of Liam's name. "Who I have nothing to do with, really," she quickly added. "We're related, but that's about it. This visit has nothing to do with him. Just, uh, just think of this as one princess consulting with another . . . about . . . tiaras. I would like Princess Briar's opinion on a tiara."

The second guard chuckled. "I'll announce you," he said. He entered the throne room and shut the door behind him. The first guard still looked like he had a mouthful of hot peppers and nowhere to spit them out. Lila tried not to make eye contact with him.

A second later, the friendlier guard reappeared and

said, "The princess will see you." He held the door open for Lila and gestured for her to come inside. As she stepped onto the red carpet of the marble-walled, art-filled throne room, Lila quickly rolled down the sleeves of her gown. She cringed when she saw how wrinkled the sleeves were. *Ugh, pretty messy for a proper princess,* she thought. *I've got to do this right. For Liam.*

She contemplated rolling her sleeves back up but decided it was too late: There was Briar Rose, in a boldly glitter-specked violet dress, sitting on a gem-studded, velvet-lined throne at the end of the long crimson carpet. Briar sat quietly, looking serene and contemplative (in a regal sort of way), watching Lila approach.

Well, Liam was right about her hair, Lila thought. *Very fluffy.*

When Lila was about twenty feet from the throne, the guard whispered from the corner of his mouth, "Stop there."

"Thanks," Lila whispered back. She glanced over to the guard with a look that silently asked, *Do I start?*

The guard nodded. Then he walked back out to his post and shut the door behind him.

Lila looked at Briar, offered a stiff curtsy, brushed back the loose ringlet, and began, "Oh, most noble and esteemed

Princess Briar Rose, I come seeking aid that Your Grace alone has the power to provide." *That sounded pretty good,* she thought happily.

"Dear, sweet child," Briar began, "my sister princess. Trust that your request will be given all the attention it is due." Briar Rose suddenly began laughing. It was more of a cackle, really. And quite loud. "Nothing! It is due nothing!" she screeched.

Lila took a small step back.

"You seek my aid? You want my help?" Briar scoffed, standing up and creeping toward Lila. "You? The sister of the man who betrayed and humiliated me? Why in the world do you think I would help you with anything?"

"But you haven't even heard what I wanted to ask," Lila tried to interject.

"Are you going to ask me to marry your brother, whom you've helpfully brought along with you, wrapped in chains out in the hallway? Because if it's anything else, the answer is NOOOOOOOOOOOOO!"

The force of that "no" nearly blew Lila over.

"You didn't bring him here, did you?" Briar asked, just to be sure.

"No," Lila said, trying to get her bearings. "Is this the way you acted around my brother? Because, if so, I'm kinda seeing why he didn't want to marry you."

"Your brother's a coward," Briar said, casually flipping her curls. "He's just not strong enough to handle pure, unadulterated Briar Rose. Which is exactly what I want in a husband, to tell the truth. And Liam *is* still going to be my husband."

"Well, you know, that's sorta why I came here," Lila said. "If you want any chance of still marrying my brother, you need to talk to the people out there and let them know that all those rumors about him aren't true."

"Why would I do that?" Briar said, with a laugh. "I started those rumors."

"You're awful. He was a hero, and you've ruined his reputation," Lila said angrily.

"He deserved it. And besides, he was coming dangerously close to being more popular than I was. No worries about that now. The man's a fool, though. Look what he wanted to give up." Briar gestured toward an elaborate stained-glass window. "Gorgeous, isn't it? Do you know how hard and long toddlers have to work to create something that beautiful? Oh, and—mmmmmmm, look at this." She sprinted over and lifted the silver lid from a plate on a small table next to her throne, revealing what appeared to be a miniature egg, sunny-side up.

"Endangered Sylvarian hummingbird," she announced. She popped the yolk with a long, painted fingernail and tasted it. "Ooh, it's true. That is simply the creamiest egg I've ever tasted. A shame there are only about ten left in the world."

"Coming here was a mistake," Lila muttered. Briar was obviously not open to negotiations. "I'll show myself out." She started toward the exit.

"Oh, no you don't, you little brat," Briar said. "You're not walking out on me the same way your good-for-nothing brother did." Briar marched toward Lila, but the younger princess had already dashed back out into the hall.

"Thanks, guys," Lila blurted as she tore past the dumbstruck guards and zipped out of the palace.

"Where is she?" Briar seethed when she reached the doorway and saw no sign of the girl. The two guards both started babbling, not sure of the best way to answer. "Never mind," Briar said. "I need to start being proactive here, or this wedding's never going to happen. Get me Ruffian the Blue."

Ten minutes later, after dodging several armed guards outside the palace, slinking behind a row of animal-shaped shrubbery, and scaling the tall neck of a giraffe-shaped hedge, Lila crouched on the sill of a window outside Briar's throne room. She inched the stained-glass casement window open and peered inside to see Briar speaking to a sour-faced man in a dark hooded cloak: Ruffian the Blue, noted to be the best bounty hunter in all the land. When it came to tracking people down and capturing them, there really was no one better. Ruffian wasn't the most sociable person, though. When he got started in the manhunting business, he wanted to call himself Ruffian the Black or Ruffian the Red, either of which had a nice intimidating sound. But Ruffian was kind of a depressing guy. And his reputation for being sad and mopey all the time got people calling him Ruffian the Blue.

". . . obviously never going to come back of his own accord," Briar was saying.

"I'll bring him to you," the man said in a flat, gloomy voice.

"Of course you will, genius," Briar snarked. "That's why I'm paying you."

Fig. 22.
RUFFIAN
the BLUE

"There's no need to be sarcastic," Ruffian said.

"Hey, if you don't want the job, I'm sure there are a hundred other bounty hunters out there who'll take it." Briar tossed a cherry into her mouth, chomped it, and spit the pit at the man. It bounced off his chest. He watched it roll across the floor.

"That was unnecessary," he said with a sniffle. "I said I'd get him."

"Stop whining and start prince-hunting, all right?"

"I'm going," the bounty hunter droned. He took a deep breath and exhaled slowly. With his head down, he shuffled out of the room.

Briar turned to a guard, who stood behind her. "That's Ruffian the Blue?" she asked. "Are we sure we got the right guy?"

The guard nodded.

"What a moaner," Briar griped.

Outside, Lila hopped down from the windowsill. She scurried to the front of the castle and watched from behind a lamppost as Ruffian the Blue mounted his dark gray steed and rode off. *There's only one way for me to warn Liam,* Lila said to herself. *I've got to follow the creepy hooded guy.*

10

PRINCE CHARMING ANNOYS THE KING

The morning after their abduction from the bandit hideout in Sylvaria, the four Princes Charming awoke inside a dusty, drafty jail cell. There were no cots or mattresses, just a cold stone floor caked with the grime of prisoners past. Liam's sword, Gustav's ax, and Duncan's flute were nowhere to be seen.

Liam, as usual, was the first to snap out of his haze. He surveyed his groggy companions with dismay. Their performance during the previous night's fight did not inspire confidence. *But we were taken by surprise; people were half-asleep,* he rationalized. *Everybody has a bad night now and then. I'm sure that's all it was.*

"Wake up, people," Liam said. "We've been captured."

"Oh, dear," moaned Frederic. "What have I gotten myself into?"

"I was just wondering the same thing," Liam muttered.

"I have to say, I'm a bit disappointed," Duncan said as he stretched his stiff arms and legs. "My very first fight, and it was over so quickly."

"We could fight right now if you'd like," said Gustav, standing up and glaring at Duncan.

"Save it for the bad guys," Liam interjected. He jumped to his feet and peered through the cell's one tiny barred window. "The first thing we need to do is figure out where we are."

"What's to figure out? We're in prison." Frederic sighed. Then, as his own words sank in, he gasped. "Oh, dear. I'm in prison. Prison! And I thought that inn that smelled like onions was bad."

"Yes, we're in a prison, but where *is* this prison?" said Liam. "Let's see, we're about three stories up. I see thick pine forests out there, and mountaintops beyond the trees to the north. One peak is very distinct—it's almost curved and comes to a sharp point at the summit. And I think that might be the spire of a tower to the south of the mountain, but it's hard to tell."

"Does it really make a difference what kingdom we're

Fig. 23
Mount BATWING

in, if we're locked behind these bars?" Frederic asked, despondent. He was beginning to believe he'd never see Ella again. Or dear Reginald. Or his father, who had apparently been right about everything. *I survived an attack by a witch and a giant,* he thought. *Why didn't I quit while I was ahead? I should have just sent Liam to rescue Ella. I don't belong here. I belong back home at the palace. In a bubble bath.*

Frederic was startled out of his self-pitying daydreams when Gustav shoved him aside in a rush to reach the window.

"This is fantastic!" Gustav announced.

"You and I must have different definitions of 'fantastic,'" said Frederic.

"That curvy mountaintop out there—that's Mount Batwing!" Gustav burst out. "We're in Sturmhagen!"

"Are you sure?" asked Liam.

"I've seen that peak a thousand times. It's pretty hard to miss," Gustav said. "We're *definitely* in Sturmhagen."

Liam breathed a sigh of relief. Perhaps he hadn't failed his companions after all. "So those bandits did us a favor and carried us exactly where we wanted to go."

"You're welcome!" exclaimed Duncan.

"You did nothing." Gustav scowled at him.

"It's just a lucky break is all I'm saying," Duncan said. "However we got here, we're here—and that's a good thing, no? I've always wanted to visit Sturmhagen. Hey, Gustav, don't you Sturmhageners have a big zucchini festival this time of year? I'm a big fan of the zukes."

"Duncan, we're still in prison," Frederic said dryly. "You're not going to see anything except this cell. Which has spiders, by the way. Have you noticed the spiders?"

"Indeed I have: Carmen, Zippy, and Dr. T," Duncan said.

Gustav glanced back out the window toward Mount Batwing. Something big was moving around at the base of the mountain, causing the trees to shift and sway. And sticking out above the highest branches—was that . . . a head? Gustav got his answer to that question when he saw a giant hand rise up and scratch vigorously at the enormous scalp.

"Hey, Cape-Face. Check this out," Gustav said.

But before Liam had a chance to rejoin Gustav at the window, the princes were distracted by the sound of footsteps along the corridor outside their cell. Neville and Horace stopped and eyed them smugly through the bars. Eyeing smugly was something the pair excelled in. They'd actually shared the title of Best Smug Eyers in their graduating class at bandit school.

"So, which of these blokes did you say you recognized, Horace?" Neville asked his burly companion.

"That long-haired piker by the window there," Horace said, pointing his boxy chin at Gustav. "He's a member of the royal family here in Sturmhagen, I know it. I seen 'im there a little while ago, while I was staking out the castle for our big you-know-what."

"Well, well, we caught ourselves a prince," Neville said with a cackle. "The boss is gonna like that, Horace, old mate. Looks like you and me are movin' up in this organization." Then, to Gustav, he added, "I don't know what you was doin' in our hideout back in Sylvaria, Yer

Highness, but many thanks. Do you know the kinda ransom we're gonna get for *you*? A real prince?"

"Ransom?" Gustav snapped back. "What you're going to get is the full force of Sturmhagen's army at your doorstep. And Erinthia's army. And Sylvaria's and Harmonia's."

Liam shook his head, mumbling, "*Why* did you just say that?"

"Sylvaria? Harmonia? Wait a minute. What am I missing here?" Neville asked. He could tell the big prisoner had just let something slip.

"Nothing!" Frederic jumped up. "He's just very bad at geography. Can't even remember which country he's from."

"There are four of 'em," Horace mused. "Maybe one of 'em's from each of those kingdoms."

"But the kings of those places wouldn't send armies for just anybody," Neville said.

"My dad certainly wouldn't," Duncan piped up. "Sylvaria doesn't even have an army."

Horace laughed. "Neville, I think we captured ourselves *four* princes."

"You're jumping to the wrong conclusion," Liam said desperately.

"Save yer breath, *Yer Highness*," snickered Neville. "Yer pal already gave you away. Come on, Horace, let's go tell the boss we gots *four* princes for him."

"Who's this boss you keep mentioning?" Liam asked.

"Our boss? Oh, I'd wager you heard of 'im. His name is Deeb Rauber," Horace said as he and Neville began to walk away. "But you probably know 'im as—"

"The Bandit King," Liam finished, with a groan. "We've been captured by the Bandit King. This is not good."

All four men's faces fell. Everyone knew about the Bandit King, whose army of thieves and thugs terrorized every land from mountain to seashore. The Bandit King and his men would heist art treasures from a royal museum just as readily as they would swipe the last loaf of bread from a family of beggars. But as vile and nasty as any of his henchmen were, Deeb Rauber himself was far worse. His wickedness was legendary. At the age of six, young Deeb locked his parents in a cupboard, filled his pockets with every piece of gold the family had ever earned, and ran off to become a professional thief.

Two years later, when he was still only eight, Deeb Rauber stole the royal jewels of Valerium by kicking the country's 103-year-old king in the belly and then snatching the crown right off the elderly monarch's head as he doubled over in pain. The boy became so infamous for this heinous act that grown men—some of the worst criminals in the land—looked to him as their leader and signed on to follow him. More recently, Deeb Rauber had led his army of thieves on a crime spree across seven kingdoms. No heist was too big or too small: One day he'd steal the giant bells from the towers of five different cathedrals, and the next he'd pluck a rag doll from the hands of a crying toddler. Villages were sometimes left without a single coin when Deeb Rauber passed through. It was because of these diabolical acts and more that he earned the title the Bandit King. And that name sent a deathly chill through the veins of anyone who heard it. The princes were no exception.

A few moments later, a contingent of armed guards showed up. They removed the princes from their cell, chained them all together at the waist, and led them to meet the Bandit King. As the princes shuffled along like a big eight-legged caterpillar, scuffing up an intricate hand-woven carpet that was probably worth a fortune in itself, they passed tons of stolen loot: grand hanging tapestries, gilt-framed oil paintings, and lifelike marble busts.

On a normal day, Frederic would have been enraptured

by the presence of such masterpieces. But today he barely noticed them. The last on the chain, Frederic leaned past Gustav to whisper to Liam, "You're going to save us, right, Liam?"

"Hel-*lo*. Am I invisible?" Gustav said.

Duncan, from the front of the line, answered for Liam: "Oh, Liam will save us, all right. And it will be *awesome*."

"It will not be *awesome*, Duncan," Frederic snapped, finding Duncan's positivity too much to take at that moment. "Look around. Nothing about this is *awesome*."

"Ha! No need to get upset," Duncan said. "We're all friends here. I mean, we were having a grand old time yesterday. Remember when that owl scared you off your horse? Good times. I don't mean to be critical, but you've become a bit of a sourpuss ever since we got captured by these evil bandits."

"Do you even listen to the words that come out of your own mouth?" Gustav snarked at Duncan. "Why did you come with us, anyway?"

"I thought it would be fun," Duncan said, and immediately regretted that answer. "Anyway, I think I can help. I've got a few tricks up my sleeves."

"Well, you've got no muscles, so there *is* plenty of room up there," said Gustav.

"Gustav, you're not helping," Frederic admonished.

"Don't act like you're my father, Cinderella Man," Gustav sniped.

Liam shushed the others. "Look, all of you, we're in far too serious a situation for all this petty bickering," he said sternly. "Follow my lead and I will get us out of this."

A thick wooden door was thrown open at the end of the hallway, allowing the princes and their guards to enter a gigantic room littered wall-to-wall with gold coins, glistening jewels, and other assorted treasures. It was perhaps the biggest stash of loot in the history of thievery. The princes' eyes all widened a bit—not just at the sight of all these mountains of riches, but also at the hundred or so armed thugs who stood, scowling, among them.

At the center of it all was a fur-lined golden throne, upon which sat Deeb Rauber, the Bandit King. He slouched back in his very expensive seat, one booted foot hooked over the arm of the throne. Aside from the oversize crown that sat, lopsided, on top of his head, the Bandit King was dressed plainly in a well-worn gray shirt, black vest, and dark blue pants. His dirty black hair jutted out messily from under the crown. His right eye squinted at the princes (the left was covered by a red leather eye patch). But the most striking thing about the Bandit King, by far, was his age. Deeb Rauber was ten years old.

"You're a child!" Gustav blurted.

"Well, that's a surprise," Duncan said. "I mean, I heard a story about the Bandit King's exploits as a young boy, but I thought it was, you know, much older. The story, I mean. Well, and you, too."

"You're a child!" Gustav repeated.

"Unbelievable," Liam muttered.

The Bandit King's squinty eye got squintier. "It seems our guests don't understand the difference between being young and being a child," he said coolly. "One's age is but a number. No matter how many years you've lived, it is your deeds that earn you respect. So there!" The boy then stuck out his tongue and blew a sloppy raspberry at his captives, much to the delight of his men.

"My friends are just very impressed!" Frederic shouted, taking a stab at diplomacy

FiS 24
The BANDIT KING

before his companions said anything they would regret. "We've heard about your many accomplishments, and we assumed you must have been further along in years. Your youth is a testament to your skill."

"Spoken like a true prince," the Bandit King said. "Yes, I know who you are. All of you." He turned to Neville and Horace, who were standing next to his throne. "You two were right. Four princes. You'll be very happy with your reward."

"I think you've mistaken us for another group of men, sir," said Liam. "We are just travelers who happened to—"

"You," the Bandit King cut in, "are Prince Liam of Erinthia. I know this, because I've robbed you. I've robbed all of you. Liam, your father's cherished sword, the jewel-encrusted one that had been passed down through twenty generations of the Erinthian royal family, the one that went missing last year—I stole it."

Liam looked like he'd been punched.

"Prince Duncan of Sylvaria," the Bandit King went on. "Remember how the hallway outside your royal library used to be lined with priceless paintings by the greatest artists of the land? They're all hanging in my outhouse now."

"That must be a big outhouse," Duncan said.

Fig. 25 SPOONS

"It is," Deeb Rauber went on. "And Prince Frederic, my silver-tongued friend from Harmonia, I bet you miss your collection of spoons from around the world."

"You beast," Frederic whispered.

"And Gustav," Rauber continued. "Gustav, Gustav, Gustav. Have you not even noticed I'm sitting on *your mother's* throne?"

Gustav clenched his fists and lurched toward the Bandit King, but was held back by guards—not to mention the chains that bound him to the other princes.

"Fine," said Liam. "So you know who we are. What do you want from us?"

The Bandit King threw his arms up and rolled his eyes. "Jeez, how slow are you people? Money! I want ransoms from your very, very, very rich families. I'm sure they will all pay dearly to make sure their precious sons are returned to them safely. Or would you have me believe your parents don't want you back?"

"What about *your* parents?" Frederic asked. "How do

you think your parents feel about the life you've chosen for yourself? What would your parents say to you today?"

"I know what they'd say," the Bandit King tittered. "They'd say, 'Help! Let us out! We've been locked in this cupboard for years!'" All the goons around him burst into laughter.

Frederic pursed his lips and nodded, not saying another word.

"Seriously, though," Rauber said, wiping a tear from his eye. "What did you fools think I was going to do with you? I'm the Bandit King. I've got a reputation to keep up. And getting four princes from four different kingdoms all in one cozy little cell is quite a coup, wouldn't you say? I can't wait to hear the next bard song about me."

"Lousy bards . . ." Liam muttered, mostly to himself. He looked up at Rauber. "How is it that all four of us here know who you are? Why does everyone know your name and no one knows ours? Why do the bards give you so much attention?"

"I'm *bad*, Liam," Rauber said as if it were the most obvious answer in the world. "Fear and loathing: That's what sells. If you want real respect, switch sides."

"You disgust me, Rauber," Liam spat.

"Call me Your Highness," the Bandit King demanded.

"I am royalty within these walls. In fact, based on what I hear, I've got more loyal subjects than you do right now. The people of Erinthia aren't very happy with you, are they?"

"How do you know all these things?" Liam asked, dumbfounded.

"I've got spies everywhere, Liam," Rauber said. "I'm very well informed."

Liam got an idea. He cleared his throat. "Well then, *Your Highness*, why don't you prove yourself worthy of all those followers? Face me in a duel. Just you and me. If I win, the four of us go free; if you win, we tell our kingdoms to hand over whatever riches you demand."

"Are you kidding?" Rauber asked. He made a fart noise with his mouth and pretended to wave away a bad odor. "Why in the world would I want to do that? You're twice my size; you'd beat me in no time. I'm evil, not stupid. Guards, take them back to their cells. Oh, and chop off their feet so they don't try to run away."

Liam was once again at a loss for words.

"Wait, what about me?" Duncan interjected. "I'm several inches shorter than Liam, the only exercise I get is running from bees, and I've never used a sword before in my life. What if you duel me instead?"

"Have you lost your mind?" Liam and Frederic both hissed.

"Don't worry," Duncan whispered. "Things like this tend to work out in my favor."

"You know what?" the Bandit King said. "Why not? That sounds like it might be fun. Let's do it." Roaring cheers rose from his followers.

"Brilliant," said Duncan. "And you'll free us all if I win?"

"No, of course not," Rauber replied. "You four are my prisoners, and that's not going to change until I get ridiculous amounts of money from your families. But I'll fight you anyway. Just for kicks. I won't kill you, of course, because I can't get a ransom if you're dead. But I think the boys here would enjoy seeing you lose a body part or two." The Bandit King started bouncing excitedly in his seat. "Ooh, and you know what else? Hey, Liam, I'm going to use your dad's sword to chop up your friend."

Duncan swallowed hard. He had an unfamiliar wobbly feeling in his stomach. Was that doubt? *No, no,* he told himself. *My magical luck will come through for me.* (Except he didn't have any magical luck.) *And besides, the risk is worth it. This will be a fantastic way to impress my new friends.*

"That's a rather fetching eye patch, by the way," he said to the king.

"Thanks," said Rauber, removing the patch and winking at Duncan with the left eye it had been covering. "Both of my eyes are actually fine; I was just wearing the patch to look scary. Okay, guards, take them away and get Prince Duncan prepped for the duel."

"On the roof, as usual?" Horace asked his boss.

"That's right," Rauber answered. "Hey, I've got an idea. Neville, why don't we ask the old lady if we can borrow one of those music men. I'd like to have this moment immortalized in song."

"Um, that was a joke, right, sir?" Neville asked with an anxious gulp. "You don't really want me to, you know, talk to 'er. Not like face-to-face or anythin'. Do ya?"

Rauber was silent for a second, during which Neville's forehead beaded with sweat.

"Nah, her place is too far from here," Rauber finally said. "I don't want to wait that long. Hey, Duncan. You had a flute with you when you got brought in here; you must have a bit of musical talent. Compose a song about your own dismemberment. But make it simple—something my doofus henchmen can remember."

Duncan was intrigued. "Ooh, I've never written a song

before." He beamed. He started humming as he and the other princes were dragged from the room in chains.

"That was odd," Liam whispered to the others as they went. "Who's the old lady Rauber was talking about?"

"His mother?" Gustav guessed. "Doesn't matter. We need to figure out how to get out of here."

"No, his mother was locked in—," Liam started to say.

"His mother is really of no concern," Frederic interjected. "We're going to be hobbled. Do you know what that means? No feet. I'm a dancer, people. *A dancer.*"

They're right, Liam thought. *We don't have time to parse out every word the Bandit King utters. There are more pressing issues at the moment. Like Duncan's impending demise.*

11

Prince Charming
Takes a Dive

The rooftop level of the Bandit King's castle had been constructed as a convenient spot from which the robbers could spill boiling oil down onto anyone who tried to break into their headquarters, but it also served as a nice place to have duels and, occasionally, to sunbathe. It was up there, with his loyal followers cheering from the sidelines, that Deeb Rauber prepared to slice and dice Prince Duncan.

Guards led the four princes, still chained to one another, from a lookout tower onto the stony rooftop. The army of bandits hissed and booed until the king raised his hand to hush them. He danced out into the center of the courtyard, waving around the most fabulous sword anybody there had ever seen. From handle to tip, the blade was encrusted with diamonds, emeralds, rubies, and sapphires. The weapon sparkled and shimmered like a sky full of fireworks. This was the legendary Sword of Erinthia. Liam gritted his teeth when he saw it and made a silent vow that he would get the sword back to his family someday. *But my first priority is to make sure that fool Duncan doesn't get himself killed,* he thought. *It's just one thing after another, isn't it? Being a hero can be so frustrating sometimes.*

Duncan's head was buzzing with adrenaline as he watched the Bandit King strut around, showing off for his followers. Duncan knew that the ten-year-old boy was soon going to stop playing around and start attacking him with that beautiful, deadly sword, and he wondered exactly how his magical luck was going to save him. One of the guards unlocked Duncan's chains, separated him from the other princes, and pushed him out into the sunny, open center of the courtyard to face the Bandit King.

Fig. 26
The SWORD
of ERINTHIA

"How's the song coming along?" Rauber asked.

"I'm thinking it can start with something like this,"

Duncan answered, and sang, "The Bandit King took Prince Duncan up to his roof. He planned to chop-chop him, and that is the troof!"

"That's terrible," Rauber said.

"Sorry. First-timer," Duncan said. "Maybe it would be better if I work on it after the duel. That way, I'll know how it ends."

"Oh, we all know how it's going to end," Rauber said with a grin. He tossed the Sword of Erinthia back and forth from hand to hand. "Ready to get hurt?"

"Would it matter if I said no?" Duncan asked.

"Nuh-uh," Rauber smirked, shaking his head. He giggled as he sliced zigzags in the air.

"Don't I get a sword, too?" Duncan asked. "I mean, you did say this was going to be a duel, not just a butchering."

"Oh, yes, of course," the Bandit King said. "Never let it be said that the Bandit King is anything but fair. Horace, let the prince borrow your weapon."

Horace stepped out of the crowd, lugging a huge two-handed sword. The blade was six feet long and weighed more than Duncan did.

Duncan let out a nervous laugh. "You know, a smaller one would be just fine." His luck was taking its sweet time to show itself. He honestly thought it would have gotten him out of this situation already, and he hoped the magic hadn't gone on vacation or something.

The next few seconds seemed to occur in slow motion. Horace tossed the enormous sword in Duncan's direction. The mocking laughter of a hundred bandits echoed in Duncan's ears as the blade flew toward him. He reached out and—surprising even himself—caught the hilt of the sword in his hands. However, Duncan was not a terribly strong man. To him, catching the sword was like being hit with a cannonball. Unable to stop the momentum of the heavy weapon, Duncan staggered backward uncontrollably—and tumbled off the edge of the roof.

That was when Liam sprang into action. He dove to save his falling companion and managed to grab hold of his ankles. But Duncan kept falling, taking Liam with him. Gustav and Frederic, still chained to Liam, yelped as they were whipped off their feet and went sailing over the castle wall with the others.

The bandits' laughter came to an abrupt stop.

"My princes!" the Bandit King screamed. He turned on Horace and Neville. "You imbeciles cost me my royal ransoms! Forget your rewards—you're about to be punished worse than I've ever punished anyone before!"

"But I didn't do anything!" protested Neville. Horace

unsuccessfully tried to hide his massive frame behind his skinny partner.

Meanwhile, many yards below, the four princes thrashed wildly as they dangled in the air. The pointed tip of Horace's sword had gotten stuck—wedged between two stones in the castle wall—and Duncan was clinging ferociously to its handle. Below him hung Liam (still gripping Duncan's ankles), Gustav, and Frederic—all connected at the waist by their prison chains.

"I can't hold on," Duncan said through gritted teeth. "I wasn't exaggerating about my lack of exercise."

"Just let go," Liam said.

"What?" Frederic yelled up to him. "Let go? Are you mad?"

"Frederic, look down," Liam said.

Frederic glanced down. His toes were a mere six inches from the ground. "Oh."

So Duncan released his grip, and the four men fell to the swampy, rain-soaked lawn below. They landed in a heap on top of one another. Duncan, aside from sore fingers, was completely unharmed. He climbed off the pile of princes, feeling pretty good about himself, and said, "Well, that was lucky."

"I don't want to hear the *L* word, Dr. Delusional,"

Gustav warned. He then pulled Frederic out of the thick, gooey mud. "You okay?" he asked.

"I'll survive," Frederic replied. "Thanks for asking."

"Hey, I just want to make sure you're not going to slow me down," Gustav said.

"Quick, let's get out of here before one of them is smart enough to look over the edge and see that we're not dead," said Liam.

"Where did those fiends put our horses?" Gustav grumbled, looking around.

"There's no time. We've got to make a run for it," said Liam. "It's not like we could ride in these chains, anyway." The four men started off down the hill, away from the Bandit King's castle, as fast as their feet would carry them.

"So . . . where are we . . . heading next?" Duncan panted.

Gustav, who was chained between Liam and Frederic, caused the others to stumble as he sprinted forward to the head of the pack. "Follow me," he yelled.

"No offense, Gustav," Frederic said, "but you've gotten us lost before. Do you know where you're going?"

Gustav smirked. "Yes, Captain Tassels, I know where we're going. Mount Batwing."

"Might we ask why?" Liam queried.

"I spotted our friend, the giant, there."

12

PRINCE CHARMING HUGS TREES

Whuddawedonow?"

"Huh?" Gustav grunted, as he and Liam clipped along through the woods, all but dragging Frederic behind them. Duncan, free of the chains, was plodding by himself several yards back.

"Whawadoo, whuwedow?" the out-of-breath Frederic tried again. He sounded like an asthmatic cat trapped inside an accordion.

"Gustav, hold up for a minute," Liam said as the trio lurched to a stop. "We're far enough from Rauber's castle. And I think our companions could use a break."

"I'm good," Duncan said cheerily as he jogged to catch up to the others. "The mud is a little hard on my felt boots, but it makes a pleasant squishy noise when I step. It reminds me of the bog walks that Snow and I take sometimes. A bog might not sound like the kind of place you want to spend a lot of time in—and the smell would back up that assumption—but when it comes to examining mosses—"

"Pipe down, Nature Boy," Gustav interrupted. "The Wheezing Wonder here is trying to say something."

Frederic had collapsed facedown in a pile of fallen leaves. He lifted his head and spit out a pinecone. "What do we do now?" he sighed.

"First order of business, we get rid of these chains," Liam said.

"What are we waiting for?" asked Gustav. He picked up a large stone and smashed it against the chain that hung between himself and Liam. But the big rock didn't break the metal links; it pulled the chain to the ground, yanking Gustav and Liam into each other violently.

Frederic shook his head. "Oh, come now. Even *I* know that's not how you do it," he said. "You've got to rest the chain on one rock while you hit it with another. It's just like what Sir Bertram did with the fob of a pocket watch in *The Secret of the Sinister Snuff Box*. Duncan, help me look for more rocks."

On his hands and knees, Frederic turned and pushed

aside the branches of a nearby shrub. He didn't see any stones, but he did see six eyes staring at him from behind the bush.

"Monster!" Frederic shrieked, and then—with more speed than he thought he possessed—he jumped to his feet and started running. Liam and Gustav were jerked into action alongside him. The three princes had no choice but to splash as one through the muddy forest.

"Why are we running?" Gustav shouted, leaping over a fallen tree limb in his path. "Let me go back and fight it!"

"Where is Duncan?" Liam yelled as he ducked one branch after another. "He's not with us!"

But fear is a powerful fuel, and Frederic's tank was fully loaded. He didn't even hear the others.

As the trio ran between a pair of thin pines, Gustav and Liam each grabbed hold of a tree trunk and pulled themselves to a halt. The sudden stop whipped Frederic off his feet, landing him on his back with a splat.

"Is the monster gone? Where's Duncan?" he cried. He saw the others glaring at him and realized for the first time that he'd ditched one of his friends. "Oh, I am so ashamed."

He scrambled to his feet, and they all rushed back to look for Duncan. But when they reached the site of Frederic's freak-out, there was no sign of the Sylvarian prince.

"The monster got him," Gustav said.

"What kind of creature was it?" Liam asked.

"I don't know," Frederic said. "I just saw eyes. Six of them."

Liam turned angrily on Frederic. "How could you leave Duncan behind? I realize you're new to this, but you never turn your back on an ally in danger."

"I know that," Frederic moaned. "Do you understand how terrible I feel about this?"

"Yeah, back off, hero," Gustav cautioned Liam. "It's obvious the guy feels awful about it."

"Yes, please don't be so hard on Frederic," Duncan said as he popped out from behind some trees, followed by a trio of grimacing dwarfs. "These fellows can be pretty scary sometimes."

Frederic collapsed into the mud again.

"Duncan, you're all right!" Liam shouted.

"Sorry if I gave you all a fright," Duncan said. "When you guys ran off, I started to follow you, but then I glanced back and saw *these guys* coming out from behind the bushes, so I had to go say hello. Fellow princes, please allow me to introduce you to some friends of mine: Flik, Frak, and Frank."

"We've met," said Frank, the largest of the three

dwarfs. Of course, "large" is a relative term when you're talking about dwarfs. He still only came up to Duncan's waist. "And we're not exactly *friends* of Prince Charming here. We're friends of his wife."

Liam looked curiously at the three bearded dwarfs, each sporting a hefty backpack and jaunty ear-flapped cap. "You're the dwarfs who were so rude to me back in Sylvaria," he said.

"Dwarves," Frank corrected.

"That's right," added Gustav. "Crumpet Boy and I met you three grumps there, too."

"I am so embarrassed," Frederic mumbled to no one in particular, as he realized there had never been any monster in the bushes. "Six eyes; three dwarfs."

"Dwarves," Frank corrected.

"How did you come to be here in Sturmhagen?" Liam asked.

"You three sounded like a bunch of weirdos with all your strange Prince Charming questions," Frank said, glaring at the men. "We were suspicious, so we followed you. And then we saw Duncan the Daring get involved with you guys."

"Duncan the *Daring*?" Gustav laughed. "You're being sarcastic, right?"

"Yes," Frank said humorlessly. "Anyway, we're not particularly fond of Duncan, but we care a lot about Snow White, and she seems to like him for some reason. So when we saw you guys get carted away by those bandits, we decided to stay on your trail to make sure Prince Pipsqueak didn't get himself killed or anything."

"You were watching when the bandits caught us?" Duncan asked, incredulous. "Why didn't you help us?"

"What do I look like? Your mother?" Frank snapped.

"Let's not worry about what anybody did or didn't do back then," Liam said. "Can you three help us *now*? We need to remove these chains."

"Dwarves are *expert* metalsmiths," Frank said, showing his first hint of a smile. "Chains are not a problem for us."

Flik, Frak, and Frank formed a little circle, and each of them dug into the backpack of the dwarf in front of him. They plucked out mallets and chisels, darted over to the princes, and whacked away at the chains with jackhammer speed. In a matter of seconds, the heavy metal links fell into the mud with a wet thunk.

"I've seen faster," Gustav mumbled.

"Show me how, Frank! Show me how!" Duncan tittered excitedly.

"How many times do I have to tell you no, Duncan?" Frank said sternly.

"Just because I'm not a dwarf?"

"That's exactly why."

Frederic, newly freed, threw his arms around Flik and Frak in an appreciative embrace. The two shocked dwarfs quickly pushed him off. "You're filthy, man," said Flik. "Show a little respect."

"So, have you overheard enough of our conversations to understand what we plan to do?" Liam asked Frank. "Are you aware that we're on a quest to rescue Cinderella?"

"Yeah, we get the gist of it."

"Will you join us?" Liam asked. He then leaned over and added in a whisper, "You've seen what I'm dealing with here. I need all the help I can get."

"No kidding. The boys and I have already talked about it," Frank said. "And we've decided you guys are far too pitiful for us to just stand back and watch anymore. So, yeah, we'll tag along. We've got to keep an eye on the Death-Defying Duncan, anyway."

Duncan rushed over. "No, no, no," he protested. "I forbid it. You fellows are not coming with us."

"You can't be serious," Frederic blurted. "They're willing to help us and you're telling them not to? Are you completely out of your—"

Liam held up a hand to hush Frederic. "What I think Frederic is trying to ask," he said, "is: Why would you send the dwarfs away?"

"I have a more important mission for this brave and worthy trio," Duncan said. He squatted down by the

Fig. 27
DUNCAN and FRANK

dwarfs and spoke to them directly. "There is something I need you to do, my friends."

"Stand up, Duncan," Frank scolded. "You know we hate it when you squat to talk to us. It's insulting."

Duncan stood up. "Sorry, sorry. Anyway, you three are

the only ones who know how to get back to my estate in Sylvaria."

"Yeah," said Frank. "Dwarves are *expert* navigators."

"Yes, and perhaps if you'd been willing to teach me any of those skills, I wouldn't have gotten lost," Duncan said.

"You're not a dwarf."

"Well, anyway, use your navigating talents to guide you back home," Duncan said. "And make sure Snow knows that I'm okay. She's probably been worried sick about me."

"Are you sure you want them to do that?" Liam asked. "I really think they'd be more helpful sticking with us."

"I don't like it, either," Frank said. "I don't know if I can trust these 'princes' to look after you." He made air quotes around the word "princes."

"Frank," Duncan said, putting on his most stern and serious face—which still wasn't very convincing—"I am the prince of your land. And this is not a request. It is a command. You will go back to Sylvaria and inform Snow White of my whereabouts. And give her this twig I found—it looks like a pony, see?"

"Fine," Frank grumbled, as he grabbed the stick. "There's no way I can stay around here, anyway. I can't bear watching you pretend to have leadership qualities. Come on, boys, we're outta here."

"Wait," said Liam. "If you really must go"—he looked hard at Duncan—"can I ask one more favor first?"

"What is it?" Frank asked impatiently.

"Do you have any weapons in those packs of yours? We can't fight a witch and a giant barehanded and expect to win."

Frank rolled his eyes. "You guys are unbelievable. Yeah, you can take our swords. They should do you fine: Dwarves are *expert* weapon makers."

As Liam thanked them, the dwarfs fished four swords out of their backpacks and handed one to each of the princes.

"They're eensy-weensy!" Gustav exclaimed. The swords, sized for dwarfs, were each only a foot long.

"Hey, buddy," Flik snarled. "You got a problem with dwarves?"

"I didn't before today," Gustav snarled back.

"The swords are great," Frederic said, slumping against a tree. "Enjoy your trip home. Even though I can't believe you're going home."

"Yes, thanks," Liam added.

FiG. 28
Dwarven
SWORD

"Don't get killed too fast," Frank said. Then he and the other dwarfs vanished into the woods.

"Seriously, how are we supposed to fight with these things?" Gustav griped.

"I have no complaints. This is a much better size for me than the last sword I tried to use," Duncan said.

"Look, these swords may be on the short side, but they're sturdy and sharp," Liam said. "I think we'll find ourselves very grateful for these weapons. Dwarfs are famous for their skills at the forge."

"Yeah, apparently dwarfs are famous for everything," Gustav muttered, shaking his head.

"Well, I guess we should move on," Liam said, sliding the miniature sword into the much larger sheath that hung from his belt.

"Sorry, I'm still kind of reeling from the fact that we sent the dwarfs away," Frederic said, somewhat testily. "What were you thinking, Duncan? You don't quite understand that going up against Zaubera will be incredibly dangerous, do you? You should be terrified. But you're acting like you're heading out to buy new tights or something."

"I know it's dangerous! That's why I sent the dwarfs away—to keep them safe," Duncan lied.

"And what about us?" Frederic said, aghast. "You're

fine if one of us dies?"

"Well, it sounds awful when you put it that way," Duncan replied.

"And you wonder why you don't have many friends," Frederic said sharply.

The remark struck a nerve.

"Well, you were the one who ran away when you thought the dwarfs were going to eat me!" Duncan exclaimed.

"I didn't think the dwarfs were going to eat you," Frederic retorted. "I thought the dwarfs were a *monster* that was going to eat *me*!"

"Enough!" Liam shouted. "We're never going to help Cinderella if we're fighting among ourselves."

"Aw, why'd you have to break it up?" Gustav said with a smirk. "I was enjoying that."

Frederic and Duncan both looked at their feet sheepishly.

"Duncan," Liam said, "why didn't you leave with the dwarfs?"

"Well, because you guys came back," Duncan said. "In my whole life, no one who has run away from me has ever come back."

Liam turned to Frederic. "Are you still mad at him?"

Frederic shook his head and blubbered a soppy "No."

"Good," said Liam. "Now let's move."

Frederic raised his hand.

"Frederic, do you, uh, have a question?" Liam asked.

Frederic sniffled and nodded. "I don't know how to use a sword."

"Oh, that's right," Duncan said. "Neither do I."

"Go team," Gustav said in a mock cheer.

"Look, men, we don't have time for fencing lessons right now," Liam said. "Just hold your weapon by the handle and swing it at the bad guys. Besides, if everything goes according to my plan, you two will only need to provide a distraction. You should never have to actually fight anyone."

Frederic raised his hand.

"You don't need to keep raising your hand, Frederic," Liam sighed.

"Sorry," Frederic said, although he kept his hand in the air. "Um, I just wanted to ask: What exactly is your plan?"

"Don't worry about it now," Liam said. To be honest, he hadn't factored the others into his plan much. He was used to working alone. He figured *he* would be the one to sneak past the giant, scale the wall of the prison, free the girl, and duel the witch if necessary. The others only needed to hang out in the shrubs and distract the giant with

some birdcalls. But something told Liam that these guys—
especially Gustav—wouldn't be satisfied with such a small
role in the mission, so he put off telling them anything.
"When we get to Zaubera's hideout, just do what I tell you
to do," he said.

Duncan raised his hand.

"What, Duncan? What?" Liam huffed.

"Where do I put the sword when I'm not using it?"
Duncan asked.

"In your belt," Liam said.

"But what if I stab myself in the leg?"

This is going to be a disaster, Liam thought.

He was right.

13

Prince Charming Is Completely Unnecessary

Lila was relieved when Ruffian the Blue stopped for a snack break. She was starving. She'd been following the bounty hunter for days, and the man barely ever rested. Every now and then, Ruffian would stop to investigate some tracks or interrogate a frightened farmer, but never long enough for Lila to scout out some food of her own. She felt grateful that at least he was a sloppy eater; she eagerly snapped up every bread crust or half-eaten apple that Ruffian left behind. But scraps like that were all she'd had since she left Briar Rose's palace.

Lila hopped down from her horse and watched from several yards away as the bounty hunter started to untie his food pack. She closed her eyes and imagined him pulling out a huge chocolate cake. She pictured him eating one small piece, deciding it was too rich, and leaving the rest on a tree stump. With a fork. Mmm, fudgey.

"Why are you following me?"

Lila's eyes popped open as soon as she heard the slow, mournful voice of Ruffian the Blue. The bounty hunter was standing right in front of her. How had he managed to get that close without her hearing? Lila let out a short gasp and darted toward her horse.

"Aw, do you have to run?" Ruffian whimpered. He grabbed a small pebble and flung it. Before the girl could reach her horse, the rock stung the animal's backside and sent it galloping off wildly.

"My horse!" Lila cried with a mixture of fear and anger. She turned to see Ruffian advancing on her. With his hood on, most of the bounty hunter's face was in shadow. All Lila

Fig. 29
LILA, IN PURSUIT

could see was his frowning mouth and pouty lower lip.

"*You're* annoyed?" Ruffian moaned. "Do you think this is how I wanted to spend my snack break?"

Lila ran. She dashed down the dirt road as fast as she could, grateful that she was not wearing the high-heeled glass slippers her mother had picked out for her. There was no noise behind her, and she thought for one happy moment that she'd managed to lose Ruffian. But then she heard the rapid clopping of hoofbeats. He was chasing her on horseback. There was no way she could outrun him now.

Lila stopped and climbed the nearest tree. Ruffian halted his horse directly underneath her. "Really?" the hooded man sighed. "Do you have to make this difficult?"

He reached up, trying to grab hold of Lila's leg. She leapt nimbly to the next tree over. Ruffian sighed and drooped in his saddle. "Kids," he complained. He nudged his horse a few feet down the road until he was under Lila again. She leapt to another tree.

"This isn't funny," Ruffian whined. He trotted another three feet and reached up for Lila once more. She jumped to the next tree.

Perching precariously on her narrow pine branch, Lila watched as Ruffian reached into a pouch at his waist. She gulped and almost lost her balance when she saw him pull out a glistening dagger. *Oh no,* she thought. Escaping from grumpy parents and absentminded tutors had not adequately prepared her for evading professional bounty hunters.

She glanced at the next closest tree, but it seemed too far off to reach with one jump. Ruffian took aim and hurled the knife. Frozen with fear, Lila watched the blade arc toward her. *His trajectory is off—it's going to miss me,* she told herself. She held her breath and prayed she was right.

She was. But the dagger hadn't actually been aimed at her. Ruffian's big knife was planted deep into the branch below her, and it was enough to snap that slim tree limb in half.

Lila felt the branch disappear from under her feet, and she tumbled down with it. She landed right in the arms of Ruffian the Blue. "I don't like children," the bounty hunter said.

"Not a surprise," Lila returned. She reached up and yanked the hood down over Ruffian's eyes. It was a slight distraction, but enough to allow the girl to slip down onto the ground and run off again.

"Aww," Ruffian moaned. He took off after her at a heavy gallop.

Lila sped, panting, around a curve in the road. *I can't keep this up,* she thought. Suddenly a pair of hands were upon her, one covering her mouth, preventing her from shrieking. The stranger who'd grabbed Lila hastily pulled her inside the dark, moist recess of a hollow tree. "Shh— I'm a good guy," a female voice whispered in her ear.

Lila and the stranger both remained absolutely still as they listened to Ruffian pound around the curve and continue speeding down the road. Within seconds the bounty hunter was far past them, most likely wondering how Lila had managed to vanish.

The stranger took Lila by the hand and led her back out into the light. Lila got her first good look at the person who had saved her. The woman was probably around the same age as Liam. Her hair was pinned back, and she was wearing a ragged blue dress. She was grinning with the same kind of wild exuberance Lila had felt when she'd won the Cross-Duchy Science Fair.

"You looked like you needed help," her rescuer said.

"Good call," Lila said, still a bit wary of this enthusiastic stranger. "Thanks."

"I'm Ella."

"Lila. Nice to meet you."

"I have been having the craziest couple of days," Ella

said. "Are you hungry?"

"Starving," Lila said, and then quickly wondered whether it had been wise to answer honestly.

"Sit down, catch your breath," Ella said. From a small sack, she produced hunks of bread and cheese that she handed over to Lila.

"Thank you." Lila sniffed the food: No telltale almondlike odor to hint at poison. Of course, there were odorless poisons, too. But she was just so darn hungry. Lila nibbled a bit of the cheese. It tasted better than the fudgiest chocolate cake she'd ever had. She took another, much larger bite. Ella offered her a flask of water to wash it down.

"Wow, thanks again," Lila said.

"No problem," Ella said. "This food and the water, I got it as a reward of sorts, I guess. I came across this little, tiny guy—the size of my hand."

"A gnome?" Lila asked.

"Uh, sure, maybe."

"Pointy hat?"   Fig. 30 GNOME

Ella nodded.

"Gnome," Lila confirmed with satisfaction. She ripped off a chunk of delicious crusty bread with her teeth.

"Okay, so yeah, a gnome," Ella continued. "And he was being beaten up by these two purply looking things with big noses and sort of bat wings—"

"Imps," Lila said.

Fig. 31 IMP

"I'll take your word for it," Ella said.

Lila smiled. "You don't get out much, do you?"

"Not until recently, no," Ella said. "But anyway, I could tell the little guy—the gnome—needed assistance, so I kicked those purple things into the river. The gnome gave me the meal as a thank-you."

"Wow, so you took on a couple of imps without even knowing what they were," Lila said, impressed. "Because imps are poisonous, you know."

"I did not know that," Ella said as a chill rushed through her. "But it will be good to keep in mind for the future. Do you want more bread?"

"Oh, no, thanks. I don't want to take the last of your food. I'm good. Really."

Lila and Ella eyed each other with a mix of curiosity and admiration.

"So what's the deal with Scary Hood Man?" Ella asked.

"Why is he chasing down a kid?"

"That's Ruffian the Blue. The notorious bounty hunter," Lila said. "He's actually after my brother. I'm trying to get ahead of Ruffian to warn him."

"That certainly sounds important," Ella said. "But I'm on a pretty important mission myself. And believe it or not, I was going to ask if you would help me. I need someone to get word to . . . well, I don't know—a king, an army? Just . . . help. There's this witch who lives at a place called Mount Batwing. She kidnapped me, and I got away, but she also has the royal bards from five different kingdoms. She's going to kill them all in front of an audience."

"Wow, you were not exaggerating. That *is* big. And that must be where Tyrese the Tuneful is." Lila brushed the dangly loose ringlet from her eyes as she pondered Ella's request. Could she really say no to a plea for help like this? There was no question which choice Liam would make. "Well, I haven't mentioned this yet, but my dad happens to be the king of Erinthia. Getting him to send an army after our bard shouldn't be too difficult. Although I'll definitely be grounded. I wonder if they've even noticed I'm gone yet."

"Does that mean you'll do it?" Ella asked hopefully. "I know you wouldn't be able to catch up to that Blue guy, but you'd be saving five lives. Not to mention the only source of entertainment for thousands of otherwise very bored people. I'd go myself, but I'm trying to find the towers that the witch put the bards in. And also, I don't really know where I am."

"Did you say towers?" Lila asked excitedly. "When I was following Ruffian, we went by this strange tower a few miles back. It was all by itself in this little meadow. Nothing else around it."

"Lila," Ella said, putting her hands on the younger girl's shoulders. "Can you take me to this tower?"

"Grab your cheese, and let's go."

14

PRINCE CHARMING FALLS FLAT

Woo-wee! That's a biggie!" Duncan shouted.

Liam quickly clamped his hand over Duncan's mouth and shushed him. They were barely a spear's throw from Zaubera's stronghold and its colossal, cloud-skimming tower.

"Sorry," Duncan whispered. "But it's *really* tall."

The four princes found hiding spots among the rock outcroppings at the base of Mount Batwing, from which they could safely monitor the big stone fortress and the meadow in which it sat.

"Is that the tallest building in Sturmhagen? It has to be, right?" Duncan asked, still mesmerized.

"Technically, we're not in Sturmhagen anymore,"

Gustav said. "As soon as we crossed to this side of Mount Batwing, we were in the Orphaned Wastes. It's a no-man's-land, a dead zone. No kingdom will claim it."

"Funny," said Duncan. "I wouldn't expect a place called the Orphaned Wastes to have such a lush lawn."

"Are those bleachers?" Frederic asked as he spotted a semicircle of raised wooden benches that sat on the lawn facing the fortress.

"I wouldn't have expected a witch's hideout to have grandstand seating," Duncan said.

"That certainly is odd," Liam said. "I wonder what she's up to."

"Well, at least we know how to get inside," Frederic added, pointing to the enormous double doors.

"You could drive a herd of elephants through those doors," said Duncan. "Why do you think they're so huge? For the giant?"

"No," said Liam. "I'm pretty sure the witch makes *him* sleep outside." He pointed off to the left of the fortress, where Reese was snoozing on the ground. Frederic gasped.

"That's him!" Frederic squeaked.

"Yes, I figured," said Liam.

"Wow, he's big, too," Duncan said in amazement. "I

mean, I know they call them *giants*, but I always thought, 'How big could they *really* be?'"

"Keep it together, Duncan," Liam cautioned. "Now, everybody listen. It's time to put my plan into action. It's all the better that the giant is asleep. That will make things much easier. I'm heading over to the fortress. You three distract the giant if he—"

But before he could finish, Gustav sprinted into the meadow with his sword drawn. "Wake up, giant!" he yelled. "We've come for the girl!"

"You've got to be kidding me," Liam grumbled.

Reese opened his eyes and spotted the charging Gustav just in time to swat at him. His enormous palm smacked into Gustav and sent him flying over the bleachers. He landed in the trees with a crash.

"Oh, dear," said Frederic. "He's dead already."

"No, look!" shouted Duncan, pointing. Gustav burst back out of the forest, roaring and running straight at the giant again. Reese scrambled to his feet and stared in astonishment at his attacker.

"Wait a minute, is this the same stupid little human who poked me in the foot a few weeks ago?" he bellowed.

"Yes, it is!" shouted Gustav. "And now I've come back to poke the rest of you!"

"He has to work on his battle talk," Duncan whispered to Frederic.

The giant kicked his foot into Gustav's chest and sent him careening backward yet again—but not before Gustav had jabbed his sword into an oversize big toe. Gustav sat on the grass, waiting for the giant to howl in pain. But it never happened.

Reese looked down at his pricked toe and wiggled it around. "Why did you stick me with a toothpick?" he asked.

Gustav turned toward the boulders that hid his companions and raged, "I told you these swords were too small!"

Reese was perplexed, wondering why his little attacker was yelling at a bunch of rocks. He became even more confused when he saw Gustav stare at his tiny sword, scream, "I hate you!" at it, and then start charging at him once again.

Liam knew he had to act fast. "Okay, I guess we need a plan B."

"You never finished telling us plan A," Frederic said nervously.

"You two go help Gustav," Liam ordered. "I'm going inside to find Cinderella. Keep the giant busy until I get back out with her."

Frederic and Duncan both opened their mouths to object, but Liam was gone before they could get a word out. When they heard a loud thump, they turned just in time to see Gustav land flat on his back for the third (or was it the fourth?) time.

"What should we do?" Frederic asked.

"Keep the giant busy, I suppose," Duncan said.

"Absolutely," Frederic agreed. "Gustav's in trouble, and I can't abandon one of my allies again."

"That's the spirit! Lead the way," Duncan encouraged. After a few seconds, he added, "You're not moving."

"No, I'm not, am I?" Frederic whimpered. "I'm scared. I can't do this. The giant will flatten me. And I don't want to be flat. Don't you understand? This is not what I was made for."

"That's okay. I do understand. Really," Duncan said earnestly. "I'll go do it. I am totally going to show these guys that they should keep me as their friend. Forget that last part, though—I didn't mean to say that out loud."

And with that, he marched out into the meadow.

Reese had Gustav by the legs and was pounding him down onto the grass as if he were beating a rug, when he heard Duncan call out, "Yoo-hoo! Giant! Over here!"

Reese looked over at Duncan, who stood there, hands

on hips, trying to look imposing and threatening (which is to say, he looked kind of silly).

"Yes, that's right, giant, down here," Duncan said. "I'm afraid I'm going to have to ask you to put my friend down. You see, *I've* got a little sword, too. No, not *little*. I didn't mean to say *little*—just *sword*. I've got a sword, too. Dwarven steel. I hear it's good. So anyway, um, prepare for your doom!" Duncan drew his sword, and in doing so, managed to slice his belt in half. It fell to the ground and his tunic puffed out, flowing loose like a nightgown. "Oh, drat."

The giant laughed. Gustav took advantage of his foe's momentary distraction, biting down hard on Reese's thumb. With a yip of pain, the giant dropped Gustav.

"Now!" Gustav shouted as he tumbled to the ground. "Get him now!"

"Get him how?" Duncan asked. He looked at the sword in his hand. Unsure of what he should do, he tossed his weapon at the giant. The sword flipped through the air a couple of times and landed softly on the grass only a few feet away.

"That was the most pathetic thing I've ever seen," said Gustav.

Duncan stepped forward to retrieve his sword, tripped

over his belt, hit his head on a rock, and knocked himself out cold.

"I spoke too soon," said Gustav. "*That* was the most pathetic thing I've ever seen."

"Duncan!" Frederic hollered, rushing out into the open.

"Another one?" Reese griped.

"What are you doing out here, Tassels?" Gustav said. "Get back behind the rocks!"

The giant took one huge step toward Frederic, bending over in an attempt to scoop the prince up. Gustav tried to stop him. Jabbing Reese with his sword was useless, so he tried a long, hard, slicing blow along the arch of the giant's foot. *That* Reese felt.

"Ow!" the giant hollered. "I have *got* to get some footwear!" He hopped onto one foot, stumbled, and fell, just as he'd done once before. This time, however, the giant did not topple into the nearby tower.

This time, he landed directly on top of Frederic.

15

PRINCE CHARMING SHOULD NOT BE LEFT UNSUPERVISED

Back in Sylvaria, Snow White was thoroughly enjoying the peace and quiet.

Out in the vast yard of her woodland estate, she kicked off her bow-tipped shoes, loosened the laces on her bow-bedecked teal bodice, and let her bow-trimmed skirt billow around her as she fell backward into the thick, cushiony grass. Flat on her back, she stared up at clouds and tree branches and giggled with contentment. This was how she'd spent much of her childhood.

She smiled at a flock of geese passing overhead, then turned her head to look at a curious bunny that approached her and sniffed at her hair. No one yelled out a strange name for the rabbit.

"Hello, little one," Snow whispered as the bunny's long whiskers tickled her cheek. She took a deep breath and sighed.

Snow rolled over onto her belly and rested her chin in her hands to watch a bluebird land on the carved wooden bench that sat by her garden wall.

"Hello, Thursday Bird," Snow greeted it. "Back again like clockwork."

She hummed a tune as she plucked blades of grass and began to weave them together into a little square. Chances are that square would have eventually become a potholder (she'd made *thousands* of them), but we'll never know for sure, because Snow White stopped when she suddenly realized something terrible.

"Thursday Bird?" she gulped, dropping her weaving project and hopping anxiously to her feet. "Wait—you can't be Thursday Bird, can you? Because I just saw Sunday Bird splashing in the birdbath right after Duncan left."

FIG. 32 BIRDS of the WEEK

MONDAY   TUESDAY   WEDNESDAY

But this was definitely Thursday Bird. She made sure by sticking her face startlingly close to the poor little thing—and getting an angry peck in return. Stepping back and rubbing her sore nose, Snow began to fret. Thursday Bird had never been off its schedule before.

She tried to think. How many sunsets had she watched since Duncan left? There was the first one, when she thought to herself how pleasant it was to watch the moon rise without accompanying flute music. And there was the one when she saw the flying kitten that might have really just been a bat. And the windy one. And the one where she remembered thinking that nothing happened, but that that was a good thing.

"Oh, dear," Snow exclaimed. "Duncan's been gone for five days!"

She began to pace back and forth, clapping her hands together nervously. He was only going for a walk, she thought. Walks shouldn't take five days. How could she

THURSDAY   FRIDAY   SATURDAY   SUNDAY

not have realized that so much time had passed?

In truth, it wasn't out of character for Snow White to be so absentminded. She was a simple girl who enjoyed simple pleasures. Most of her life had been spent happily alone, admiring shrubbery and chuckling at wildlife. Without Duncan's manic energy stealing her focus, Snow easily slid back into that quiet, solitary state—and managed to lose track of her husband.

Now she was worried. While Snow loved Duncan, she had no more faith in his abilities than anyone else. She pictured all manner of strange and awful things that might have happened to him out there on his own. He might have climbed onto the roof of a house and not known how to get down. He might have tried to count the teeth in the mouth of a sleeping wolf. He could have passed out somewhere after trying to see if he could hold his breath and count to a million. With Duncan, the possibilities for calamity were endless.

Snow waved her fist angrily in the air. "Where are you, Monday Bird? Why didn't you warn me when the first day had passed?"

Just then she heard approaching footsteps. Her heart leapt. She ran to the garden gate.

"Duncan!"

"No, it's us," said Frank the dwarf, as he, Flik, and Frak entered Snow White's yard. Snow slumped miserably when she saw them.

"Thanks for the enthusiastic welcome," Frank said.

"Sorry, I don't mean to be rude," she said drearily. "You know I'm always happy to see you fellows. But I was really hoping you were Duncan. He's been missing for five days."

"Jeez, has it been that long?" Flik asked grumpily. "No wonder I'm tired."

"What do you mean?" Snow asked. "You know he's missing?"

"Don't worry," Frank said. "We've been watching out for him. And if we really thought those bandits were going to kill him, we would have done something about it."

"Bandits!" Snow was aghast. "What bandits?"

"I don't know," Frank said with a shrug. "Just some bandits. They're gone now. And they didn't kill him. So what's the big deal?"

"Where is Duncan now?" Snow demanded. She was beginning to get irritated.

"The Idiot Prince didn't want to come back with us," Frank replied gruffly.

"Hey," Snow said. "You know I don't like it when you call him the Idiot Prince."

"Sorry," said Frank. "The Idiot didn't want to come back with us."

Snow bent over and pressed her forehead against Frank's. "Enough with the insults," she said with a quiet intensity that shook the normally unflappable dwarf.

"O-okay," he muttered. Beads of sweat ran down his forehead and pooled at the tip of his bulbous nose. Flik and Frak tried to subtly inch away.

"Where is Duncan *now*?" Snow growled.

"Sturmhagen. He's with a bunch of other guys who all call themselves Prince Charming," Frank said. "They're planning to rescue Cinderella from some witch's tower or something."

"Prince Charming rescuing Cinderella from a witch's tower?" Snow repeated, backing off a bit. "What, are they doing a reenactment? I think they're getting their stories mixed up."

"No, this is for real. Real Cinderella, real witch."

"Duncan will be killed," Snow said. "I can't believe you three left him there."

"He ordered us to go," Frank explained. "He thought it was most important for us to get word to you about where he was. And to give you this stick." He handed Snow the odd twig he'd gotten from Duncan. "He thought it looked like a pony."

Snow was flabbergasted. "I can't believe you listened to him. The man has no sense!"

"But—"

"Listen, I love Duncan dearly, but he *cannot* be left unsupervised," Snow said. "What was he thinking? Storming a tower? Facing a witch? And this stick is *obviously* shaped like a *cat*."

"Um, I hate to say this," Frank mumbled. "But I think they mentioned something about a giant, too."

Snow was breathing in and out in short, rapid bursts of air, her normally pale white cheeks now pinker than the dwarfs had ever seen. Then, quite suddenly, she regained control of herself. She stood up tall and straight, stared icily at the dwarfs, and cleared her throat. She calmly slipped her feet back into her shoes.

"Gentlemen, get my wagon ready," she said authoritatively. "You're taking me to Duncan."

In earlier times, the meek and quiet Snow White would never have been so demanding. But there was something about living with Duncan that brought out the ferociousness in her.

16

PRINCE CHARMING MEETS A PIECE OF WOOD

In order to make sure she'd be taken seriously as a villain, Zaubera had carefully noted the props and set pieces that appeared in every famous witch story she'd heard—cobwebs, broomsticks, jars of dried dead things—and then proceeded to fill her headquarters with as much of that stuff as she could find. Her stronghold was so cluttered with these bits of highly unoriginal witch decor that Liam had to be careful not to trip over a pumpkin or bump into a basket of poisoned apples as he snuck along the winding stone corridors.

Wall-mounted torches cast dancing shadows all about Liam as he dashed from floor to floor, peeking into one empty prison cell after another. Finally, on the tenth story, he peered through the small barred window of one wooden cell door and spotted a figure leaning up against the wall.

Liam rammed his shoulder against the door, busted it open, and charged into the cell.

"I'm Liam of Erinthia. I'm here to rescue you," he announced triumphantly. He then added, with less enthusiasm, "And you are not Cinderella. You are a tree branch wrapped in a sheet."

But how? he wondered as he paced the small cell. There was no sign of a struggle, nothing broken, no evidence of an escape tunnel, and the door had been locked. There was only one possible exit Cinderella could have used: the window. *Gutsy move,* Liam thought, impressed that the girl had freed herself, if a bit disappointed that there was nobody for him to rescue.

He walked over to the window to see

Fig. 33
NOT ELLA

how far down it was to the ground, assuming Ella must have climbed, jumped, or somehow soared to freedom. From there, he got a perfect view of Duncan cutting his own belt off. "Cripes. Never mind the girl—I have to rescue *those guys*."

Liam retraced his steps back downstairs. Or at least he tried to. The interior of Zaubera's fortress was far more mazelike than he'd recalled, and he soon began wondering if he was on the right path. Many of the rooms were nearly identical.

"Okay, this is the room with the cauldron," he said to himself. "So those stairs over there should lead down to the room with the skeleton on the wall."

He darted down the steps.

"Crud," he sputtered. "This one's got a cauldron, too. How many cauldrons does one witch need?"

He ran like this, from corridor to room to staircase, until he turned a corner and found himself in a chamber that was stocked floor to ceiling with maps. There were framed maps hanging on walls, rolled maps sticking out of barrels, flat maps displayed on easels, and a huge map suspended by hooks overhead.

"I definitely didn't pass through here before," Liam said. He turned to dash back out of the room but stopped when one particular map caught his attention. It sat unrolled on a large desk with an open bottle of red ink and a still-wet feather quill lying next to it, as if it had been recently marked up. At its center, the map showed Zaubera's enormous fortress, right at the foot of Mount Batwing. Southeast of that, the picture of a small tower was scratched out.

"That must be the tower the giant knocked down," Liam said. "But what are all these others?" Several more towers were marked on the map, each in a different area of the surrounding forests and mountains. Scrawled beneath five of them was the word *prisoner*.

"Oh, this is excellent. There are *more* prisoners," Liam murmured as a delighted awe washed over him. "This isn't over yet."

He rolled up the map and took it with him as he ran out to renew his search for the exit. At the end of the hall, he spotted a familiar-looking staircase and darted down to what he was pretty sure was the ground floor.

Aha! he said to himself. *That chandelier was the first thing I saw when I came in.* The large wrought-iron fixture suspended above the center of the room must have held seventy or eighty lit candles, but even so, it wasn't bright enough to properly light a room so large. Liam rushed across the chamber, toward the exit. He hurtled past shelves lined with voodoo dolls and dead ravens. Past cabinets loaded with crystal balls. Past a life-size stuffed dragon. *Hmm,* Liam thought, *don't know how I managed to miss* that *before.*

That was when the steam-spouting red dragon—which wasn't stuffed with anything other than the yak meat it had eaten for lunch—lurched forward and snapped its gigantic jaws at Liam. He dove to the side just in time and instinctively reached for his sword. Unfortunately, in doing so, he lost his grip on the map.

As the parchment fell from Liam's hand, the dragon's big claw swatted it up into the air, where it unrolled and hovered kitelike above them. Liam jumped for the fluttering map, but the dragon whomped its tail hard against the floor, creating a gust of wind that sent the flying paper sailing across the cavernous chamber—over tables arrayed with beakers of glowing green liquids, past a dangling mobile of mummified monkey hands, and finally into a corner so dark and distant that it was practically in another kingdom.

"Oh, give me a break," Liam yelled, and stomped his foot in anger. "Why is there a dragon here? Nobody mentioned a dragon!"

The dragon breathed out another whiff of flame, and Liam crouched behind some crates labeled EYE OF NEWT. The dragon darted its head forward and chomped through the crates, crushing them and sending an avalanche of tiny eyeballs spilling out onto the floor. Liam threw himself back against the wall. The beast snapped again. Liam spun to avoid those deadly jaws and took a stab at the dragon's head with his dwarven sword. The monster was quicker than he expected, and it deftly bit down onto Liam's blade.

"Hey, give that back!" Liam shouted as he tried to tug the weapon free. But the dragon wrestled the sword from his hand and spit it into another far-off corner of the chamber. Weaponless, Liam tried to make a run for it. But he slipped on the sea of newt eyeballs and slid across the floor until he was directly under the dragon's belly.

"I could have done this by myself!" he yelled in frustration. "But of course Gustav had to run around like a lunatic!"

From below, Liam kicked both his feet up into the dragon's gut.

"And Frederic is scared of his own shadow!"

The dragon craned its neck downward, trying to see under itself.

"And Duncan is cutting his own clothes off!"

Liam scrabbled across the floor and crawled out from underneath the dragon's backside.

"And the girl turned out to be a tree!"

The dragon spotted him and swung its massive tail. The tail caught Liam in the chest, knocking him down, but he rolled to the side before it could come down on top of him for a second blow.

"And then somebody went and put a DRAGON in here!"

This was not Liam's finest hour. The frustrations of the past several days had been slowly eating away at him and muddying his mind. On a normal day, had Liam been confronted by a fire-breathing dragon, he would have come up with a brilliant tactic for defeating the beast. He would have lured the dragon into a tight spot to trap it, or maybe found some clever way to make the huge chandelier overhead fall down onto the monster. But this day? This day he decided to kick the beast in the tail and yell, "Take that, dumb dragon!"

The dragon, as you might suspect, was not impressed. It roared, spun around to face him, and let loose a wide plume of fiery breath. Liam leapt to the side, but not fast enough to keep his long cape from catching fire.

"Bad move! Bad move!" Liam panted as he ran in circles, trying desperately to remove his burning cape. When untying the cape proved too much of a challenge, he dropped to the floor and rolled to extinguish the blaze—

Fig. 34 Red DRAGON

narrowly avoiding another chomp of the dragon's jaws in the process.

There's nothing like being engulfed in flames to snap you out of a daze and get you focused on the task at hand. Once his cape fire was out, Liam dodged a swipe of the dragon's claws, then ran straight at the beast and leapt up onto its head. As the startled dragon coughed out a cloud of black smoke, Liam spun himself around and straddled the monster's thick neck. Holding on tightly, he spoke directly into the dragon's ear: "That's right, dragon, I'm in charge now. Let's get that map."

Placing his hands on the dragon's horns like they were handlebars, Liam kicked his heel hard into the dragon's neck and attempted to steer the great beast into the corner where the map had landed. Alas, Liam overestimated his dragon-riding skills. The monster galloped at high speed directly toward the big doors that led back outside—back to the other princes. And honestly, those guys didn't need any more trouble than they already had.

17

Prince Charming Still Has No Idea What's Going On

Well, there it is," Lila whispered.

She and Ella pulled whiplike branches aside as they worked their way through the bramble toward the tower. Like the one that Ella (and Rapunzel before her) had been held in, this tower was about ninety feet of white-streaked gray stone sticking straight up out of the ground. And again, there were no doors—just one small window at the top. Ella tiptoed closer.

She froze when she heard voices from behind the tower. They were high-pitched, burbling, almost wet-sounding voices that, had Ella gotten around more, she would have immediately recognized as goblin voices. Goblins always sound as if they are talking with a mouth full of gelatin.

As awful sounds go, there's nothing quite as disgusting as being serenaded by a goblin choir. But like I said, Ella didn't realize she was hearing a goblin conversation; she heard the sloppy gurgling sounds and thought somebody was drowning.

"Someone needs help!" Ella shouted. "Don't worry, I'm coming!"

"Wait," Lila said. "Those are—"

But Ella was already tearing around to the back of the tower. She came to an abrupt stop when she noticed that: (a) there was no body of water in sight, and (b) there *were* three smallish green-skinned creatures with wooden spears pointed in her direction.

"Oh, my goodness," Ella said. "What are you?"

"What *are* we?" one of the goblins gurgled. "Do you know how insulting that is?"

"Of course I know what you *are*," Ella lied, realizing she'd offended a group of creatures with very sharp sticks. "You didn't let me finish. I was going to ask, 'What are you . . . *doing here*?' I think *you* were rude for interrupting me."

"You paused," the goblin said. "I thought you were done."

"That's no excuse," Ella said haughtily. She decided to

simply act as if she belonged there and hope the creatures would buy it. "And you still haven't answered my question."

"We're guarding the tower," a goblin said. "Who are *you* supposed to be, anyway?"

"She is Ruffian the Blue," Lila said as she ran up next to Ella. "The infamous bounty hunter. See her blue dress."

"Ruffian the Blue?" the head goblin questioned. "I figured he was a man."

"Why?" Ella said, narrowing her eyes. "You think a woman can't be the world's best bounty hunter?"

The two smaller goblins shook their heads rapidly.

"Who's the little human, then?" the lead goblin asked.

"Oh, she, uh . . . she captured me," Lila offered.

"That's right, I work for the witch," Ella said. "I'm delivering my new prisoner to this tower."

"Prisoner?" the head goblin asked skeptically. "But she's not even tied up or anything. And she was running about twelve yards behind you."

"She doesn't need to tie me up," Lila said quickly. "I'm totally terrified of her. If you saw the things this lady could do, you would not try to run either."

The two goblins in the back goggled at Ella in trepidation. Their eyes bulged audibly, making a rather disgusting sucking sound. Their leader, however, was still doubtful. He squinted at Ella. "If you work for the witch," he asked, speaking at a slow and deliberate pace, "can you tell us her name?"

Lila shot Ella an expectant look. Ella took a deep breath. She had no idea what the witch's name was. But she was willing to bet that these loopy little creatures didn't have the information either. "Can *you* tell me her name?" she asked.

The three goblins, who had only met with their boss for about five minutes before she screamed at them and sent them away to guard the tower, huddled together and whispered among themselves. It sounded like a pug snuffling into a pot of stew. After a minute or so—and several instances of one goblin slapping another in frustration—they broke the huddle and faced Ella again.

"Um, we're gonna go with . . . Wendy," the first goblin announced.

"Excellent," Ella said, having no clue whether they were correct or not. "She'll be very happy to hear that you got that right."

The three goblins all sighed with relief.

"But she's not going to be very happy to hear that I found the three of you on the wrong side of the tower,"

Ella continued in a sinister tone, doing her best impression of her stepmother. The goblins jumped to attention. "You were supposed to be guarding the tower. Why weren't you on the side with the window?"

"Well, the prisoner—," the first goblin started.

"The *bard*, you mean," Ella prompted, hoping the goblin would confirm what she already believed about the witch's plot.

"Yep, that's right, the bard," the goblin said. "He wrote that famous song. You know the one." He signaled the other goblins, and the trio began singing, "Listen, dear hearts, to the tale I confess, the tale of a girl who needed a dress—"

It was the most horrible sound Ella and Lila had ever heard.

"Stop! Stop!" Ella cried. "Yes, I know the song. Just finish telling me why you're not out there keeping an eye on him."

"Well, the bard kept shooting these weird little thingies at us," the first goblin said sheepishly, avoiding eye contact with Ella.

"I'm not sure how he was doing it, but they flew real fast and stung real hard," the second goblin added. "He must have a slingshot up there or something." The creature handed Ella a tiny ear-shaped piece of carved ivory.

Ella had seen enough private concerts with Frederic to recognize the tuning knob of a mandolin when she saw one.

"We didn't want to get hurt anymore, so we moved to this side," the first goblin finished.

"That is so irresponsible," Ella scolded. "How do you know the prisoner hasn't escaped while you've been back here?"

Lila shook her head sadly. She pointed at Ella with one hand and made a throat-slashing motion with the other. One of the smaller goblins fell flat on his back and had to be helped up by the others.

"We're going to have to check," Ella said. "How do we get up there?"

Anxious, the goblins retrieved an extremely tall ladder from the nearby trees. They dragged it to the front of the tower and, groaning under its weight, stood it up until its top rested against the lone high windowsill. The first goblin began to climb, but Ella put her hand on his head to stop him. She quivered a bit at the damp-rug feel under her palm, but stayed in character.

"Where do you think you're going?" Ella snapped. "I'll go first."

"Yes, sir, Miss Ruffian, sir," the goblin said, and he

hopped down out of her way. Ella began to climb the tall ladder.

"Should we, uh, keep an eye on your new prisoner here?" one of the other goblins asked, bringing the point of his spear dangerously close to Lila's chest.

Ella paused. She didn't want to leave Lila alone with these creatures. But Lila nodded to her reassuringly. *I'm okay,* the younger girl mouthed to her.

"Yes, watch her," Ella said. "But do not harm a hair on her head, if you know what's good for you." Lila grinned.

Ella continued up the ladder. As she neared the top, she saw a floppy-hatted man appear in the window. He was holding a mandolin as if it were a bow, with the low E string pulled back and ready to launch another tuning knob. *Pennyfeather!*

When the bard saw who was coming up the ladder, he lowered his makeshift weapon.

"Lady Ella?" he asked, thinking he must be hallucinating.

Ella held her finger to her lips to shush Pennyfeather and motioned for him to get away from the window. Below, the goblins were circling Lila with their spears.

Ella climbed over the windowsill into the small tower cell.

"Don't say a word," she whispered to the bard, trying not to be distracted by his glistening silver pantaloons. "We can trick them and get you out of here."

"What do you plan to do?" the musician whispered. "I've only got one string left."

"Give me your mandolin and step back," Ella said. The minstrel handed over his instrument, and Ella yelled out to the goblins, "Uh-oh, Wendy is not going to be happy about this. You three had better come in here quick."

The panicked goblins started to flee. "Don't run," Lila warned. "It's pointless. No one escapes Ruffian the Blue. She'll find you in minutes."

"But—," the first goblin began.

"Your only chance is to get up there and fix the mess you've made," Lila said.

In a tizzy, the goblins handed their spears to Lila. "Hold these," one said.

The goblins hustled to the top of the ladder, and as each stepped in through the window, Ella clobbered him over the head with the mandolin.

"That takes care of that," Ella said once all three goblins lay in a heap on the floor of the cell. She and the bard made a speedy exit, practically sliding down the ladder on their way out. Then they pulled it away from the tower and let it fall to the grass with a thump, ensuring that the goblins would be trapped up there for quite some time.

"Oh, and there's another lovely young lady," the bard said.

"Lila. Big fan. Pleasure to meet you." She shook his hand. "Oh, darn. I probably should have curtsied, right?"

"Think nothing of it," the former prisoner said with an over-the-top bow. "Pennyfeather the Mellifluous is forever in your debt, young lasses. Though I must admit, I'm quite baffled by your presence here, Lady Ella."

"I was a prisoner of the witch myself," Ella said.

"Oh, so you know that the fiendish woman has my brethren bards locked away as well?" Pennyfeather asked, as he fluffed out the puffy sleeves of his shimmery gold blouse-shirt. "Aid must be procured for the others. As much as there's a part of me that would love to see my competition languish away in that garishly decorated fortress—especially Lyrical Leif and his lackluster rhymes. Can you believe the man rhymed 'Rumpelstiltskin' with 'crumpled napkins'? I don't even know how that got past the Bards' Board of Acceptable Rhymes. But I digress. As I was saying, even those lesser tunesmiths don't deserve to be at the whim of that horrid sorceress. When she took us from her stronghold, I had no idea what manner of nightmarish plans she had in store for us. To be honest, I was rather relieved when she deposited me in this smaller tower and left me with those goblins."

"Is that what they were?" Ella asked. "Goblins?"

"Don't mind her," Lila said, patting Ella on the back. "She's apparently new to the outside world."

"Pennyfeather, did you by any chance see where the other towers are?" Ella asked. "The ones the rest of the bards are in?"

"No, I was the first of us to be dropped off," Pennyfeather said. "But if my fellow troubadours are all in similar towers, I think there may be a map that reveals their locations. I heard the goblins talking about it when they showed up for guard duty, complaining that the witch wouldn't let them take the map and wondering if maybe they were at the wrong tower."

"That's great," said Lila. "So the map must be back at that Batwing place. I'll tell my dad to send his army straight over there."

"Yes, you should do exactly that," Ella said. "But I need to continue back to the witch's fortress now."

"By yourself?" Lila cried. "Why?"

"Because that witch is unstable," Ella said. "She may try to kill the bards before any assistance can arrive. I have to act now." What she didn't tell Lila was that she had no desire to sit back twiddling her thumbs while some platoon of men with swords swooped in to save the day. She wanted to be right in the thick of things.

"Well, good luck, I guess," Lila said. "Maybe I'll see you again someday?"

"I guarantee it." Ella pulled a brass pin from her own hair and used it to pin back Lila's annoyingly loose ringlet. "Sorry," she said. "It's been bugging me."

"It's okay," Lila said.

Ella turned to Pennyfeather. "Oh, here's your mandolin back, by the way." She handed him the shattered instrument, the cracked body of which was completely separated from the neck, dangling only by the frayed E string. "My apologies for that," she added. "I hope you have a spare."

"Thirty-five, actually," Pennyfeather said, flashing a very white smile. "Thank you again for the rescue. I'm going to write another song about you."

"*Another* song?" Lila wondered aloud as Ella ran off into the woods.

18

Prince Charming Gets Battered and Fried

Outside Zaubera's fortress, Gustav was pounding mercilessly on the fallen giant.

"Get off him!" Gustav screamed as he kicked, punched, and poked. Groaning, Reese rolled over, revealing poor Prince Frederic, who'd been smashed facedown into the soil. Gustav peeled Frederic up from the sloppy, wet muck.

"Are you alive?" he asked his limp companion.

"I don't think so," Frederic said weakly.

Gustav dragged him over to the still-unconscious Duncan.

"Stay here by Mr. Mini-Cape," he said. "I'm going to finish off this extra-large pain in the neck."

Reese was sitting on the ground, rubbing his various

injuries. He groaned when he saw Gustav marching back toward him.

"This job doesn't pay enough," wailed the giant.

Suddenly the doors of the stronghold burst open, and the dragon charged out into the clearing with Liam astride its serpentine neck. Liam's eyes grew wide as he saw Gustav walking directly in the dragon's path.

"Gustav, look out!" he yelled.

Gustav had only enough time to look in the direction of Liam's voice and say, "Oh, starf it all," before he was engulfed in a ball of dragon fire. His armor protected most of his body, although its fur trim disintegrated instantly, and Gustav's long blond hair sizzled into nothingness. He dropped his sword and crumpled to the ground, beating on his head to put out the fire.

Relieved to see that Gustav was still alive (if slightly scorched), Liam began tugging on the dragon's horns, trying to steer it in the giant's direction. Instead of following directions, the beast surprised him by unfurling a pair of broad, leathery wings and taking to the air.

"Where were you hiding *those*?" Liam cried as the dragon circled the open sky above the fortress. Trying to keep his wits about him, he pushed the horns to angle the dragon's head ground-ward. "Down! Down!"

It seemed to work. At tremendous speed, the dragon began to dive straight down toward the giant. Wind whipped at Liam viciously, threatening to tear him from his perch on the dragon's neck, but he held on tight. Reese saw the dragon zooming toward him and hid his face in his hands.

During all of this, Zaubera had been planning and plotting up in the observatory at the top of her fortress's tallest tower, where she often went to think. Her Supreme Scheme for Infamy was moving along nicely. She'd procured Cinderella, the ultimate hero lure. She had each of the bards hidden away in a separate location, safe from any mass rescue attempts before the grand finale. And she'd already taken the precaution of hiring extra security for the big day.

Three weeks earlier . . .

Surrounded by wary bandit henchmen, Deeb Rauber sat upon his stolen throne and gave a steely-eyed staredown to the bone-thin, sunken-eyed old woman who'd burst, uninvited, into his headquarters.

"Let me see if I've got this straight," Rauber said. "You want me, the infamous Bandit King, and my entire army to work as security for some show you're putting on?"

"Not a *show*, a massacre," Zaubera scoffed. "I'm going to be obliterating people."

"And how are you going to do that, old lady?" Rauber asked. "Spook 'em to death with your creepy grandma stare?"

"No," said Zaubera. "I was thinking something more like this." She flexed her fingers and sent an arc of mystic blue lightning across the room and directly into Neville's chest. The lanky bandit let out a high-pitched shriek and hit the floor, twitching.

"Neat," said Rauber. He stroked an imaginary beard. "But if you can do *that*, what do you need us for?"

"As I explained earlier, I'm expecting a rather large audience," Zaubera said. "It would be helpful if you and your men could, shall we say, keep them in their seats. I don't want anybody leaving before the big finale."

"Well, this all sounds like tons of fun," Rauber said, reaching into a bowl of gumdrops beside his throne and popping one into his mouth. "But what's in it for me?"

"How about a kingdom?" Zaubera said. The Bandit King leaned forward, listening intently. A little droplet of drool slipped past his lower lip. "Once my entire plan has worked its course, five of the biggest kingdoms in the land will be left utterly defenseless. You can take whichever of them you'd like."

Rauber found it hard not to bounce in his seat, but tried to sound cool and professional. "I think this might be a

Fi9. 35
Zaubera's
HOME OFFICE

mutually beneficial arrangement," he said. "You can count us in, old lady."

The only thing left for Zaubera to figure out was the best way to inform the world about her bardnappings. Whatever method she chose, it had to really grab people's attention. It had to be spectacular.

Zaubera sat down at her desk in the center of the large round observatory. The dark stone pillars that ringed the room and the bloodred roof above had a way of making her feel extra evil. The witch moved her human skull candleholder and cage of tarantulas out of the way and unrolled a yellowing parchment. She dipped her vulture-feather quill into an inkwell and began to brainstorm.

— *Notes tied to rabid bats?*

— *Release wild boars with message*
  shaved into fur   ~~*Too time consuming*~~

— *Learn telepathy*

— *Carve into side of mountain*   <u>*maybe*</u>

— *Teach birds to say "Cinderella must die!"*

She heard a commotion outside and ran to the window. A handful of armed men were storming her fortress.

"Well, those fools took their time getting here," she said. "How hard is it to track someone who makes ten-yard footprints?" She scurried downstairs as fast as her spindly legs would carry her.

Zaubera emerged from the front door of her stronghold just in time to see the dragon hurtling toward Reese.

"Freeze!" she rasped.

The dragon abruptly stopped in midair. Liam, however, did not. His own momentum was so great that he lost his grip on the monster's horns. He flew off the dragon's neck, sailed over its head, and barreled into the giant's hefty belly. With a loud *oof!* Reese doubled over, and Liam bounced to the ground, dazed and bruised.

"Shake it off, you colossal wimp," Zaubera rasped at the giant. "I think I might have to let you go, Reese. I don't think you're working out. I got you a *dragon* and you still can't handle a handful of ridiculous little humans."

"At least they didn't free the girl," Reese said, hoping the witch had not yet discovered that the only prisoner inside her fortress was a hunk of lumber.

"True," Zaubera said. "But *these* sorry losers were

getting the better of you, Reese. You're bigger than the four of them combined."

"I'll do better next time, ma'am," Reese said, lowering his head.

"And *you*," the witch said, turning to the dragon. "You let one of them *ride* you?"

The creature licked its claws, pretending not to hear her.

"Ach, never mind," Zaubera spat. "Reese, you want to make it as a force of evil in this town? Watch me. I'll show you how you do *evil*. Just keep that dumb animal out of my way."

The giant called the dragon to his side, where it plopped itself down and began licking its wings.

"Okay, now," Zaubera said, looking out upon the four princes. "There are more of you than I expected. Who are you? Who is it who thinks he can defeat the all-powerful Zaubera?"

Liam rose shakily to his feet. "We are the men who are going to put an end to you."

"Wrong," Zaubera said. She raised her arms into the air, her ragged red-and-gray robe fluttering around her as a sudden wind began to blow. A bolt of glowing blue energy burst forth from her hands and blasted into Liam. He landed in a heap. "Any of you others have a better answer?"

Frederic shook Duncan awake.

"Eek! A mud-man!" Duncan shrieked when he opened his eyes. "Oh, wait. Frederic, that's you. Sorry. You're very dirty."

"Duncan, pay attention," Frederic instructed soberly. "The witch is here. And a dragon."

"Giant, too?"

"Yes. And the witch just blasted Liam with some kind of magic lightning."

Duncan sat up and looked around.

"There's nothing good about any of that," he said flatly.

"We've got to do something, Duncan. Use your luck."

"But I don't *use* my luck," Duncan said apologetically. "It just happens. I'm sorry."

"I'm waaaaiting," Zaubera called in a singsong voice. "Who *are* you?"

"We are the men who are going to put an end to you." This time it was Gustav, who had managed to stagger to his feet.

"Ooh, you're repeating what the last guy said," the witch mocked. "Nice dramatic effect. Still, however, not a good enough answer. I'm looking for names, people."

Gustav started to charge at Zaubera. Only a few steps

into his attack, a massive blast of blue lightning stopped him in his tracks. Zaubera cackled as she watched Gustav writhe on the ground before her.

"I know I'm impressively terrifying, but enough with the slack-jawed staring," Zaubera continued. "One of you had better speak up soon. I'm just going to keep zapping your bald friend here until someone tells me who you all are." She pummeled Gustav with one blast of mystical energy after another.

Duncan popped to his feet. "Princes!" he blurted. "Prince of Sylvonia. I mean Harmaria. No, that's him. I mean we're all princes. The song says Prince Charming, but that's not the real name. I mean we all have real names. Is that what you want to hear? We know *your* name. Something with a Z. Did you know I'm magic?"

Duncan continued to babble, but Zaubera stopped listening after the words "Prince Charming." One of these fools was Prince Charming? It was too perfect. Prince Charming would make the perfect addition to her finale. But which one was he?

Liam, in the meantime, was taking advantage of the distraction Duncan provided. Crawling on his belly, he made his way to Gustav's fallen sword. He grabbed the weapon and began twisting it until its glimmering blade caught a ray of sun and reflected the glare directly into the dragon's eye.

As Liam had hoped, the big creature recoiled from the sudden eyeful of bright light. The dragon growled and thrashed, and smashed into the unsuspecting Reese.

Out of the corner of her eye, Zaubera saw Reese's tremendous form falling toward her. "You oaf!" she screamed, and quickly cast a magic bubble shield in time to protect herself. Taking advantage of the distraction, Liam grabbed Gustav's arm and tugged him, staggering, toward the trees.

"What's happening? Are we running away or going back to fight some more?" Gustav asked. "I can't see."

"Gustav, are you blind again?" Liam asked.

"Not like before," Gustav said. "I just can't—argh! All I see are colored lights."

"Just go where I pull you," Liam said. "We're heading into the woods. The witch is . . . busy for the moment."

Back at the foot of the tower, the three villains were embroiled in chaos. The witch, still in her protective bubble, was screaming at the giant to get off her, which he was having a hard time doing, thanks to the dragon, which had jumped, snarling, onto his chest.

As Liam dragged Gustav to safety, Duncan and

Frederic ran alongside them.

"What's going on?" Frederic panted. "What about Ella?"

"Just run, Frederic," Liam said. "Ella's gone!"

"She's dead?" Frederic gasped.

"Not dead," Liam clarified. "*Gone.* As in: not in the fortress. She escaped."

Frederic's mind was reeling. Ella was free, the princes were all still alive (somehow), and this adventure was over. He should have been feeling nothing but relief. But more than anything else, he was depressed. This entire sorry episode had proven one thing: He was *not* a hero.

19

Prince Charming
Needs a Bath

"Come, Your Young Highness. Castle Sturmhagen lies not a full day's trek from here," Pennyfeather said, as he and Lila stood at the foot of the tower that now held a trio of very sad goblins. "The venerable King Olaf and Queen Berthilda can no doubt provide a formidable rescue party for my fellow bards."

"I don't know," Lila hedged. "I mean, I may be a princess, but I'm not so great when it comes to dealing with other royals. I think we should still just go back and tell my mom and dad."

"Tut-tut," Pennyfeather said. "I shall do all the talking. No worries there."

"Well, maybe," Lila said.

"Then it's settled," Pennyfeather said as he straightened the feather on his floppy cap. "And once we've done our civic duty by informing the authorities about the witch, then we can see to it that Sturmhagen's courtiers get you properly fixed up, Your Highness. We'll get you a new gown— with unwrinkled sleeves. And new footwear. Have you tried those new glass slippers that are becoming so popular among the aristocracy these days? I hear they're simply darling. I'm sure we could even get your hair recurled if we ask the right people. Worry not, Your Highness: With my input, you'll be looking like a proper princess again in no time. Now let us be off. Your Highness? Your Highness? Where did you go? Your Highness?"

Elsewhere in the same forest, the four princes pushed their way through the underbrush until they came to a dirt road several miles from Zaubera's stronghold. They stopped to catch their breath and gripe about one another.

"Gustav, let me take a look at you," Liam said.

"Go ahead," Gustav said. "*You've* got working eyes."

"I think you'll be okay," Liam said, ignoring Gustav's jibe and checking him out anyway. "Between the sparks and the fire, it was probably just too much bright light at one time. A similar thing happened to me once when I

was fighting a Zenocian strobe spirit. Your vision should return to normal."

"How do I look?" Gustav asked.

"Bald," said Duncan. "But on the bright side, you don't look as bad as Frederic."

"Starf it all," Gustav cursed, fingering his scorched, virtually hairless scalp. "You pathetic losers cost me my manly mojo."

"Well, wait," said Duncan. "I tried to help—"

"Too late!" Gustav burst. "That little comedy act you call 'helping' was *too late*. And a lot of good it did anyway."

"*You* shouldn't cast blame, Gustav," Liam said sternly. "You set that whole mess into motion by ignoring my plan."

"You said, 'Distract the giant,' so I did!" Gustav retorted.

"There was more to the plan than that!" Liam barked back.

"You cooked my head! Was that part of your plan?"

"I didn't know you'd be standing right in my way," Liam snapped defensively. "I did what I could. It's not like anybody else was going to get the job done." He glared at Duncan and Frederic.

"Are you referring to us?" Duncan asked. He was genuinely unsure.

"I don't know why you're looking at me," Frederic said. "You knew I was no hero. I had no business even being there."

"You're right," Liam snarled. "My biggest tactical error was not doing this alone. Why in the world did I ever think I could do this with a coward, a clown, and a guy whose only claim to fame is being beaten by the very witch we needed to stop?"

With that, Gustav leapt at Liam, tackling him and knocking him to the ground. The two princes rolled in the dirt, each fighting to get on top of the other.

"Looks to me like you can see fine," Liam said as they wrestled.

"It's still blurry," Gustav yelled. He smashed Liam into a tree trunk.

"I'm glad it's improving," Liam grunted as he planted his feet into Gustav's chest and kicked him backward.

"You're lucky I can't see perfectly yet," Gustav snarled. "Or I would have crushed you by now." He reached out and tried to yank Liam down by the cape, but most of Liam's cape was gone. Gustav's hand closed on empty air.

"O-ho! What happened to your beloved cape, Fancy Man?" Gustav laughed.

"The dragon burned it up. Just like your hair."

"Hch-hch. You lost your cape. That's good enough for me." Gustav walked away chuckling and took a seat on a tree stump. Liam leaned back against a nearby pine, panting and shooting dirty looks at Gustav. A long, uncomfortable silence followed.

"Well, from where I stand it's been a pretty good day," Duncan finally said, drawing some odd looks from the others. "I got to see my very first giant, my very first dragon, *and* my very first witch, all in one shot!"

"What about the witch who poisoned Snow White?" Frederic asked.

Duncan shook his head. "Never met her."

Liam took a deep breath. "Okay, everyone, let's follow this road and see if there's a town nearby," he said. "Maybe we can stop for food and a little first aid."

"And a change of clothes, maybe?" Frederic added. "A change of clothes would be *so* nice."

"Which direction did we run from the witch's place?" Gustav asked.

"East, I believe."

"Then there should be a town about five miles down this road to the north," Gustav said. "Flargstagg, it's called. I've always meant to go there."

"Why?" Frederic asked.

"Because my brothers always told me to stay away from Flargstagg," Gustav replied.

"Flargstagg," Duncan said. "Sounds exciting! Let's go." And he started heading south.

Gustav leaned over to Frederic. "I still can't see great," he said. "Please tell me he's not skipping."

Lila strode purposefully down a muddy road, on her way back to Erinthia. She stuck to the path and kept a constant watch for any movement among the trees. While she felt pretty sure she'd know what to do if she ran into any dangerous wildlife—she'd read *Native Beasts of Sturmhagen* five times—she still flinched every time she noticed a scurrying rat or heard the sharp caw of a passing crow. Occasionally she came across a fork in the road, and while she was reasonably certain which path she'd come along, she found it hard to shake the fear that she was becoming lost. She began to question the wisdom of ditching Pennyfeather.

A long-drawn-out howl echoed among the trees.

Wolf, Lila thought. *What did the book say about wolves? Oh, yes. You're supposed to bathe yourself in tomato juice to disguise your scent and keep the wolves off your trail. Crud. That's not helpful.*

Then she remembered another piece of advice from

Native Beasts of Sturmhagen: "When all else fails, run."

And that is what she did. She ran as fast as her legs would carry her, looking down to make sure she didn't lose her footing or trip over a stray rock or tree root. She never even saw Ruffian the Blue until she ran smack into his horse.

"Crud," Lila muttered as the bounty hunter pulled her up onto his horse and quickly looped a rope around her.

"Finally," the bounty hunter sighed. "Do you know how much time I wasted looking for you? So inconsiderate." His eyes grew misty.

"Are you about to cry?" Lila asked.

"It's hard being the best at something," Ruffian sniffled. "People expect so much from you. It's a lot of pressure. I'm just glad I finally have you and I can get back to my job now."

"You could have just kept going after my brother," Lila said. "You didn't have to come back for me."

"Yes, I did," Ruffian said. "You were going to get in the way. You're a way-getter-inner, I can tell."

The bounty hunter rode off with a tied-up Lila lying across the back of his horse. "Besides, you never know what kind of nasty things might step out from behind those trees," he said.

* * *

An hour later . . .

"So what are you doing now?" Lila asked.

Ruffian was crouched on the ground, examining a set of footprints. "Why do you keep asking me questions?" he moaned without looking up.

"I just want to know what you're doing," Lila said. "It seems interesting."

Ruffian sighed. "Four people went this way. Three of them were chained together."

"How can you tell?"

"The angle. Plus, some of the prints are deeper at the toes than the heels. Guys toward the back of the chain were being dragged by the one ahead of them. There are knee- and handprints, too. One of them fell down a lot."

"Can I see?"

"No. I tied you up for a reason." Ruffian climbed back onto the horse and sat in front of Lila. He gave the animal a kick and started trotting off the road into the forest.

"So, why are we following these prints?" Lila asked.

"*We* are not following anything," Ruffian said. "*I* am. And I'm following them because your brother is part of the group that made them."

"You can tell that from the footprints?" Lila asked, very impressed.

Ruffian shook his head. "There's a bandit hideout not far from here. Your brother was there, but he escaped. With three other men."

"Fascinating," Lila said. "So where do you think he's headed now?"

"These tracks are cutting a very straight line from the bandit castle. These guys are heading very specifically to the Orphaned Wastes. Mount Batwing. Now stop asking questions. My throat is starting to hurt from all this talking."

Lila lifted her head, shocked by the realization that suddenly dawned on her.

"Ruffian," she said with urgency in her voice. "You need to turn your horse around."

"Why are you addressing me by my first name?" the bounty hunter groaned. "Don't you kids have any—"

"Ruffian, listen to me, you're never going to be able to bring my brother back to Briar Rose, because very soon, my brother's going to be dead. He's on his way to fight a witch who will very likely kill him."

Ruffian remained silent, his expression downcast.

"It's the only thing that makes sense," Lila said. "Why else would he be going to Mount Batwing? He must have heard about the kidnapped bards, and he's going to try to save them. That's exactly what Liam would do. But if the witch is as dangerous as Ella says, Liam has no idea what he's about to go up against."

"Am I supposed to know what you're talking about?" Ruffian grumbled. Lila filled the bounty hunter in on everything she'd learned from Ella.

"You've got to turn around right now and go back to Avondell, Ruffian. You know it," Lila said. "Briar Rose wants to marry Liam. She's not going to be happy if he's dead. This is your only way to avoid her wrath and possibly still earn your pay." Lila hated the idea of alerting Briar Rose to her brother's whereabouts, but seeing him in her clutches would be far preferable to seeing him toasted into a piece of charcoal.

"I just can't get a break," Ruffian said with a long, slow exhale. Lila saw a tear run along the deep creases of the bounty hunter's weatherworn face.

He turned his horse around. "You're lucky I know a shortcut."

The exhausted quartet of princes staggered onto the cobblestone main street of Flargstagg. Cozy thatched-roof cottages lined the narrow avenues of the town, with colorful flower gardens in front. Children chased one another in giggly games of tag; cuddling couples sat on carved wooden benches, enjoying the clear blue sky.

"This place is adorable!" Duncan gasped.

"Yes," said Frederic. "I think I can handle this."

Gustav started laughing.

"What's so funny?" Frederic asked.

"I can see better now," Gustav said. "And you all look *terrible*."

As they passed one of the quaint little houses, a villager emerged—a crookbacked old man, carrying a bucket of food scraps. Several cats darted out from under bushes and meowed at his feet.

"Patience, patience, my little whiskered ones," the old man chuckled. "I've got some tidbits for you." He stopped when he caught sight of the princes. "My goodness, what happened to you young men?"

Liam stepped to the front of the group. "Hello, kind sir," he said. "We've traveled a very long and difficult way, and we could use a place to clean up and get some rest. Would you be able to lend a hand?"

"Of course, of course," the man said. "Please, use my house as you wish. I'll ask my wife to make some hot tea for you all."

"Thank you," Liam said.

"Oh, it's no trouble at all," the man said. "The people of

Flargstagg take pride in offering kindness to any stranger who happens upon our town, be he beggar or be he prince."

"Lucky for us, huh?" Duncan said cheerily. "Since we happen to *be* princes."

A sudden panic overcame Liam. The last thing he wanted was for these villagers to know who the four princes really were. Luckily, the old man laughed, assuming Duncan's comment to be a joke (the princes looked like they'd just crawled out of a sewer). But Duncan kept right on going.

"No, really, we're princes. And famous ones, too," Duncan insisted. He put his hand on Liam's shoulder. "This man right here is Prince Liam of Erinthia. But you might know him better as Prince Charming. "

"Charming, eh?" the old man said, and curled his lip in disgust. "You're the Prince Charming from Erinthia? I heard about your wicked deeds just the other day. You're the scoundrel who dumped poor Sleeping Beauty."

"Dumped? What? No, Charming is the hero of that story. The hero!" Liam said, shocked and confused. "He has nothing to do with that guy from Erinthia."

"Nice try, prince, but someone as awful as you can't hide behind an assumed name," the wrinkled old man scoffed. "We *all* know who you really are."

"Who do you mean by *all?*" Liam asked. His gut felt like it was turning inside out.

"Everyone," the old villager said. "The minstrels might have no new songs, but they haven't been quiet, either. They've given us the news about you—news that comes straight from that lovely Sleeping Beauty herself, Briar Rose of Avondell. Honestly, I don't know how you live with yourself after you pelted such a sweet girl with pumpkin innards. And then you painted a mustache on her mother?" (Since Briar's rant about Liam didn't rhyme and wasn't set to music, people had a hard time remembering exactly how it went. Almost every minstrel around was telling a slightly different version of it. And when their listeners decided to retell the tale to friends and neighbors, details tended to change even more. Always for the worse.)

"You *did* that?" Duncan asked, aghast.

"No, of course not!" Liam protested. "Mustache on her mother? What are you even talking about? Look, sir, everything you've heard about me is a lie. I dumped that girl because she was awful."

"I'll show you a good dumping," the old man scowled, and proceeded to overturn his bucket of garbage directly onto Liam's head. The other princes gasped.

"Now get out of my sight," the man snarled. "And take

your ugly henchmen with you."

Gustav stepped forward. "Henchman?" he scowled. "I am *your* prince, foolish man. I am Gustav of Sturmhagen. And you will treat me with the respect I deserve from my subjects."

"Oh, really? And what respect do *you* deserve?" the old man snickered. He cupped his hands around his mouth and shouted out to his neighbors, "Hey, everybody! Look who we have here! It's our little Prince Gustav, who doesn't even know how to rescue a maiden! And guess who he's with? That brute from Erinthia who dunked Sleeping Beauty in a barrel of pickles!"

"Barrel of pickles? Are you insane?" Liam cried. A crowd started to gather around the princes.

"Hey, he's right! It *is* that useless Gustav! Why can't he be more like his sixteen brothers?"

"I'd like to give that Prince Charming a good smack for what he did to Sleeping Beauty!"

"Ha-ha! Look how tiny that other guy's cape is!"

"Hey, everybody! They're friends with a mud-man!"

Liam looked to the other princes. "Let's go, shall we?"

The four of them fought their way through the mob of people and ran as fast as they could, farther into town.

"Well, I always wanted people to connect the real me

to the Prince Charming in the story," Liam huffed as they ran.

The princes zigzagged around corners, scrambled behind houses, and darted down narrow alleyways, until they were sure they'd lost the mob.

"Wasn't it daytime just a minute ago?" Frederic asked.

The princes surveyed their surroundings. They stood in a part of town that bore no resemblance whatsoever to the quaint and colorful Flargstagg they'd just seen. The buildings on this side of the village were dark, with boarded-up windows. The cobblestone streets ran thick with slimy green sewage. Rats skittered along the gutters. Even the sunlight had vanished.

"I can't even manage to get us a little rest without something going wrong," Liam muttered.

"Look up ahead." Duncan pointed toward a rather sketchy-looking tavern at the dead end of a dead-end street. The princes approached.

"Hmm, the Stumpy Boarhound," read Duncan. "Not a great name for an eating establishment. What is a boarhound, anyway? Some kind of pig? Some kind of dog?"

"Either way, it sounds ugly," Frederic said, peering in through a smudgy window. "I don't like the looks of the customers. They seem a bit rough around the edges."

"Where else are we going to go?" Liam asked. He opened the door and entered the Stumpy Boarhound. Which you knew he would do. Because you read the prologue.

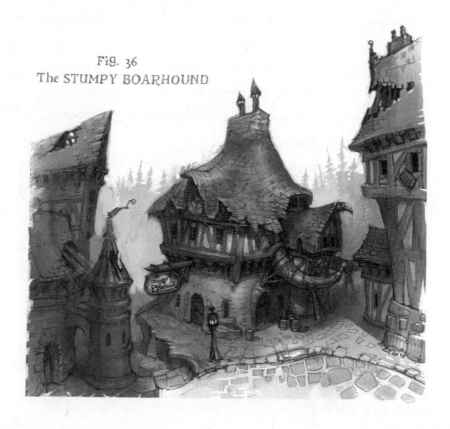

Fig. 36
The STUMPY BOARHOUND

20

PRINCE CHARMING
WALKS INTO A BAR

A t a small table in the back corner of the sticky-floored, body-odor-scented dining room of the Stumpy Boarhound, the four princes quietly picked at the rattlesnake kebabs that they'd purchased with a few coins Duncan found stuck to the bottom of his boot.

"I've never eaten snake before . . . and apparently, I haven't been missing much," Frederic said, squinching up his face in disgust.

"Well, it was either this or something called 'critter-bit casserole,'" Liam said. "At least with this, we know what *kind* of animal we're eating."

"I don't think this is actually rattlesnake," Duncan said, rolling a piece of the grayish meat around on his tongue.

"Tastes more like pit viper to me."

"If you're not going to eat yours . . . ," Gustav said, eyeing Frederic's mostly untouched meal.

Frederic glumly pushed his plate over to Gustav. How had he ended up in a place like *this*? Ghastly dead-animal decor graced the walls: moose heads, elk antlers, rabbit ears, bear bottoms, gator claws. Directly below Frederic's seat, the wooden floor was stained with what he hoped was red wine. Rough-looking criminals spat and swore at nearby tables. The bartender had been robbed three times since they'd started eating.

"Well, this is where I call it quits," Frederic said. "I'm amazed I've stayed alive this long, and seeing as Ella is safe, I don't see why I should push my luck. I'm heading back to Harmonia."

"Wait, Frederic, you can't leave now," Liam said.

"What's left to do?" Gustav asked.

"How can you ask that?" Liam said in an irked tone. "I told you all about that map in Zaubera's fortress. That witch has at least five more prisoners out there."

"Maybe," said Frederic. "You don't know that for sure."

"I'm done following other people's hunches," Gustav said. "I work better alone. If I get killed, I want it to be because of my own stupidity, not someone else's."

Fig. 37
Boarhound DECOR

"You should probably return home, too, Duncan," Frederic said. "I'm sure you miss Snow, no?"

"Yes, I do, but . . ." Duncan's words trailed off sadly. His group of friends was dissolving before his eyes.

"People!" Liam barked. "Did you not hear me mention the other prisoners?"

"Why do you assume they need our help?" Frederic asked. "Ella got out on her own; maybe these other folks could, too. Maybe they already have."

"Phht!" Gustav spat grumpily. "Cinderella Man's probably right. Apparently, stupid maidens don't need rescuing anymore."

"You people are looking at this all wrong!" Liam exploded. His hands trembled as he spoke in breathless spurts.

"We are going to rescue those people because we are heroes, and that's what heroes do," Liam said.

"*You're* a hero, Liam," Frederic said. "But the rest of us aren't like you."

"You are," Liam shot back. "You *all* are. We were all Prince Charming. We were all faceless, no-name whoevers. And then we found each other, and now—"

"And now what?" Frederic cut in. "We're some kind of unstoppable super-team? Have you noticed how poorly we've fared since we've been together?"

"He's right," Gustav said. "We don't do teamwork well."

"Fine! I'll do it myself!" Liam shouted, standing up and slamming both hands down onto the table. "Everybody else go back home! I'll just go run around thousands of miles of forest—on foot—and fight off all sorts of trolls and giants and dragons to rescue those people *all by myself*. Bare-handed. And I'll probably die in the process. Because it's an insane suicide mission for one person to attempt alone. But that's okay! That's totally fine! Because you guys are scared. Or you're tired. Or you're too proud, or you want to play your flutes, or whatever. And that's all fine with me. Fine, fine, fine!"

"Aww," mocked a gruff voice from behind the princes.

"Sounds like someone's having a pity party and didn't invite the rest of us." A large, thickly bearded pirate had swaggered over to their corner table. He was flanked on either side by scar-faced thieves twirling daggers between their callused fingers.

"Are you guys villains?" Duncan asked with wide-eyed wonder.

"You fellers ain't regulars around here," the pirate said. "We just like to make newcomers feel welcome is all."

"That's right," said a bare-bellied barbarian who strolled up to join them. He ran his hand up and down a gnarled wooden club. "And we couldn't help hearing a whiny guy who wants everybody to feel sorry for him."

A half-ogre thug in a ragged fur vest popped up alongside the others. He swung a spiked ball on a chain. "So we jus' thought we'd help out by givin' ya enough of a hurtin' to make peoples feel real bad for ya."

"Oh, and by taking yer money, too," said the pirate. "It's best if you hand it over now before we start with the beating."

The princes noticed that every rogue in the room had gotten out of his seat. They surrounded the princes' table, scowling menacingly and thwapping assorted weapons into their palms. Ready for the fight of his life, Liam put his hand on the dwarven sword in his belt.

"You know that's actually *my* sword," Gustav said, eyeing Liam's weapon.

"And you're going to ask for it back *now*?" Liam gaped.

The pirate cleared his throat. "Ahem, money, please. We're waiting."

"Starf it all!" Gustav grunted. He hurled himself at the nearest dagger-twirling thief and knocked him to the floor. Seven other hooligans piled quickly on top of him.

Almost instantly, everything went crazy.

In a place like the Stumpy Boarhound, with its quick-tempered and conscience-free customers, fights broke out on a regular basis. All you'd need is a burglar to accidentally spill a drop of grog onto some pirate's treasure map and before you knew it, everybody in the place would be throwing punches. So when Gustav took the extra step of actually *attacking* one of the Boarhound's resident thieves, it took less than a second for the entire tavern to devolve into total bedlam. The princes found themselves at the heart of a classic barroom brawl (Duncan's *very first* barroom brawl, as he was sure to let everybody know).

Liam stood up and kicked his chair at the half ogre, while swinging his sword to block the barbarian's club. The crowd of criminals climbed over one another as they tried to land a blow on one of the princes. Mugs and bottles started flying, glass shattering here and there. Chairs were smashed against people's backs. A stuffed moose head was torn off the wall and eaten.

Duncan tried to cause a diversion. "Anybody want some critter bits? They're on me!" he shouted to no avail. He was hoisted in the air and passed from one thug to another over the crowd.

Frederic put his hand to the hilt of his dwarven sword but stopped before drawing the weapon. *No,* he thought. *I'm not a fighter. I need to handle this a different way.*

Frederic spotted Liam being held in a headlock by the sweaty barbarian.

"Liam, we have to tell them who you are," Frederic blurted.

"What? No!" Liam squeaked, the barbarian's arm wrapped around his throat. "That's a terrible idea! Do you remember what just happ—"

Frederic ignored Liam, climbed on top of the table, and shouted, "EVERYBODY STOP!"

Amazingly, everybody did stop. In mid-punch, in some cases.

"Do any of you people know who you're attacking?" Frederic asked.

"No, do tell," the bearded pirate called to him, amused. "Whom exactly are we kickin' the tar out of?"

Frederic gestured to Liam. "This man is Prince Liam of Erinthia," he said. There was a murmur of recognition from a few among the crowd. "Yes, that's right," Frederic went on. "He's the guy who dumped Sleeping Beauty."

Liam closed his eyes, incredulous that Frederic could have somehow managed to make this dreadful situation even worse.

"Hey, I heard about that guy. He spit in the princess's milk," shouted one of the thugs.

A roar of laughter rose from the mob.

"That's right," another criminal called out. "And he threw rotten eggs at the royal family's prize poodles. And wiped his dirty feet on the Avondellian flag!"

"Someone told me he sprinkled hot red pepper flakes into Sleeping Beauty's goldfish bowl," another thug cried.

"Ooh! That's wicked!" someone shouted.

"I heard this guy drew a mustache on the queen's portrait!" the bearded pirate said.

"No," Frederic corrected, "he actually drew it *on* the queen!"

"Classic!" somebody yelled.

By now the entire mob had given up on fighting. The

barbarian released his grip on Liam.

"Didya really do all that?" the pirate asked.

Liam had to admit Frederic's plan was pretty ingenious. "If you can't believe a random rumor, what can you believe?" he said coyly.

"Oh, Liam's just being modest," Frederic said. "Did you hear that after he tore down the flag of Avondell and wiped his feet on it, he ran a pair of Sleeping Beauty's bloomers up the flagpole?"

More laughter sounded throughout the tavern.

"Oh, yes," Frederic continued. "My friend Liam here may not be a regular at your establishment, but believe me, he's quite at home in a place like this. And he's not the only one." Frederic scanned the room for Duncan and spotted him stretched across the bar with a funnel in his mouth (and a grinning burglar about to pour a jar labeled PICKLED TENTACLES into it).

"That man back there," Frederic announced, "is Duncan the Daring."

"Never heard of him," someone called out.

"Not yet, maybe. But you will," Frederic said. "Duncan recently faced Deeb Rauber—the Bandit King—in a duel. And he won."

The burglar backed off.

"Yer makin' that up," the half ogre growled.

"No, he's not," said one of the thieves. "I think it's true. My cousin works for the Bandit King, and he was just telling me that Rauber set up a duel with a prisoner of his, but that it didn't go very well and the guy got away." The thief pointed to Duncan. "Was that really you?"

Duncan spit out the funnel, stood up on the bar, and took a bow. "Absolutely!" he exclaimed with delight. "Got out without a scratch on me! Ta-da!"

"Oh, yeah?" the big barbarian challenged. "What about that big bump you got there?"

"Oh, this?" Duncan said, touching the bruise on his forehead. "The Bandit King didn't do that to me; that was from the battle with the giant and the dragon."

Gasps were heard from around the room.

"It's all true," Frederic said. "And if I might introduce you to the next member of our formidable team . . . Gustav, where are you?"

Gustav burst out from under a pile of brawny buccaneers. In his burned and battered armor, with his heaving, hulking muscles and scalded bald head, he looked downright terrifying.

"What?" he growled.

"This is Prince Gustav, from the royal family right here

in Sturmhagen," Frederic announced.

"Wait a minute," said an assassin. "He's the Rapunzel guy, isn't he? He didn't do *anything!*"

"Oh, didn't he?" Frederic asked. "He got thrown out of a ninety-foot tower, got his eyes scratched out, and walked away from it all alive and well. If that's not an impressive feat, I don't know what is."

Some of the hooligans murmured softly as they considered this point.

"When I first met Gustav," Frederic continued, "he had just been thrown through a fence by a troll—and he was in good enough spirits to start insulting me the moment he saw me. I've seen this man get pummeled by bandits, pulled off the roof of a castle, whipped around by a raging giant, and magically sizzled by an evil witch. I watched him get hit full-on by a blast of dragon fire. Heck, you've all been beating on him for the past five minutes. And look at him! He's just waiting for more. Gustav is unstoppable! Believe me, he's not a man you want to mess with."

All the villains silently stepped away from Gustav, giving him plenty of space. He grinned at Frederic.

"Maybe your friends aren't so bad, after all," said the bearded pirate. "But what about you? Who are *you* supposed to be?"

"Me?" Frederic asked. It hadn't been difficult to figure out how to spin each of his companions' stories in a way that would appeal to this rough-and-tumble crowd, but how could he do that for himself? What about him—what trait of his—could he possibly use to impress this tavern full of ruthless criminals? He was stumped. He smiled at the villains to buy himself some time to think. A few of them grinned back, in spite of themselves.

And suddenly he knew exactly what to say: "I'm Prince Charming. People like me."

21

PRINCE CHARMING JOINS A GANG

Frederic, you were *brilliant*," Liam said.

The four princes were once again sitting by themselves at the table in the corner of the Stumpy Boarhound. Once the tavern patrons realized they had celebrities in their midst, they oohed and aahed for a few minutes—the big barbarian asked Frederic to autograph his belly—and then they respectfully agreed to leave the famous quartet to their own business. The bartender, a jowly, stubble-faced man who went by the name of Boniface K. Ripsnard, even supplied the princes with a few rags and a basin of soapy water so they could clean up.

"Yep, nice job, Harmonia," Gustav chimed in.

"Thanks," Frederic said with aw-shucks boyishness.

"I usually hate it when the dwarfs call me Duncan the Daring," Duncan added. "But I liked when you said it. It sounded different."

"Because I meant it," Frederic said. "You volunteered for a duel with the Bandit King, you stood up to a giant twenty times your size—of *course* you're daring."

Ripsnard the bartender approached their table and set down four big mugs. Each was filled with some sort of thick, foamy, yellow-brown liquid.

"Compliments of the house," Ripsnard said.

"Thank you, sir," Frederic said as the man walked away.

"I'm not drinking that," Liam said as soon as the bartender was out of earshot.

Duncan sniffed the drink and shivered. "Eew! What is it?"

"I have no idea," said Frederic, grimacing as he watched bubbles rise to the surface of the drink. "Something's swimming in mine."

Gustav grabbed his mug by its oversize handle and downed the entire beverage in one huge gulp. He slammed the empty mug back on the table and wiped his mouth on his sleeve.

"That was awful," he said, wincing.

The other three laughed, and even Gustav himself smiled.

"So tell us, Liam," Frederic said. "What's the new plan?"

"Wait, wait! Don't tell me," Duncan said. "Can we take guesses first? I'm thinking it involves flying monkeys."

"Alas, Duncan, I don't believe those exist, so we'll have to make do without," Liam said. "But I *have* been thinking about a new plan, if you men are really willing to hear it. It would include all four of us, so I need to know: Are you all with me?"

"I am," Frederic said. "Now that I know I can serve a purpose."

"I never wanted to leave to begin with," Duncan said, beaming.

"Gustav?" Liam asked.

Gustav shrugged. "I know when I'm outnumbered."

"No, you don't," Frederic laughed. "Only ten minutes ago you threw yourself into a mob of about thirty people."

"Yeah, yeah, yeah," Gustav said dismissively. "I'm still here, all right?"

"You know, Frederic's got a point," Liam said. "You *don't* know when to hold back, Gustav. But that's who you are. I should have taken that into account. You see, my biggest error was in not recognizing the individual strengths of everyone in this group. It took Frederic here to help me realize what those strengths are.

"Gustav, you can take a ridiculous amount of punishment. We need to use that. Frederic, you're a talker. You're the diplomat of our group. And Duncan, well, you can always be counted on to do something utterly insane. And I mean that in the best possible way. You're not risk-averse."

"No offense taken," Duncan said.

"So how do we use these, um, talents?" Frederic asked.

"Okay, but please hear me out before you start complaining," Liam began. The others leaned in. "First thing we need to do is go back to Zaubera's tower and get that map. Unless there's some new bit of craziness thrown at us, we have three obstacles to deal with: The giant, the dragon, and the witch. Frederic, the giant is yours."

"The giant?" Frederic asked. He was feeling more game than ever, but the thought of facing the giant by himself seemed both terrifying and unwise.

"Yes," Liam said. "You need to keep him distracted. I don't want you to fight him. I want you to *talk* to him. Play mind games with him; keep him listening to you. Just make sure he's not paying attention to the rest of us."

"I'm supposed to walk up to the giant—the same giant that almost squashed me—and start up a conversation with him?" Frederic was skeptical. "You don't think he'd find that suspicious?"

"Of course he would," Liam said. "We have to make sure it's believable. That's why I want you to let him capture you."

Frederic gulped.

"I don't like it," said Gustav.

"Frederic can handle this," Liam said. "I trust him."

"If anything happens to him, I'll pop your head like a tomato," Gustav said.

"Gustav, it's okay," Frederic said, putting a hand on Gustav's shoulder to calm him. "I want to try. Besides, I'm sure you'll have an important part in this plan yourself."

"Yes, Gustav, I want you to take care of the dragon," Liam instructed.

"Now you're talking." Gustav perked up.

"The goal here is distraction," Liam said. "Same general idea as with Frederic and the giant. The dragon is an animal; if it sees something it wants, it will chase it. Get it to go after you; then just keep moving. If it knocks you down, get back up. But don't let it stop you, and don't let it give up on you. Keep it busy." *And please try not to die,*

Liam thought. He knew Gustav's portion of the plan was the riskiest, but Gustav was the only one of them cut out for it.

"I don't know," Gustav said skeptically. "I usually run *at* stuff, not away from it."

"It's always good to try new things," Liam said.

"All right," Gustav mumbled. Then after a pause, he added, "Can I kill the dragon?"

"Please don't," Liam said, humoring him—Gustav actually defeating the dragon was not something he was worried about. "We need it for another part of the plan."

"If you insist," Gustav said grudgingly.

"While the two of you have the giant and dragon occupied," Liam said, "Duncan and I will sneak into the fortress to get the map. Now, last time I was in the witch's stronghold, I got hit with a big surprise: the dragon. And in case there's another surprise waiting this time, I've got you, Duncan. You're my wild card."

"Wild card, got it," Duncan said. "Just like in Crazy Eights. I can be a diamond; I can be a spade. Whatever you need me to be, I'm that thing. That is *so* me."

"Once we have the map, we'll head back out and help Gustav," Liam said. "Between three of us, we should be able to redirect the dragon and get it to attack the giant like it did last time."

"How do we do that?" Duncan asked. "With steaks?"

"That could work," Liam agreed, pleasantly surprised to hear a logical a suggestion. "Then, while the giant is dealing with the dragon, we grab Frederic and run off. Then we use the map to track down the prisoners and free them. So, everybody ready?"

The other three nodded and mumbled.

"Not good enough," Liam said. "I expect a bit more enthusiasm from my teammates. I am a hero, and I know I will succeed."

He stood up, pointed to Duncan, and dramatically posed the question: "Duncan, what are you?"

"Human!" Duncan cried, trembling with excitement.

"More specific," Liam said, still dramatically.

"A five-foot-two human!"

"I'm going for *hero* here," Liam hinted under his breath.

"Hero!" Duncan shouted. "I'm a hero!"

Liam pivoted. "Frederic, what are you?"

"I am a hero," Frederic answered, proudly puffing out his chest. "A different type of hero, perhaps, but still. . . ."

Liam pivoted once more. "Gustav, what are you?"

"Too corny. Not doing it," Gustav said, crossing his arms.

"You're a hero, Gustav," Liam said. "We all are. And maybe I didn't completely believe that when I said it an hour ago, but I do now. We may be unsung heroes, but give us time. That'll change. So, come on. Let's do this. We're a team." He held his hand out over the center of the table, waiting for the others to rise and place their hands on top of his.

Duncan jumped up and slapped Liam's outstretched hand hard. "Too slow!" he shouted giddily.

Frederic and Gustav laughed. "Fine, we're a team," Gustav said.

"Well, all right, then," said Liam. "We need to equip ourselves. The Bandit King took pretty much everything we had that was of value, though. I'm not sure what we can use to barter with."

Frederic dug deep into a hidden inner pocket of his jacket and came out with a diamond ring. "Well, the bandits missed this. I had planned to give it to Ella after I found her, as a way to woo her back," he said. "But I suppose it would be of more use to us here and now."

"Thank you, Frederic," Liam said, and gave Frederic's shoulder a grateful squeeze. "Let's go visit the bartender."

The four princes used Frederic's ring to trade for supplies with Ripsnard, who loaded their arms with

changes of clothing and
a rucksack full of rancid-
looking muskrat steaks ("It
doesn't have to look tasty to
us," Liam reminded them. "Just
the dragon.").

"We could use some new
weapons, too," Liam said to
the bartender.

"Can't help you there, Prince,"
Ripsnard replied apologetically.
"I don't allow implements of
violence in my establishment."

FiG. 38
MUSKRAT
STEAKS

"But everybody in here is armed. How can
you say—," Liam protested. "Ah, never mind." At least
they still had two dwarven swords.

"Hope ya enjoyed your lemonade," the bartender
added as Liam walked away.

"That was lemonade?" Liam gaped.

He joined the others in the tavern's back storeroom,
where they changed into their new garb. The quartet drew
stares when they strode back into the main dining room.

"Heh-heh," Ripsnard laughed. "I still can't believe
you lot are famous princes. You certainly don't look very

Prince Charming, do ya?" The four princes, clad in black, looked like a band of thieves.

"That's okay," said Liam. "We're off to handle some very unprincely business."

The tavern's tough-guy customers looked the princes up and down. "Don't worry," said the bearded pirate. "Cutting a picture the way you fellers do right now, I don't think anybody'll be getting in your way."

"I think we actually look scary," Frederic whispered excitedly to Gustav.

"*I* look scary," Gustav said.

"Toodle-oo," Ripsnard said, waving them off. "You and your league of princes will always be welcome at the Stumpy Boarhound."

"League of Princes," Frederic echoed. "I like the sound of that."

"Ooh, how about the League of Princes *Charming*?" proposed Duncan.

"No," Liam and Gustav said in unison.

"League of Princes," Liam said. "Just League of Princes."

"It makes us sound like we should be bowling," Gustav complained.

* * *

The four princes exited the Stumpy Boarhound. As they stepped out into the waste-strewn alleyway, they were nearly bowled over by a burly black-clad stranger who was on his way into the pub.

"Oi, am I late?" the grizzled stranger asked, eyeing the outfits of the men he'd just bumped into. "Didya give up on me so soon?"

"Come again?" asked Frederic.

"We were supposed to meet inside the tavern, right?" the man said. "You four are the witch's other couriers, right?"

Duncan stepped forward, struck a pose, and began to announce, "We are the League of—"

Liam bumped him out of the way with a quick hip-check. "Couriers," Liam said. "The League of . . . Evil Couriers. That's right."

"Oi, I didn' know you were part of the League," the stranger said. "I'm jus' freelance, myself. I wouldn'a kept ya waitin' if I knew." He reached into a satchel that hung over his shoulder and pulled out five scrolls. "Anyway, here's the messages."

The courier handed each of the princes a rolled-up scroll. "This one goes to Sylvaria. This one to Harmonia. Um, Avondell for you. And . . . you get Erinthia. I'll deliver the one to Castle Sturmhagen myself."

The princes took quick peeks at their parchments, scanning for the main points of the messages within: "Your bard is mine . . . Mount Batwing . . . sundown on Midsummer Day . . . slaughter unlike anything the world has ever seen . . . Yours abominably, Zaubera."

"I should have the Sylvaria one," Duncan said to Frederic. "Wanna trade?"

Gustav gave Duncan a shove to shut him up.

"We'll get these notes to where they have to go," Liam said. "Gustav, you want to give our friend a tip?"

Gustav socked the witch's courier with a powerful fist to the jaw. The man fell instantly unconscious. Gustav grabbed the fifth scroll from his hand and shoved his limp body into a nearby barrel, which he then tossed through an empty window into an abandoned building across the street.

"Um, people?" Frederic said, a look of dread creeping across his face. "You all understand what these notes mean, right?"

"Yeah," Gustav said. "It means there's a change of plan—I'm going home. There's no way I'm running out there to save the guys who ruined my life."

"Gustav," Frederic scolded. "None of us may be too

happy with the treatment we got from those bards, but they're innocent people!"

"I don't know about innocent," Gustav grumbled.

"We're not going to abandon them, though," Frederic said. "Liam, please back me up on this."

Liam was silent, mired in thought. He was never one to hesitate when a life was in danger—but he'd never been called upon to rescue *bards* before. And not just any bards: One of them was Tyrese the Tuneful, the man who'd ignored Liam's heroics for years and then robbed him of his deserved fame by turning him into a generic Prince Charming. *This is a test,* Liam thought. *I can't think of anybody I like less than Tyrese.*

"Liam?" Frederic tried again.

"Given the information in these notes, I see no choice but for us to change our plan," Liam said.

"You *want* to leave the songbirds with the witch?" Gustav asked, incredulous. "I honestly wasn't expecting that."

"No," Liam said. "We have to make sure those prisoners are freed, no matter who they are. But it's midsummer eve; the witch is planning on killing them tomorrow. Even if we get the map as planned, we won't have time to reach all those towers before noon."

"That's a good point," Frederic said. "So what do we do?"

"We get help," Liam said. "And the nearest place to get it will be Castle Sturmhagen. Once we have the map, we take it to Gustav's brothers. There would be twenty of us then; we can split up and hopefully get to all the towers in time."

"You want me to ask my *brothers* for help?" Gustav gasped. "The only worse thing would be to ask Rapunzel for help."

"We need the extra manpower," Liam said. "It's our only chance."

"Our only chance to save the lives of people we despise," Gustav sighed.

"Gustav, I know you feel that your brothers get more attention than you," Frederic said. "But look at it this way: They've simply had more time to build their reputations. Most of them are much older than you, I assume."

"Only by a year or two!" Gustav said.

"All sixteen of them?" Liam asked. "How is that possible?"

"My mother had two sets of octuplets and then me," Gustav stated bluntly.

"Eesh," Liam winced.

"Gustav, we need you to be on board for this," Frederic said. "Please."

"Look," Liam said, "sometimes being a hero isn't about getting the glory. It's about doing what needs to be done."

"I understand that, but this is where I put my foot down," Gustav said. "I'll help you rescue the tune-chuckers, but just the four of us."

"Okay. If that's the way it has to be," Liam said.

"Hey, guys," Duncan burst in. "I think I figured out who the witch has in those towers: the bards!"

"Nice detective work, Duncan," Liam said. "Now, let's get out of here before the real couriers show up. We're the only hope those bards have."

"That is correct, Your Excellency," Pennyfeather said, bowing before King Olaf and Queen Berthilda in the fur-carpeted throne room of Castle Sturmhagen. "The witch will smite Lyrical Leif in a manner most dastardly. Three other of my fellow music masters as well."

"We can't have that now, can we?" the hefty king said, patting his cloudlike beard. He shifted his glance to the sixteen statuesque, heavily armored men who were standing by in a long, well-organized line. "Henrik, make sure all your brothers are armed and suited up;

then head to Mount Batwing."

"We're all ready to go," said Henrik, the eldest of the Sturmhagen princes. "Well, except Gustav. He's off playing by himself again somewhere, I suppose."

"No matter," King Olaf said. "You sixteen will be enough. Head out."

With Henrik at the lead, the brothers all turned and marched from the room with military precision.

Meanwhile, in a different royal palace:

"I still can't believe you came back here without my prince!" Briar Rose snarled. She picked up the golden bowl of dried figs that sat beside her throne and flung it angrily. It crashed through a stained-glass window, sending a rain of colored shards onto the marble floor. "You had one simple job! One! Bring me Prince Liam. And instead you show up with his bratty little sister."

Ruffian the Blue moaned and stared at his feet. "I've already explained why," he mumbled.

"Briar, get a grip," Lila said. "Believe me, the last thing I want to see is my brother in your arms. But if you don't get your army out to Mount Batwing immediately, Liam's going to end up dead. Do you get what that means? No wedding."

Briar wrinkled her nose at Lila. "I know that, you annoying flea. I'm just having a tantrum, which is my royal right as a princess." She turned to a nearby guard. "I want Avondell's entire army mobilized in ten minutes. And have my carriage waiting as well."

"Your carriage?" Lila asked.

"Do you think I'm going to risk Ruffian the Whiner failing again?" Briar said, arching her brow. "I'm riding along to see to it myself that Liam comes back home with us. And so are you."

Ten minutes later, five hundred armed cavalry men rode off in unison under the Avondellian flag (which Liam had never wiped his feet on, by the way), cutting through forests along Ruffian's secret shortcut to the Orphaned Wastes. And at the head of the military force: a ridiculous gold-plated carriage, in which a sweating Lila sat sandwiched between Briar Rose and Ruffian the Blue.

Ruffian locked Lila's wrists into a set of shackles. Briar snatched the key from the bounty hunter's fingers and tossed it out the window. Ruffian just stared at her, puzzled.

"I don't trust this brat," Briar said.

"This is going to be a long ride," Lila sighed.

* * *

On another road, in another kingdom, Henrik of Sturmhagen and fifteen of his equally brawny brothers marched cheerily along, twirling battle-axes, flexing muscles, and singing war songs.

On yet another road, another army was on the move—an army of men in black, some on horseback, some on foot. They pulled wagons loaded with pikes, clubs, and swords, cooking pots and sleeping bags. Deeb Rauber, the Bandit King, perched up on the roof of a supply wagon, giggling maniacally as he launched walnuts into his followers' backsides with a slingshot.

Not too far away, a smaller wagon rumbled through the woods. Flik, Frak, and Frank said nothing as they rode along. They never even changed expressions. Inside the vehicle, Snow White was feverishly weaving her forty-seventh potholder of the day, trying desperately to keep her mind off Duncan.

In a different section of those woods, though far from any road, Ella was sprinting as fast as she could to outrun a hungry wolf. She hurdled a thick gorse bush and shimmied into a hollow log to avoid the animal's scratching claws. The muscular beast tried to squeeze itself in after her and promptly got its head stuck. Ella laughed, slid out the other end of the log, and kept on running.

On still another road, a green-haired man wobbled by on peppermint-stick stilts; a fiery-plumed bird of paradise perched on his shoulder. But he's not in this story, so don't pay any attention to him.

Ignoring roads altogether, Zaubera meandered through the forest, flash-frying any squirrels or baby bunnies that dared to cross her path. Behind her floated a large but cramped green bubble, holding four terrified bards. They'd witnessed her anger upon discovering that the goblins had let Pennyfeather escape. None of the four bards ever thought he'd be able to eat bacon again.

The witch was heading to Mount Batwing—just like everybody else. It was midsummer eve.

22

PRINCE CHARMING IS A SNEAK

The princes were in high spirits as they tromped through the forest. Duncan serenaded the others with his favorite dwarven campfire song, "Flames and Beards Don't Mix." As he finished with a flourish—"So don't bend over the cooooooooals!"—Liam and Frederic applauded.

"Thank you, Duncan," said Liam. "I actually kind of liked that."

"Yes, marching off to a deadly showdown has been much more enjoyable this time around," Frederic said. "I really do wish we'd been able to get our horses back, though."

"Me too," Duncan said.

"You didn't lose a horse," Gustav reminded him.

"Not on *this* trip," Duncan said. "But I lost one a few months ago. His name was Papa Scoots. I rode him down to the stream to look for shiny stones one day, and while I was naming some trout, he took off. I think I embarrassed him."

"My horse had been with me through all my greatest adventures," Liam said. "If I didn't have him during my battle with the evil fairy, I don't know if I would have made it out alive. Mark my words: If I get the chance to go back to Rauber's castle and look for Thunderbreaker, I will." He was interrupted by snickering. "What, Gustav?"

"It's a bit over the top, isn't it?" Gustav said. "Thunderbreaker?"

"He's a powerful warhorse. What's wrong with giving him a powerful name?" Liam replied.

"Warhorse—pah!" Gustav scoffed. "*Mine* was a real warhorse. Did you see the size of its haunches?"

"And what, may I ask, is the oh-so-perfect name of your horse?" Liam inquired coolly.

Gustav mumbled something.

"What was that?" Frederic asked with a smirk.

"Seventeen," Gustav grumbled, a bit more audibly.

"Seventeen what?" Duncan asked.

"*Seventeen*," Gustav repeated. "That's the horse's name. I didn't name him. Every child in our family was given a horse when he came of age. And the horses were named according to our birth order. So mine is Seventeen."

"My horse's name was Gwendolyn," Frederic said. "It's not like I had any kind of history with her, though. I only met her the day I left on this journey. But considering the way she tolerated my poor riding skills so well, I have to say I grew quite fond of her. I do hope I get to see her again someday."

"Isn't that her there?" Duncan asked, pointing at a tan mare that was grazing just beyond the trees ahead of them.

The four princes stopped in their tracks. Indeed, the Harmonian crest was emblazoned upon the horse's saddle. The four men crept closer.

"It really is Gwendolyn," Frederic said in a stunned whisper.

"Seventeen!" Gustav beamed as he spotted his own horse. He caught himself grinning giddily, and quickly spat on the ground before anybody noticed.

"All of our horses are there," Liam said.

"Well, except mine," Duncan added, with some disappointment. If the others' horses had returned, he expected his magical luck to deliver Papa Scoots as well.

The princes' three horses (plus several dozen others) were tied to a row of trees in a makeshift corral.

"That's a lot of horses. What are they all doing out here?" Frederic asked. "Do you think the Bandit King sold our horses to a trader or something?"

"No, I think Rauber and his men are using our horses themselves," Liam said. "Look over there. And be absolutely quiet."

He ushered the men farther off the trail and pointed out a drab canvas tent beyond the trees.

"You think some of the bandits are over there?" Duncan asked. The four men crouched low to the ground and slunk closer. As they approached, they could see that this wasn't the only tent that had been pitched in the nearby field. An entire *city* of tents lay before them; too many to count. At the heart of the crowded camp flew a flag that depicted an old, bearded king being kicked by a giant boot: the flag of the Bandit King.

"I think *all* the bandits are over there," Liam said.

They watched as brutish-looking men—several of whom they recognized from their time in the Bandit King's castle—emerged from their tents and milled about, chatting and occasionally punching one another. As the sun started to set, a few of the bandits started campfires and warmed up blackened pots of gruel.

"They're busy making dinner," Gustav said. "Let's steal our horses back before they notice."

"No," Liam said. "Leave the horses for now. This is our chance to find out what the bandits are up to. In these black thieves' outfits, we're perfectly dressed for stealth work. Let's see if we can eavesdrop."

"Look!" Frederic gasped. "It's Horace and Neville!"

"Who?"

"The two guys who captured us back at that house in Sylvaria," Frederic said. "The big one who threw the giant sword at Duncan and the little guy with the ratty mustache."

"Oh, yeah," Duncan said. "There they are." Horace and Neville were deep in conversation, walking along the outskirts of the camp only a few yards away.

"Huh. I figured Rauber would have knocked them off by now," Gustav said.

"Come on," Liam whispered. He squatted and crept off until he was only a few feet behind Horace and Neville. The others followed, holding their breath.

"Whuddaya suppose he wants to do to us now?" Neville wheezed in his pinched nasal voice.

"Give us our old jobs back, I hope," Horace said. "I'm more'n ready to be done cleanin' up after the horses."

"That's unlikely, though, don't ya think?" Neville asked. "He's been torturing us for days. I'm still sore from all the noogies. Frankly, I'm happy to be alive. I'll gladly scoop some you-know-what if it means my head stays attached."

"You know, I never seen the kid *kill* anyone," Horace said. "You do realize we're workin' for a child, right?"

Neville came to an abrupt stop. Liam did as well, causing the other princes to smack into one another and pile up behind him. The four men wobbled but grabbed one another's shoulders and managed to stay up.

"Don't mention that!" Neville barked in a harsh whisper. "You got a death wish or somethin'? We're right near his tent. What if he heard you sayin' how he's a . . . a . . . *you know*."

"A little kid," Horace said.

"Aagh! Shut up, shut up, shut up!" Neville took off his black felt cap and started beating Horace with it. Horace snickered. He enjoyed watching Neville get scared.

"Let's go see what the tyke wants," Horace said, and he started singing, "Snips and snails and puppy dogs' tails, that's what *little boys* are made of." Neville smacked his hands to his head in despair.

The two bandits turned and entered a large tent. The princes sidled over and placed their ears against the drab, dirt-colored canvas to listen.

"You wanted to see us, sir," they heard Horace say. As much as Horace liked to joke about the Bandit King for Neville's benefit, he always showed total respect in the presence of the diabolical tween. He did not want to end up on the wrong side of one of Deeb Rauber's tantrums. He knew a guard who'd once made the mistake of nicking a cookie from Rauber, and was subjected to a solid week of spitball torture.

"You know I like you two, right?" Rauber asked in his reedy voice.

"Uh, yes, sure," Neville said.

"We do what we can," Horace added.

"Now, I still haven't forgiven you for that fiasco on the roof the other day," Rauber said. "But I need a couple of right-hand men, and in this army of losers, you guys are sadly the best I've got."

"Happy to hear it, sir," Neville said.

Horace bumped him and whispered, "That wasn't a compliment."

"And so, it is with much displeasure," Rauber continued

in an overly formal tone, "that I hereby name you two Sir Horace and Sir Neville, my first official knights."

"An honor, sir," Horace responded.

"As my knights," Rauber said, "you will manage the daily business of our new castle. I'm sure it will be a much larger castle than our old one, so I imagine it'll need a lot more cleaning. You'll need to get the kitchen in running order; make sure everybody—but especially me—stays fed and happy."

"If ya don't mind me sayin' so, sir," Neville hedged, "if me and him are knights now, shouldn't we be doin' something a bit more, I dunno, excitin'?"

"Shall I ready the spitballs, Sir Neville?"

"No, sir."

"Now, as I was saying," Rauber went on. "You two will also deal with visitors. I'm sure all sorts of important people from faraway nations will be knocking on my door once I've got a kingdom of my own. So you will invite them in for a banquet and—I don't know—diplomatic negotiations or something. Then we steal all their stuff."

As Rauber laughed, the princes glanced at one another with disbelief.

"I gotta say, sir," Horace added, "this is a pretty genius deal you worked out."

"I know!" Rauber shouted with glee. "A couple hours of guard work and we get an entire kingdom in return. I tell you, being a king is going to be a lot more fun when I have innocent people to push around and not just you bozos."

"The witch said ya could take whichever of the five ya wanted," said Neville. "Have ya decided which one yer takin'?"

"Yes. I think this kingdom right here suits me well," Rauber said. "I'm taking over Sturmhagen."

"Okay, that's enough," Gustav hissed through clenched teeth. "We crush them right now."

"Gustav, no," Liam warned. He grabbed hold of Gustav's arm and prevented him from standing. "There are four of us and, oh, I'd say about two hundred of them— far more than we saw back at the castle. This throws a huge snag into our plans. We need to change tactics. We'll never even get the map if we have to make it through Rauber's entire army. We need to leave and run to Castle Sturmhagen *first* to get reinforcements."

"No, we should crush them now," Gustav sneered.

"Gustav, listen to reason," Liam said. "The four of us cannot take out an entire army. With your brothers, though, and your father's guards—"

"We're wasting time talking about it when we could just chop our way through this canvas and take care of the little brat right now," Gustav growled.

Frederic and Duncan both made shushing noises.

"Rushing into things hasn't helped much in the past, has it, Gustav?" Liam spat.

"So tell me a better idea, Professor Brainstorm," Gustav said.

Frederic and Duncan tried to shush them again.

"I just told you a better idea: We go to your family," Liam insisted.

"That's pointless!" Gustav argued. "We've got the opportunity to take Rauber out now. Without the little bully, his army will fall apart."

"It's too risky!" Liam snarled. "I don't want any dead princes on my conscience!"

"Guys," Frederic hissed. "You're being a little loud."

"STAY OUT OF IT!" Liam and Gustav shouted in unison.

"What was that?" they heard the Bandit King call out from inside the tent.

"Crud," muttered Liam.

Rauber burst out of the tent with Horace and Neville at his side.

"Holy cow!" Rauber giggled. "I can't believe you dolts were dumb enough to come back!" He started dancing around and hooting with wicked joy.

"Split up," Liam said, as bandits began running toward them from all around. He grasped Duncan's arm and pulled him in one direction; Gustav grabbed Frederic by the collar and ran off in the other.

"Boys!" Horace bellowed loudly, his voice echoing through the city of tents. "We've got some princes to catch!"

"Ow! Both my feet fell asleep," Frederic wailed as he hopped along awkwardly. "Ow-ow-ow-ow-ow!" Huffing, Gustav hoisted Frederic off the ground, slung him over his shoulder, and kept running. Bandits lunged toward him as he ran, but each time one got too close, Gustav would pivot and let Frederic's booted feet swing around to kick the man in the face. "Ooh, this is waking my feet up," Frederic said.

Neville darted ahead of Gustav. He planted himself in the big prince's path and pulled out a sharp, glinting dagger.

"Please don't run toward the man with the knife," Frederic pleaded.

"Just hold on," Gustav said as he barreled toward the sneering Neville. Gustav yanked one of Frederic's boots off and pitched it at the wiry bandit. The heel of the boot smacked Neville right between the eyes and knocked him flat. Without ever slowing his pace, Gustav reached down with his free arm, plucked the boot up from where it lay next to the groaning bandit, and slapped it back onto Frederic's foot. He also stepped on Neville's hand for good measure. With Frederic still over his shoulder, Gustav continued his juggernaut run out of the camp and disappeared into the trees.

Meanwhile, Horace bounded after Liam and Duncan. "You fellas must have really missed us," the big bandit called out. "I'm touched you came back to see us again."

"You've completely misunderstood!" Duncan yelled back to Horace, as he and Liam hopped over a series of staked tent ropes. "We didn't miss you at all! That's not why we're here!"

"Sarcasm, Duncan. Sarcasm," Liam said as he dodged a diving bandit.

"You might as well slow down, you've got no place to go," Horace said.

Liam stopped as he saw a wall of bandits closing in ahead of them. He glanced left and right to see an impenetrable tangle of tents, wagons, and supply crates. They were trapped. Horace began strolling lazily toward them, casually swinging a huge wooden club—a weapon that looked large and strong enough to flatten a human head into a crepe.

"Throw me at him," Duncan said. "Let's see what happens."

"That's insane," Liam replied, but he considered the idea. Liam generally wrote off Duncan's belief in his "magical luck" as just another of his quirks, but every so often, such as when they survived that fall from Rauber's roof, he couldn't help but wonder a little. Duncan looked to Liam expectantly. "Okay," Liam shrugged.

He took hold of Duncan and heaved the small man straight at Horace. The bulky bandit caught Duncan neatly in his one free arm and held him tight.

"Heh," Horace chuckled. "Well, thank you. I honestly didn't expect it to be *that* easy."

Liam simply shook his head in disappointment. He made no attempt to defend himself as ten large bandits pounced from behind. One ripped Liam's sword away as the others held his limbs down. Fighting was pointless, especially when Duncan was completely at the enemy's mercy.

Duncan hung limply in Horace's grasp, his mind reeling. Nothing remotely good had happened. Horace hadn't had a sudden heart attack. The ground hadn't opened up and swallowed the bandits. No, Duncan just got caught by the bad guy. *There's no question about it anymore,* he thought. *My luck has run out.*

23

Prince Charming Takes the Wrong Seat

The sun had fully set by the time Gustav slowed his retreat and put Frederic back down on his own two feet. They were miles away from the bandit camp, surrounded by thick, gnarly underbrush.

"Footsies all better?" Gustav asked.

"Yes. Thanks for the lift," Frederic replied. "Do you think they're still following us?"

"No." Gustav shook his head. "We can catch our breath."

"Oh, Gustav, before I forget . . . ," Frederic said. "I've been thinking: You lost your sword, and I still have mine. That feels just plain wrong to me. I want you to have my sword. We'd both be better off."

He reached to his belt to grab the dwarven blade but realized, with a gasp, that it was not there. "Oh, no. It's—"

"Don't panic. I already have it," Gustav said. "I thought the same thing you did, so I snagged the sword from you hours ago."

"You stole my sword?"

"You just said you wanted me to have it!"

"I wanted to *give* it to you. I didn't want you to swipe it."

"What difference does it make? I have the sword, we're fine."

Frederic sighed. He felt his way through the near blackness, until he found a big tree to lean against.

"It is really, really dark," he said. "I wish we had Duncan with us right now. He'd probably pull a lit torch out of his pocket or something."

"Yeah, and a bed, and a pillow, and an all-flute orchestra to play him a lullaby," Gustav snickered. "But seriously, you need to stop encouraging the little guy. *You* don't honestly think he's magic, do you?"

"I don't know. I'm less skeptical about such things ever since I saw a coach turn into a pumpkin," Frederic said earnestly. "Do you think Duncan and Liam got away, too?"

Gustav shrugged. "We can't go looking for them now. We should try to rest until dawn and start searching then."

"That makes sense." Frederic looked around. Little moonlight could make its way through the thick forest canopy overhead. All he saw were the outlines of trees. He slid down to the ground but popped back up, squealing. "Nettles! Pointy nettles all over the ground," he moaned.

Gustav swiped his feet back and forth. "Just kick them out of the way."

"Can't we see if there's a better place to lie down?" Frederic peered into the shadows and spotted a soft-looking patch of green. "Gustav," he called. "There's a nice bed of moss over here."

Gustav glanced over just in time to see Frederic snuggling into the tangled green fur of a sleeping troll. "No!" he yelled.

But it was too late.

"What sit on Troll?" the monster bellowed, and jumped to its feet. Frederic was sent flying to the ground—and got a backside full of nettles when he landed. "Ouch-ouch-ouch-ouch-ouch-ouch-ouch-ouch-*ouch*!" he moaned, as he rolled back and forth. The troll scooped the prince up into its arms.

"Drop him, troll," Gustav growled, drawing his sword.

"Ha-ha! Round-Head Man have toy baby sword!" The

troll's laugh was guttural, as if it were trying to cough up a hairball.

"This is no plaything, troll," Gustav said. "It's dwarven steel. And I will ram it right through you if you don't put that man down."

"But Ouching Man sit on Troll," the monster said. "Ouching Man is Troll's prisoner now."

The troll cupped one furry, clawed hand by its mouth and gave a loud shout that reverberated through the trees: "Troll has prisoner!"

Trees moved and quivered all around Gustav. Within seconds, half a dozen more trolls appeared.

"Troll has *two* prisoners!" one of them noted pleasantly.

Gustav flexed his fingers around the hilt of his sword. Despite being greatly outnumbered and barely being able to see his enemies in the darkness, he was, as usual, prepared to leap into battle.

"Don't do it, Gustav," Frederic pleaded from within the tight troll bear hug. "Don't make a mistake we'll regret."

For once, Gustav held back. He slipped the sword under his belt and raised his empty hands up in the air. The trolls swooped in, lifted him high over their heads, and marched off into the blackness with a chant of "PRIS-O-NERS! PRIS-O-NERS!"

Gustav shot a wary look at Frederic, who was slung over the shoulder of the first troll. "Bed of moss—humph!"

When dawn broke the next morning, Frederic and Gustav awoke to find themselves in a wooden cage in the center of a troll village. At least they *assumed* it to be a troll village. What trolls refer to as a "village," most humans would refer to as a "big mess of sticks."

Trolls are not great builders. Most of their "houses" don't resemble buildings at all; they consist of three to five logs haphazardly leaned up against one another. A fancier troll home might have a "door," which would actually just be one more log resting against the others—except you were supposed to move it out of the way when you entered.

FiG. 39
TROLL "HOUSE"

The cage that the princes were in was constructed just as poorly. The "bars" were long, thin sticks that even Frederic could have easily snapped in half. Not that he would have needed to, because the sticks were spaced far enough apart to easily step between. And there was nothing holding the sticks together. No ties, no paste—nothing. Frederic figured the entire structure would probably collapse if he breathed on it too hard.

"Do they really think we can't get out of here?" Frederic asked.

Big, swampy-green trolls strolled about casually, acting as if the two princes were securely locked away.

"The heck with this," said Gustav. "Let's go." He strolled out, between the bars, into the village square, and Frederic scurried after him. They'd taken only a few steps away from the cage when the big troll who had captured them the night before ran over.

"Where going? Round-Head Man and Ouching Man are prisoners," the troll said. "Back in cage."

"Why should we?" Gustav said, with a steely-eyed squint.

"What my friend is asking," Frederic offered, "is why we can't just talk this out."

"You're not going to be able to negotiate with trolls, Señor Sweet-Talk," Gustav said to him. "They're not very bright."

"Back in cage now!" the troll ordered.

"No!" Gustav yelled back in its face. "Now get out of our way, troll, or you'll meet the business end of my blade."

"Look, Mr. Troll," Frederic said. "Why exactly do you want to keep us here?"

"Ouching Man sat on Troll," the monster said, crossing its arms.

"And I am terribly sorry about that," Frederic said. "It was an accident. It was very dark, and I couldn't see you there. Surely you can forgive an honest mistake like that. I mean, it's not like sitting on someone is against the law."

"Is for trolls," the troll said bluntly.

"Sitting on a troll is actually *illegal* under troll law?" Gustav asked.

"Yes."

"What's the punishment for it?" Frederic asked.

"Troll not sure," the creature said, scratching its chin. "Trolls very careful not to sit on other trolls. No one done it before."

"Well, then why don't we just say that one night in jail was enough and we'll be on our way?" Frederic suggested.

"No. It very important for trolls to follow rules of troll law," the creature said thoughtfully. "Now back in cage, while Troll find out punishment for sit on troll."

"You're stupider than you look, troll," Gustav barked,

"if you think we're going to wait around patiently until you decide to eat us."

The troll threw its arms up in frustration. "Why humans never remember trolls is herbivore!" it cried. The monster lowered its shaggy, one-horned head and howled angrily into the princes' faces. "Trolls is vegetarian! Last time Troll looked, Round-Head Man made of meat! Oh, Troll is *so tired* of closed-minded humans!"

Gustav and Frederic were too taken aback to respond. They simply stood there as the monster's heavily scallion-scented breath dampened their faces.

"Argh, Troll get so frustrated!" the creature continued. "Round-Head Man is just like Angry Man that think Troll eat Shovel Lady's children! Troll just wanted some beets!"

Gustav's eyes widened. "Criminy," he muttered, turning to Frederic. "I think this is the same troll I fought at that beet farm the day I met you."

"What?" Frederic and the troll both said together.

"This is really the same troll from the beet farm?" Frederic asked.

"I'm pretty sure," Gustav replied.

"Troll fight *Angry Man* at beet farm," the troll said. "Not Round-Head Man."

"Um, Mr. Troll," Frederic tried. "I think Round-Head

Man *is* Angry Man."

"But Angry Man have long hair like dead grass."

"He did," Frederic explained. "But his long, dead hair went bye-bye. And now he has a round head."

The troll examined Gustav's face carefully. "Uh-oh," it exclaimed. "Troll think Ouching Man right. Troll not recognize Angry Man with no grassy head. Humans all look alike to Troll."

"Oh, and *now* who's being closed-minded?" Gustav shouted with smug satisfaction.

"So Troll captured Angry Man, huh?" the troll retorted. "This change things. Troll *hate* Angry Man. Maybe Troll turn carnivore for just one day."

"Now, wait," Frederic said quickly. "Just because he beat you in a battle doesn't mean you need to take revenge. We can always—"

The troll let out one of its retching laughs. "Ha-ha! Angry Man not beat Troll. Troll beat Angry Man."

"No, no," Gustav said, trying to save face in front of Frederic. "I definitely beat you."

"Angry Man not beat Troll. *Shovel Lady* beat Troll."

Gustav twirled his finger next to his head. *Loony,* he mouthed.

"You know, it doesn't matter who beat who," Frederic

said. "Mr. Troll, you have to understand that my friend here was only fighting with you because you were stealing crops from that family."

"Trolls *have* to steal food. How else trolls supposed to eat?" The troll's gritty voice began to quiver slightly. "Like Troll say, trolls vegetarian. But trolls live in forest. Forest dirt not good for making veggies grow. Trolls starve unless trolls take veggies from humans."

"So all you need is some workable farmland," Frederic said, getting the picture. "Mr. Troll, why don't you and your people move out of the forest?"

"Every time trolls try leave forest, humans fight trolls and send trolls back. Greedy humans want land for humans only."

"Well, that's just wrong," Frederic said earnestly. He understood the trolls' dilemma. The people of Sturmhagen thought of them as monsters—which technically they were, but that's beside the point—so any attempt by the trolls to move out of the forest and onto decent farmland was viewed as an attack. This was Frederic's chance to broker a peace treaty.

"Lucky for you, you've got someone right here who can help," he continued. "Mr. Troll, do you know who Angry Man really is?"

"Angry Man is Angry Man," the troll replied. "Says mean things 'bout trolls and stops Troll from getting food."

Gustav frowned. He eyed Frederic cautiously.

"No," Frederic said. "This man is the prince of Sturmhagen. His family rules this kingdom. He can arrange to have some farmland set aside for the trolls."

Gustav tugged at Frederic's elbow. "I don't have the authority to—" Frederic gave Gustav a swift kick.

"Angry Man can really do that?" the troll asked, with a tinge of hopefulness in its voice.

"Yes, he can," Frederic said definitively. "And he will."

The troll raised its arms in the air and called to its fellow monsters, "Trolls, come here! Angry Man is *Prince* Angry Man! Angry Man give trolls land to grow trolls' own vegetables!"

About seventy trolls, nearly the entire village, came bounding over. They looked like rolling waves of collard greens, and Frederic thought momentarily that the idea of these creatures eating vegetables seemed almost cannibalistic.

The troll villagers cheered and howled. Random shouts of "Yay, Angry Man!" and "Yay, veggies!" rose from the crowd.

"Glad to hear you're all so excited about it," Frederic

said. "His real name, by the way, is Prince Gustav of Sturmhagen. And I am Frederic."

"Troll will call you Angry Man and Ouching Man," the lead troll stated matter-of-factly. "It is troll way: Trolls name humans after first thing troll notices about humans."

"Fair enough," Frederic said. "But we'd love to know *your* name, Mr. Troll."

The troll furrowed its shaggy brow. "Ouching Man and Angry Man already know Troll's name. Call Troll by Troll's name whole time now."

"I'm sorry, I'm confused," Frederic said.

"Troll's name is Troll," the troll said, flashing a toothy smile. "All trolls' name is Troll." He pointed to a number of other trolls in the crowd. "That's Troll. And that's Troll. And that's Troll. . . . All Troll."

"Every troll is just named Troll?" Gustav asked in disbelief. "It must be impossible to keep track of who's who."

"Yeah," Troll said with a sigh. "It not easy."

"So, Troll . . . ," Frederic began.

"Say 'Mr. Troll,'" Troll interjected. "Troll like sound of it."

"Very well . . . Mr. Troll," Frederic continued. "What are your plans for us now? Are you going to keep us locked in your prison? Or will you let Prince Angry Man go back to his castle and work out a sweet land deal for you and your people?"

"Angry Man can go!" Mr. Troll loudly declared, and a cheer rose up from the troll villagers. Mr. Troll then turned to Frederic with a somber look on his face. "But Ouching Man must stay. Ouching Man break troll law. Ouching Man needs be punished."

"But look, Mr. Troll," Frederic pleaded. "Gustav needs me to go with him. If I have to sit in this cage for ages, you won't be able to get your land."

"Ooh! Ooh! Troll found it!" came a cry from the back of the crowd. A squat three-horned troll moved to the front. It held a pile of large floppy leaves that were pinned together by one sharp stick. "Troll found troll law book!"

Frederic and Gustav exchanged worried glances. Frederic braced himself for the news that he would be expected to spend a hundred years in a troll prison, or worse.

The squat troll shuffled through the leaves of its "book," sending several fluttering free, until it found the page it wanted. The creature pointed to a bunch of squiggles that we have to assume were words, and read, "Punishment for human sit on troll is . . . troll sit on human."

"Great!" Gustav said. He looked at Frederic. "Well, get

on the ground and get it over with."

"Ouching Man heard Angry Man," big Mr. Troll said. "Lie down."

Frederic took a deep breath and lay down in the dirt. He hadn't quite finished positioning himself when Mr. Troll plopped down on him. Frederic let out a big *oof!* and Mr. Troll stood back up.

"Okay," Mr. Troll said. "Ouching Man can go now."

"That wasn't so bad," Frederic said, dusting himself off. "Once you've been squashed by a giant, a troll doesn't even seem nearly as heavy."

With the entertainment over, the trolls dispersed, shuffling back off to do whatever it is that trolls do—steal vegetables, growl at humans, pile two rocks on top of each other and call it a gazebo . . . stuff like that.

"Wait, trolls!" Frederic hollered, waving his hands over his head. The creatures paid him no attention, so he bumped his hip against the cage. The entire structure crashed to the ground in a heap. This had the desired effect, as most of the trolls turned back to look at Frederic and Gustav standing among the scattered sticks.

"Hey, Ouching Man break cage! That going to take *minutes* to rebuild," Mr. Troll complained. He considered the task for a second and then waved his big, furry hand dismissively. "Eh. Troll fix later. Don't need cage anyway unless Ouching Man sit on troll again."

"Never mind the cage, I have something very important to tell you," Frederic said, addressing all the villagers. "This will affect all you trolls. Yes, even you, Troll. And you, too, Troll."

One troll in the crowd leaned over to its neighbor and said approvingly, "Personal touch is nice."

"Now as I said," Frederic continued, "my friend Gustav here is a ruler of Sturmhagen, and he can help you trolls get some farmland of your own. He will do that because he likes trolls. He knows that trolls are good . . . people." Many of the trolls nodded in appreciation. Frederic glanced over at Gustav to make sure he wasn't going to interrupt, but Gustav quietly stood by with his arms crossed, curious to see what Frederic was up to.

"However, not every human is as nice as us," Frederic said. "Some don't like trolls. There's a group of humans in the forest not too far from here right now who *hate* trolls." Angry grumbles arose from the crowd.

"And those nasty, anti-troll humans are planning to take over the kingdom of Sturmhagen. If the Bandit King and his men do this, Angry Man won't be able to help you trolls."

"Trolls will not let this happen," Mr. Troll declared unequivocally. "Trolls will stop Bandit Man!"

"He's really more of a Bandit Boy," Gustav said.

"Boy, man—it no matter to trolls," Mr. Troll said. "Angry Man is trolls' friend now. If Bandit Boy want to do bad things to Angry Man, trolls will do bad things to Bandit Boy." A chorus of troll roars sounded from all around them.

"Where are bad humans?" Mr. Troll asked. His already unattractive face twisted itself into a frightening mask of fur, teeth, and angry glowing eyes. It sent a shiver through Frederic, and even Gustav flinched a little at the sight.

"They've set up camp in a big field to the west of here," Frederic told them.

"Come, trolls!" Mr. Troll bellowed. "Trolls attack!"

With one hand, Mr. Troll hoisted Frederic up onto his shoulders. A gangly, hunchbacked troll grabbed Gustav and did the same. As they rode atop their trolls, Gustav glanced at Frederic.

"This could get very ugly, you know," he said.

Frederic nodded.

"It's the best idea you've had yet," Gustav said gleefully.

And with that, the ground began to rumble as the entire troll village started marching westward.

24

Prince Charming Hates Children

"H ey, kid," Liam taunted.

He and Duncan were each tied to a tree trunk on the edge of the bandit camp. They'd spent the whole night there. And throughout that long, sleepless night (well, sleepless for Liam, at least—Duncan, exhausted by self-doubt, had been out for hours), Liam had come up with a plan for dealing with the Bandit King. From what he could gather, Rauber had one major weakness: He was sensitive about his age. As soon as Liam saw the Bandit King walking by that morning, he started in. "Little boy, I'm talking to you."

Rauber and his small entourage stopped. The Bandit King poked Horace, who was right by his side (Neville, having let the other princes slip away, had been demoted to the role of spitball target, and was busy dangling upside-down from a flagpole).

"Did you hear that, Horace?" Rauber smirked. "The prince called you little." All the bandits laughed.

"That's really funny, kiddo," Liam said. "But you know I'm talking to you, right, squirt?"

"You want me to punch 'im?" Horace asked Rauber.

The Bandit King shook his head. "You know, I'd taken you for the smart one," he said to Liam. "But maybe your snoozing buddy over there is the real brains of your outfit."

Duncan, who'd been snoring softly, stirred and opened his eyes a crack. "Hmm, what's that?" he muttered. "Time for flute lessons?"

"Or maybe not," Rauber snickered.

"No, Duncan, we're in the bandit camp, remember?" Liam said.

"Oh, yes, that's right," Duncan said glumly. "I tried something dumb and ruined everything. My luck is gone. I remember now. So, Liam, you were saying . . ."

"I was just trying to get the attention of the runny-nosed baby over there who likes to play bad guy," Liam sneered at Rauber.

"What's with all the insults?" the Bandit King snapped. "What are you playing at?"

"He's tryin' to make you angry, sir," Horace advised. "You sure you don't want me to punch 'im? I got a pretty big arm span—I can probably sock both of these princes in the face at the same time."

"Might as well go ahead," Duncan moped. "I'm sure any swing you take at me will land good and hard, since I've got no luck left."

"No, Deeb, I'm not trying to make you angry," Liam said. "I'm calling it like I see it. The same way your big man Horace does."

Horace raised his eyebrows.

"Okay, Prince, I'll bite. But only because I'm curious to see where this is all going," Rauber said. "What are you saying about Horace?"

"Oh, just that he understands you're nothing more than a weaselly little brat," Liam said. "You should hear the way he talks about you to the other bandits—saying how ridiculous it is that they're working for a child . . ." Several of the bandits gasped.

". . . laughing at all those grown men who are frightened of a little boy," Liam went on, "joking about how easily he could crush you if he ever wanted to . . ."

Horace broke into a panicky sweat. "It's not true, sir. He's making it all up."

Rauber gave Horace a hard kick in the ankle. "You know, I *thought* I heard the puppy-dog-tails song outside my tent last night," Rauber screeched. "I figured I must have imagined it, because no one would be *idiotic* enough to sing that song at my camp. You traitorous buffoon!" He kicked Horace twice more, the big man wincing with each blow. The Bandit King's strikes didn't hurt Horace, but the big man knew full well what it meant to be on the wrong end of one of Deeb Rauber's tantrums.

"That wasn't me," Horace cried. "It was Neville!"

"Yeah, right! Neville faints if I flick a booger in his direction. He doesn't have the guts for treason," Rauber retorted. "*You're* the one who thinks he's better than me—*meaner* than me. I'll show you who's mean. I'll hang you up by your back hair!"

Duncan was perking up. He was inspired watching the way Liam was manipulating Rauber. *He's a master,* Duncan realized. *He's a planner, a doer, a man of action. Liam doesn't rely on luck. Liam* creates *his own luck.*

"Hey, kid," Liam shouted, eager to pile on. "I've got an idea. Instead of beating up on

FiG. 40
DEEB
RAUBER

your henchman yourself, why don't you make him fight me? I'm sure a bullying brat like you would get a kick out of seeing the two of us pummel each other."

"Oh, hey, that's a fantastic idea!" Rauber declared, dripping with over-the-top sarcasm. "I'll untie you and put a weapon in your hand—nothing could go wrong with that idea! It's not like you've ever escaped from me before by suggesting a duel!" He ran over to the tied-up Liam and glared up at him. "I AM NOT STUPID!"

"What was that?" Liam said casually. "You're so short. I can't hear you all the way down there."

Furious, Rauber marched off to the crowd, grabbed a random bandit by the sleeve, and dragged him back to Liam's tree. Rauber shoved the bandit down onto his hands and knees and stepped up onto the henchman's back so he could get nose-to-nose with the prince.

"CAN YOU HEAR ME NOW?" Rauber screamed into Liam's face. "I AM NOT STUPID!"

That's when Liam thrust his upper body forward and head-butted the Bandit King as hard as he could. Rauber toppled backward off the kneeling henchman and lay unconscious on his back in the grass.

The bandits were stunned. "Now's your chance, Horace!" Liam said, shaking off the ringing in his ears. "Get him while he's down. Take control while you can."

Horace's head was spinning as well—metaphorically, that is. "I don't get you, Prince," he said cautiously. "First you try to get me in trouble, then you try to help me."

"I've been *helping* you the whole time," Liam said. He knew he had to talk fast and get himself and Duncan out of there before Rauber woke up. "Let's team up here, Horace. I'm on your side."

"My side, huh? The heroic prince wants to join the Bandit Army?" Horace asked suspiciously. "Not likely."

"Of course he doesn't want to join you," Duncan chimed in. "I've gotten to know this man pretty well in the past several days, and believe me, there's nothing more important to him than being a hero."

"Hey, Horace, don't listen to this guy," Liam said. He prayed that Duncan would not ruin his strategy. "Duncan— or whatever his name is—barely knows me."

"Don't be so modest, Liam. You're the biggest hero there is," Duncan went on, flashing his friend a wink. "Or at least, he used to be. Everybody hates him now, ever since he dumped Sleeping Beauty."

"Oh, that's right; that was you," Horace said with a bemused smile. "Maybe you *should* join us. Heh-heh."

"But it tears him apart that people don't treat him like

a hero anymore," Duncan said. He was through standing around and waiting for his imaginary luck to save the day. From now on, he was in command of his own destiny. "Liam's been looking for some way to make everybody love him again. And what could be a greater victory for any hero than to capture the notorious Bandit King? My pal, Prince Liam, wants to be the one to get the glory for tossing Deeb Rauber in a dungeon. You see? So we have a little proposition for you."

"Oh, I get it," Horace said with a knowing nod. "You want me to give you the Bandit King, all wrapped-up-like, with a shiny bow an' everything. But what could you give me in return that's gonna be better than the whoppin' ransom I could get for you?"

"Well, first of all, in case you weren't paying attention: Everybody hates me," Liam said. "You're not going to get much of a ransom from my people—that's for sure. And besides, wouldn't you trade a few loads of ransom money for an *entire kingdom*? Because that's what I'll give you in return: Sturmhagen."

Horace chuckled. "The old lady's already going to give us Sturmhagen."

"The old lady's dead," Liam said.

Horace's eyes widened. "Explain."

"Look inside my right pants pocket, the long one on the side," Liam said.

Horace seemed skeptical.

"You'll find the witch's ransom notes in there," Liam said. "We intercepted them."

Horace motioned for one of the other bandits to check Liam's pocket. "It's true," the bandit reported, rerolling the scroll he'd checked and slipping it back into Liam's long pocket.

"We found out about the witch's plan, snuck into her fortress overnight, and slew her in her sleep," Liam said. "Why do you think we were back in these woods, wearing these black clothes?"

Horace was dumbstruck.

"So, you're not taking over Sturmhagen anytime soon," Liam said. "At least not with the witch's help. But I can offer you another way in the door."

"Whaddaya got?" Horace said, scratching his stubbly scalp.

"If I show up at Castle Sturmhagen with Rauber as my captive, I'll be the biggest hero they've ever had. They'll worship me. And they'll sure as heck send their entire army with me if I tell them there's a massive threat in, say, Frostheim or some other far-off place. Do you see what I'm saying? I'll empty the castle for you. All you and your men need to do is waltz in there and kick out the royal couple. Voilà! You're the new ruler of Sturmhagen. It's a win-win: I get the glory, you get the kingdom. So do we have a deal?"

Horace scratched his large, squarish chin. "That's a plan worthy of the little man himself. You're even more vicious than those stories about you let on. If you're tellin' the truth, that is. Why should I believe you?"

"Because I need an enemy, Horace," Liam said. "People have short memories. In a matter of time, they'll forget all about the Man Who Captured the Bandit King. I'll need to perform some new heroic feat to get their attention again. And those opportunities are harder to come by than you think. That's why I want you out there, being as villainous as you can be. I can't be a hero if there's no one left to fight. So, after you're seated on the throne of Sturmhagen, am I going to come after you? The answer is yes. You need to ask yourself if you can beat me when I do."

Horace twirled his massive club in the air. He was grinning from ear to ear. "Cut 'em down, boys. And tie up the *ex*-Bandit King. Good and tight."

Several bandits quickly swarmed over to the trees and severed the ropes that held Liam and Duncan. Back on the ground, the princes stretched their stiff limbs.

"Thank you, Duncan," Liam whispered to his friend. "You said exactly what he needed to hear to believe I would turn traitor."

"I had no idea that was what he was going to think," Duncan whispered back, his eyes agog. "I was about to challenge him to another duel."

"Well, I'm sure that would have worked, too," Liam said, and breathed a sigh of relief. Maybe it had been safer when Duncan was saving the day *unintentionally*.

"And Liam," Duncan began sheepishly, "we're not really going to . . ."

"No, Duncan. We're not. Don't worry."

"Whew. I figured that. It's just that, you know—lying, sarcasm—there are so many new ways of talking that I have to get used to."

"Nice doing business with you, *Your Highness*," Liam said, as they approached Horace. "So, you're going to let us leave here peacefully?"

"I'm a man of my word," Horace said as he laid his massive club down on the ground and walked over to shake Liam's hand. "See you in a few months, eh?" Horace added with a wink.

A low rumble rose up in the distance.

"Funny. Doesn't look like rain," Duncan said, holding

out a hand to feel for drops.

The rumbling grew steadily louder, and the ground started to tremble. Liam, Duncan, Horace, and all the other bandits stopped what they were doing to peer toward the eastern edge of the field.

"What's going on?" Horace asked.

Suddenly a wave of flapping, flowing greenness burst forth from the trees.

"It looks like a big, angry salad," Duncan said in awe.

"Trolls. Scores of them!" Liam said.

"And look! Two of them are carrying dolls shaped like Gustav and Frederic," Duncan shouted.

"It *is* Gustav and Frederic," Liam said. "Unbelievable."

"Backstabber!" Horace growled at Liam. "You tricked me."

"Ha! *He's* a backstabber?" a reedy voice called out from behind Horace. "Look who's talking!" It was Rauber. He'd woken up while several bandits argued fearfully over which of them would have to tie him up. With everyone distracted by the trolls, nobody noticed him get to his feet and grab Horace's enormous wooden club.

"But, sir—!" That was all Horace had a chance to say before Rauber swung and smashed the club into the side of his head. With a sickening thud, the hulking man collapsed at the feet of the wickedly grinning ten-year-old boy. Rauber stuck out his tongue, just to rub it in.

"That boy is dangerous, Liam!" Duncan cried in horror. "I think he killed Horace!"

The trolls thrashed their way into the camp, trampling tents and toppling big wooden wagons. The monsters overturned pots of gruel, ripped flagpoles from the ground, and punched holes through barrels of ale, howling madly as they wreaked their havoc. Within seconds, they were clashing with the bandits, tossing them about mercilessly. Poor Neville, still dangling from his pole, was batted back and forth by two trolls in an impromptu game of human tetherball.

"Forget about Rauber," Liam said to Duncan. "Just get ready to run."

"Where?" Duncan asked (and Liam was proud of him for thinking to ask that question).

"To the horses," Liam urged as Rauber charged toward them with the club raised over his head. "Go. Now!"

Duncan sprinted away as Liam turned to face Rauber. The Bandit King was about to clobber him, when Liam thrust a booted foot forward and kicked him square in the chest. Rauber fell to his knees and doubled over.

"Ow!" he yowled, clutching his chest. "I can't believe

you kicked a little kid! Real noble, man." He let out a pitiful moan. Liam saw a tear come to Rauber's eye, and he felt a twinge of guilt. He stepped forward and offered the boy his hand.

"Can you stand?" Liam asked.

"Sure, I can. Can you?" Rauber sneered, and whipped his club into the side of Liam's knee. The painful jolt sent Liam to the ground, clutching his leg. Rauber jumped to his feet, cackling with glee. He raised the club for another blow, but before he could strike, a raging gang of trolls barreled into him. Before Liam had a chance to blink, the Bandit King was gone.

A second later, another mob of trolls tramped by. Liam wiggled out of the way, narrowly dodging their clomping footsteps.

"Troll, stop!" came a shout from above.

One troll came to a halt mere inches before stepping on Liam. Liam looked up to see Gustav mounted on the creature's shaggy shoulders.

"Troll no step on Squirmy Man?" the troll asked.

"That's right, Troll," Gustav said. "Squirmy Man is with us."

The troll reached down and hoisted Liam up to Gustav's level.

"Having a good time?" Liam asked.

"I would normally respond with something sarcastic," Gustav said. "But you know, this is really pretty awesome."

"Where's Frederic?" Liam asked.

"He's on Mr. Troll somewhere."

"*Mister* Troll?"

"You heard right," Gustav said. He leaned down. "Hey, Troll, can you get this guy a ride, too?"

Gustav's hunchbacked troll tapped a passing five-horned troll. "Troll," it called to its fellow monster. "'Nother human need ride. His name Squirmy Man."

The five-horned troll flipped Liam onto its back.

"Thank you," Liam said, "but my name's not Squirmy Man."

"Too late," Gustav said with a chuckle.

From atop the troll's shoulders, Liam could see that the bandit army was nearly decimated. Terrified criminals were being hurled through the air left and right.

Mr. Troll loped over. He himself had an unconscious bandit in each of his big, clawed hands—and Frederic clamped onto his shoulders in a piggyback of terror.

"Ouching Man, this the other *nice* human you talk about?" Mr. Troll asked, pointing at Liam.

"Ouching Man, huh?" Liam asked.

Frederic inched his ashen face out from behind Mr. Troll's head to sneak a peek. "Yes, that's one of them," he confirmed. "Hi, Liam."

"Look, I can't begin to understand what's happening here, but I think I'm happy about it," Liam said. "I sent Duncan over by the horses. But now I see horses everywhere. We should go find him." Dozens of horses were indeed running wild, adding to the commotion in the camp.

"Come on, trolls," Gustav said.

"Please try not to bounce so much," Frederic squeaked, and buried his face back into Mr. Troll's fur.

The three trolls pummeled their way through the remaining bandits over to the row of trees where the horses had been tied. Doing his part to help thwart the bandit army, Duncan had set every single horse free. It occurred to him too late, though, that he probably should not have untied the princes' horses as well. Now, so as not to lose track of Thunderbreaker, Gwendolyn, or Seventeen, he was attempting to ride all three of them at once.

"Oh, good," Duncan cried when he saw his friends. "I'm so glad you're here. I don't think I can keep this up much longer." He was lying across the backs of all three horses, with one set of reins wrapped around his hands, another around his waist, and the last around his feet.

"Somehow, that is exactly the position I imagined we'd find him in," Gustav said.

The trolls set down the grateful princes, and Frederic and Gustav helped Duncan untangle himself. Rauber's army was in really bad shape. Most of the bandits were curled up on the grass with dislocated shoulders, twisted ankles, broken legs, or worse. The luckier ones were out cold. All around them, the trolls were still joyously smashing things. They tore open wardrobe crates and played tug-of-war with all the black leather pants they found. They dashed weapon racks to bits and shredded bandit flags. A few of them found the camp's food storage and ran off, giggling, with armfuls of stolen leeks.

"Well, that's one problem taken care of," Liam said.

"Yes, trolls will keep broken bandits locked up, so broken bandits not bother Ouching Man and his friends," Mr. Troll croaked happily. "Then trolls just wait for Prince Angry Man to give trolls land."

Liam looked at Gustav (who he easily guessed was Prince Angry Man).

"We'll explain later," Gustav said.

"I just wish I knew what happened to Rauber," Liam said. "I don't see him anywhere."

"Oh, guys, look what else I grabbed," Duncan called out,

holding out four new swords. In a welcome change of pace, these blades were sized for normal human hands. "The bandits didn't seem to need them anymore."

"And we've got our horses back," Frederic said, petting Gwendolyn.

"And muskrat steaks," Duncan added, holding up a drippy backpack. "Although I'm not sure if that's something to be happy about. They smell even worse than before."

"So, gentlemen," Liam said. "I believe we have some bards to rescue."

The men mounted their horses.

"I don't know why you didn't keep one of the bandits' horses for yourself," Liam said as Duncan nestled in behind him on Thunderbreaker.

"It was hard enough keeping three together. I don't think I could have ridden four."

The princes waved good-bye to the trolls and galloped off for their climactic showdown with Zaubera. Together again, and having had a little taste of victory, they were more optimistic than ever—which they probably wouldn't have been if they'd known that one of them was not going to walk away from that battle.

Oops, sorry about that. I probably should have said, "Spoiler alert."

25

PRINCE CHARMING REALLY NEEDS TO FIGURE OUT WHAT'S GOING ON

As the princes galloped toward Mount Batwing, Ella—who was headed to the very same destination—was making great time on foot. She'd found running through the woods a whole lot easier since she'd performed a little creative tailoring on the skirt of her dress, slitting it up the middle and retying the loose fabric around her legs to create a pair of makeshift shorts.

She couldn't wait to get her hands on the witch's map. As she ran, she envisioned rescuing one poor prisoner after another, and getting that same wonderful rush each time. She imagined the different kinds of bizarre monsters she might find standing in her way: Giants? Goblins?

Giant goblins? (Her experience with monsters was pretty limited.)

As Ella came within a few miles of Mount Batwing, she spotted a figure staggering awkwardly through the bushes. The stranger was on the small side, and she wondered at first if it might be another goblin. She saw a large stick lying nearby and grabbed it—just in case. But as the mysterious figure hobbled out into the open, Ella soon realized that it was not a goblin at all; it was a child. And not just any child.

"Deeb?" Ella asked in disbelief. "Cousin Deeb?"

Yes, Deeb Rauber was Ella's cousin—well, step-cousin really. And he was just as surprised as Ella. The last person he expected to come across in the forests of Sturmhagen was his ugly aunt Esmeralda's annoying stepdaughter. And she was wearing such strange pants.

"You don't look so good," Ella said—and she was putting it mildly: The boy's clothing was shredded, he had a black eye, and he was limping, favoring a right leg that was badly bleeding.

Rauber's first instinct was to throw a rock at Ella, but he quickly thought better of it. He was hurting pretty badly and needed some first aid. And from what he remembered about Ella, she was good-hearted and naïve—a perfect mark. *Time for the Bandit King to work his sinister charm,* Rauber thought.

"That *is* you, isn't it, Deeb?" Ella asked gently, stepping up for a closer look. "You were a lot younger the last time we saw each other, so I don't know if you remember me, but . . ."

"Of course I do, Cousin Ella," Rauber said with feigned sweetness. "I could never forget you. You were always so nice to my mother and me when we visited Aunt Esmeralda's house."

Ella was surprised. She had always been pretty sure Deeb didn't like her. Her only real memory of him was watching him cackle as he dumped out the ash bin she'd just spent the entire morning on her hands and knees filling up. But that naughtiness had occurred years ago. Maybe her cousin had changed.

"What are you doing out here in the woods all by yourself?" Ella asked, as she helped Rauber sit at the foot of a tree. "How did you get hurt?"

"I fell off my horse," Rauber said, with tears brimming. "It was *so* scary. Oh, Cousin Ella, please help me. Please."

"Here, let me take a look at you," Ella said. "I'll do what I can. Don't worry, little Deebie."

"Don't call me that," Rauber said, trying to remember

to sound sad and not angry. "Um, please," he added.

"Wasn't anyone with you?" Ella asked. "Where are your parents?"

Rauber started to laugh, but caught himself and turned it into a cough. Ella unwrapped a small bundle she'd been carrying with her. Inside were several strips of fabric that had been ripped from her skirt, some leftover bread and cheese, and the flask of water. She handed the flask to her cousin, and he took a few long, greedy swigs.

"I was alone," Rauber said, wiping his mouth on his sleeve. "Foolish of me, I know. You should always ride with a buddy."

"That's true, especially at your age," Ella said as she took the flask back and tipped it to dampen a piece of cloth. She used the wet rag to wipe down the big gash on his leg, as well as several other cuts and scrapes on his limbs. "Are you even old enough to be riding?"

Rauber crinkled his nose angrily and crossed his eyes at Ella.

"Oh, did that hurt?" Ella asked. "Sorry if it stings a bit, but I've got to get these boo-boos cleaned up. Especially this nasty cut on your shin. We've got to get you fixed up so you can go run and play with the other little boys again."

Rauber took a deep breath. If this girl didn't stop

treating him like a baby, he was going to lose it. "Is that cheese?" he asked.

"Go ahead, take a bit," Ella replied, as she bandaged his leg. She used the big stick she'd found as a splint and tied it to the injured limb. Rauber snatched up Ella's remaining cheese and bread and shoved it all messily into his mouth.

"Hey, cuz," Rauber called. When Ella looked up, the boy opened his mouth wide and showed her the disgusting glob of half-chewed food on his tongue. "Ha!"

Ella shook her head. "Sheesh. You used to do that when you were six. I would hope you'd be a little more mature by now."

"Oho!" Rauber said with a spray of crumbs. "So which is it? Am I supposed to be a *sweetie widdle* baby? Or am I supposed to be mature? You can't have it both ways."

"Whoa, there, Deebie," Ella cautioned.

"How thick is your skull?" Rauber snapped. "I told you not to call me that! I mean, *asked*. I asked you not to call me that."

Ella stared at him sternly.

"Please," he added.

"Not much in the manners department, are you, Deeb?"

"No, ma'am. I guess not. Sorry about that. I've got a lot to learn." He flashed a smile, hoping it would disguise the sarcasm that he was finding increasingly difficult to stifle.

"You certainly do. Do you talk to your mother like that?"

Rauber couldn't hold back. "No," he snickered. "I talk to my mother by slipping notes under the door of the cupboard *I locked her in*." And then he burst into a big belly laugh.

"Boys are so strange. I don't even get that joke," Ella said drily as Rauber continued to guffaw.

Rauber waved his hand at her dismissively. "Eh, what would a grime-wiper like you know about funny, anyway?"

Ella stopped wrapping up a scrape on her cousin's knee and stood up. "You know, I think you're fine now," she said tersely, crossing her arms and glaring down at Rauber. "You're just as bratty as I remember. Get up and see if you can walk."

Rauber pulled himself to his feet. He tested his injured leg and smiled.

"All better?" Ella asked, still annoyed with her cousin, but pleased with herself for a successful first-aid job.

"Oh, yes," Rauber said, a wicked grin spreading across his face. "I'm just perfect." He leaned in toward her. "Because you fell for my trick!"

"Come again?" Ella said. She was growing extremely tired of his childish nonsense.

"I *tricked* you into fixing me up," Rauber continued in a melodramatic tone. "You thought I was just your sweet, innocent little cousin—"

"Actually, I thought you were a brat, but go on."

"You assumed the person you were helping was nothing more than a cousin in need, but really, you were assisting . . . THE BANDIT KING!"

Ella stared at him quizzically.

"I am the Bandit King!" Rauber proclaimed again.

"That's cute," Ella said. "But I don't really have time for games right now. Do you need me to get you back to your parents' house or not? Because I've got important things to do."

Rauber limped up to her, getting as close as he could. "The *Bandit King*," he said once more. "Scourge of seven kingdoms. Most feared man in the known world. He is me!"

"I'm going to take that as a *no*," Ella said, shaking her head. "You seem pretty intent on playing Knights and Robbers—and that's fine. You're a kid. That's what kids do. But I've got to go."

"I'm not playing, cuz," Rauber said, a bit of a whine

creeping into his voice. "I'm *deadly* serious."

Ella couldn't help laughing.

"Come *on*," Rauber grumbled. "You can't tell me you're not afraid of the Bandit King."

"Am I supposed to be? I don't think I ever read that story."

"Agh! It's not a story!" Rauber pounded a nearby tree with his fist. "It's everything I've worked for my entire life!"

"Ha," Ella chuckled. "Your entire life? What are you? Nine?"

"Ten!" Rauber hissed. He was practically vibrating with rage. "And I've accomplished more in ten years than you will in your entire life. How can you not know about the Bandit King? I'm infamous! *In*famous!"

"Look, Deeb," Ella said, patting his shoulder. "You've got quite an imagination, but there are people whose lives are in danger, and I need to go help them right now. I'm going to trust that you can get back home by yourself. Please be careful out there. And say hi to Aunt Prudey for me."

Ella bent over to rewrap her pack of supplies, only to discover there was nothing left to take. She let out an annoyed sigh and tossed the empty cloth at Rauber.

"How dare you disrespect the Bandit King!" he shouted.

"Bye, Deeb," Ella said, turning on her heel and walking away. Rauber tried to go after her, but realized that with the wooden splint tied to his leg, he couldn't move very fast. He waved his fists madly and stomped his good foot.

"You won't get away with this!" he screamed, his cheeks burning red. "Kings cower at my name! Armies run when they see my shadow! I am a master of evil! Eeeeeeeee-vil! You can't just walk away from me!"

But Ella did just walk away. It was quite possibly the Bandit King's greatest defeat.

26

PRINCE CHARMING GIVES UP

Frederic tiptoed slowly across the big lawn outside Zaubera's fortress, past the tiered-bench seating, a couple of booths with GET YOUR GROG HERE signs, and several large banners that bore the witch's name. Of course, Frederic was actually hoping to be captured—all in keeping with Liam's plan. He'd never considered himself a human-bait type of guy. But there he was, aiming to distract a giant long enough for his partners to steal a map. *I guess I really will do anything for Ella,* he thought. Then he stopped himself. *No, it's not just Ella, is it? I'm doing this for Liam and Gustav and Duncan, too. I don't want to let any of them down.*

The giant, Reese, was standing a few yards from the

tower, picking his teeth with a wheelbarrow (its dual handles allowed him to scrape between two teeth at once). Frederic "sneaked" by, peering up from time to time to see if the giant had noticed him. No luck. Reese was very much engaged in a battle with a boulder-size hunk of yak meat that was wedged between a pair of molars.

So Frederic coughed. And then he coughed louder. Reese paid the sound no notice. Then Frederic began whistling. Reese continued to ignore him. Eventually, the giant freed the pesky morsel from his teeth, but instead of looking down and seeing Frederic—who was now performing a handstand—he just kept studying the grotesque lump of meat, staring at it sitting on the wet tip of his giant finger, contemplating whether or not to put it back in his mouth.

Down on the ground, Frederic was jumping around and waving his arms. He tried a cartwheel. At last he decided to borrow a proven tactic that had worked in the past. "Stuuuurm-hayyyyyy-gennnnn!" He hollered Gustav's battle cry as he ran at the giant, wildly waving his new sword.

That did it. Reese dropped his chunk of meat to the ground. "No way," he muttered in astonishment, as he reached down and snatched up Frederic. "You can't be back *again*." Frederic, for his part, was grateful that he hadn't needed to stick the giant with his sword in order to get noticed. Trying to charm someone is never easy once you've stabbed him.

Reese examined Frederic. "Hey, wait. You're not the one who keeps coming back and poking me."

"No," said Frederic. "That would be my friend, Gustav."

"Is he here, too?" The giant frowned and scanned the field.

"No!" Frederic said quickly. "He . . . he got eaten by trolls." It was the first thing that came into his head. And he immediately regretted saying it.

"I thought trolls were vegetarian," Reese said suspiciously.

"Normally, uh, sure," Frederic said, his mind scrambling. "But Gustav annoyed them so badly, they made an exception and ate him anyway."

"I can believe that," Reese said. Then, feeling a bit contrite, the giant adopted a more agreeable tone. "Well, I can't say as I'll miss the little pest, but I assume you must be a bit sad about it, seeing as he was your friend. So, uh, you have my sympathies. I am very sorry for your loss."

Sitting in the giant's rough-skinned palm, Frederic

sheathed his sword. Etiquette! This was a giant who understood proper manners. "Thank you," he said. "Your kindness is much appreciated. I don't know many people—of any size—who would treat a prisoner with such respect."

"Your appreciation is much appreciated as well," said Reese. With his free hand, he scratched his stubbly chin. "Why'd you come back here, anyway? You must have known you couldn't get past me."

"Oh, absolutely. I fully expected you to stop me. You're enormous, obviously very powerful, and the last time we met, you proved yourself to be a determined and tireless opponent. But I had to come back here to honor the memory of my dear friend. He very badly wanted something that's inside that fortress, and now that he's digesting in a troll's belly somewhere, I felt the need to fulfill his final wishes. I was a little afraid of the dragon, though—it's not still here, is it?"

"It's around back," Reese said. "I hate that thing."

"Likewise," Frederic said. "Dragons can't be trusted, but *you* . . . I was pretty sure that when you captured me, you'd treat me well."

"How'd you know I wouldn't just crush you?"

"I had a good feeling. When we clashed last time, you

seemed like a noble sort."

"I like to do my mum proud."

"That's what I figured. And so far my initial impression of you has been borne out. You've been quite pleasant. It makes me wonder why you associate yourself with someone as wicked and awful as that witch, Zaubera."

The giant's body shook as he began to laugh, and Frederic had to wrap his arms around an enormous pinkie to make sure he didn't tumble off. "What did I say that was so funny?" he asked.

"I may be polite, but I'm no fool," Reese said. "I'm not going to fall for the same trick twice."

Frederic began to panic. Was his strategy backfiring? "It's no trick! I meant every word. And, um, what do you mean by 'same trick twice'? You and I never even spoke the last time we met."

"Not you," Reese said. "The brown-haired girl. She did the same exact thing: complimented me, harped on how terrible the witch was, got me to trust her. And then she scampered off. Oh, yeah, she got me good. But it's not going to work again."

"You're talking about Ella, aren't you?" Frederic asked. A warm wave of happiness washed over him. Ella had escaped with the very same tactic he was trying to use.

Maybe the two of them did have a few things in common.

"Oh, man, I shouldn't have told you that," Reese muttered, glancing around nervously. "The witch doesn't know the girl is gone."

"She doesn't?" Frederic was intrigued. Maybe things hadn't taken a bad turn after all.

"I made a wonderful little dummy and put it in the tower," Reese explained. "Frankly, I didn't know I had such artistic talent in me. But that's beside the point. Look, you can't tell the witch. I don't want to be a pile of bacon."

"I don't quite understand the last part of what you said," Frederic began, "but it appears that you're asking me for a favor." Yes, he thought, this was all going to work out just fine.

A few moments earlier, Liam, Duncan, and Gustav watched Frederic and the giant from among the rocks at the base of Mount Batwing.

"Stuuuurm-hayyyyyy-gennnnn!" they heard Frederic yell.

Gustav turned to the others and smiled. "He got that from me."

"I liked that little dance he was doing," Duncan added.

"I have to remember to ask him about the choreography later."

"Shhh! They're talking," Liam scolded. "Pay attention."

"I was a little afraid of the dragon, though," Frederic was saying. "It's not still here, is it?"

"It's around back."

"Okay, I'm off to go play," Gustav said. "You two had better get that map. I don't like risking my life for nothing."

Liam snorted. "You *always* risk your life for nothing. It's like a hobby."

Gustav ignored him, drew his sword, and ran toward the back of the fortress.

He was looking forward to this. None of his brothers had ever fought a dragon. Harald (brother #8) got all those kudos for skewering a couple of goblins; Lars (#12) got a feast after he caught a wild dog-man; and Henrik (#1) and Osvald (#5) were showered with praise after they took down one measly bog-beast. But those creatures were nothing compared to a dragon. No, if Gustav held his own against a dragon, it would be, hands down, the most impressive feat any of the princes of Sturmhagen had ever pulled off. Gustav was sure he could do it, too. In fact, he had no doubt he could slay the monster and be done with it. But a dead dragon wouldn't fit into the plan.

They needed the dragon to scare off the giant later. And for once, Gustav was determined to stick to the plan.

This was going to be his moment for redemption—the moment he would show everybody what he was capable of.

But the dragon was asleep.

"Seriously?" Gustav threw his arms down and kicked a rock in frustration. "I was supposed to have a fighting job. Not a pet-sitting job."

He looked at the beast, snoozing peacefully in the shadow of the stronghold's tall tower, and was strongly tempted to wake it up. One jab of his sword would do the trick.

But he held back. He was going to follow the plan and do what was best for the group. Using all the willpower he could muster, he sat on the grass and simply stared at the sleeping dragon.

This is the most boring moment of redemption ever, he thought.

A few moments after Gustav ran off to meet the dragon, Liam and Duncan darted over to the large wooden doors of the fortress. The giant was laughing at something Frederic said, and it seemed like the perfect time to sneak in without raising any alarms.

Duncan began to laugh, too, and Liam shushed him.

"Sorry," Duncan whispered. "Frederic must have said something pretty funny to make the giant laugh like that. So I was trying to imagine what it might have been, and—ha!—it was even funnier than I thought."

"Duncan, focus."

Duncan nodded in response, and Liam tugged at the big round iron door handle. It cracked open, and he and Duncan slipped inside.

They were in the cavernous main chamber where Liam had first faced the dragon (and lost the map). Duncan surveyed the vast collections of ancient runic tomes, the skeletal owls and dried snake skins, the buckets of slime and the bowls of shrunken heads. "It's like a scary-story museum," he said in hushed wonder.

"This plan is working out perfectly so far," Liam said softly, occasionally glancing at the front door to make sure no one was coming. "I don't like it."

"What do you mean?" Duncan asked. "It's *your* plan; of course it's going to work."

"I'm glad one of us is so sure of that," Liam whispered. "I had a plan last time, too, you know. At least, in my head I did. And look how that worked out."

"Nobody's perfect, Liam," Duncan said, putting his hand on Liam's shoulder. "You're the best hero among us. If anybody can stop this witch and save those people, it's you. I consider it a privilege just to be by your side."

Liam smiled weakly. He didn't quite share Duncan's faith in him after all that had happened, but he appreciated it nonetheless.

"You're a good friend, Duncan."

"That's what I've been trying to tell people for years!"

"Okay," Liam said. "Stay here and watch the doors. I'm going to check that corner over there." He headed across the big room to the last place he'd seen the map. He crouched down into the dark corner. Almost immediately, he saw the map, just lying there on the stone floor.

"Oh, that's not good," he muttered. "That was too easy."

He grabbed the map and anxiously rolled it up. "Something is going to go wrong any second now. I can feel it. Duncan," he called out. "Let's get out of here."

But when he turned around and looked back toward the exit doors, Duncan was gone.

When Liam had said, "Watch the doors," Duncan wasn't sure if he'd meant the *front* doors. There were, after all, lots of doors in that room. So Duncan thought about it for a second and decided that the big exit doors probably didn't need much watching—they were hard to miss. Some of these smaller, more out-of-the-way doors were another matter entirely.

He slunk along the wall until he came to the first of the doors. He slowly opened it, poked his head inside, and saw nothing but a chamber pot, which made him giggle. He closed the door and moved down to the next one. Behind that door, he found a small room lined with broomsticks. He briefly considered trying to ride one, but the risk of inner-thigh splinters was too unappealing, and he opted against it. The third door opened onto a long, torch-lit corridor. He was about to shut it, when he heard footsteps around the corner. If it was the witch, he needed to warn Liam. But maybe it wasn't the witch. . . .

He tiptoed down the corridor, turned the corner, and was shocked to find himself face-to-face with a brown-haired girl in interesting pants. Ella was equally surprised. Each jumped away from the other and took a defensive stance—Ella in a martial arts crouch, Duncan standing on one leg with his hands in front of his face.

"Who are you?" both asked in unison.

"Oops, sorry. You first." Duncan was unfailingly polite, even when suspicious.

"Are you one of her guards?" Ella asked. Her jaw was clenched tight. She looked ready for a fight.

"Whose guards?"

"The witch's."

"No. Are you?"

"Of course not. If I was one of her guards, why would I ask you if you were one of her guards?"

"To trick me, I guess."

"Well, I'm not."

"And neither am I."

"Are you a bandit, then? You're dressed like one."

"Oh, I borrowed these clothes from the Stumpy Boarhound."

"Who's the stumpy boarhound?"

"The Stumpy Boarhound is not a who; it's a what."

"Well, what is it then?"

"A place with terrible lemonade."

"You're trying to confuse me."

"No, I'm not. I like your pants."

"Stop distracting me. Tell me who you are."

"Duncan. Pleased to meet you."

"Likewise. Why are you here?"

"To get a map."

Ella gasped. "I need that map!"

"You can't have it!" Duncan said defensively.

With both hands, Ella grabbed Duncan by his collar. "Give me the map!"

"I don't have the map!" Duncan squeaked. "It's still missing."

Ella loosened her grip on his shirt. "I really need to get that map. I risked my life to come back here for it."

"So did we."

"You did? Wait. Who's 'we'?"

"Me and Liam and Gustav and Frederic."

"Frederic?" Ella let go and stepped back, shocked to hear the name. She'd begun to wonder if that incident with Frederic back at Rapunzel's tower had been some sort of witch-induced hallucination. "Frederic from Harmonia? He's here?"

"You know Frederic?"

"We were supposed to get married."

"You're Ella?" Duncan shouted with excitement. "I thought you were a piece of wood!"

"Huh?"

"Oh, this is fantastic," Duncan said. "Come with me!" He grabbed Ella's hand and pulled her along with him as he ran back to the main chamber.

"Duncan! Thank goodness," Liam said as he saw his

friend emerge from behind the door.

"Look who I found," Duncan cried. "It's Ella!"

"Ella? What? She's here?"

Ella popped out of the corridor behind Duncan, and Liam was instantly enchanted. Ella's hair was a tousled mess and her dress was torn and muddied, but to Liam, she looked radiant. More than anything else, he was struck by her eyes. Ella had that same devil-may-care look that Liam had seen in only one other place: a mirror. "Wow," he breathed.

"Wow?" Ella echoed, a bit confused.

"He means, '*Wow*, we can't believe we found you,'" Duncan interjected.

"Of course," Liam said, playing innocent, although he was still gazing moony-eyed at Ella. "We thought you escaped days ago."

"You were right. But I came back for the map," Ella said. "Please tell me you found it."

"I did." Liam showed them the rolled-up parchment.

"Do you know what's on that map?" Ella asked. "The witch has prisoners in those towers."

"Aha! Just as I suspected!" Liam said.

"Well, it didn't take much guesswork," Duncan said. "She'd written 'prisoner'—"

"Just as I suspected," Liam repeated, cutting him off. "So with you free, we have five more people to rescue."

"Four," Ella said. "I already rescued one."

"You did?" Liam leaned his elbow on a nearby sarcophagus and brushed his fingers through his hair, trying to look casually dashing. "You're a very impressive woman."

"Thanks. But, anyway, her prisoners are all bards," Ella said. "The witch is striking at the very heart of our world's entertainment industry. She's planning to kill the bards as part of some huge demented spectacle."

"I know. She's going to do it today," Liam said. "That's why *I* insisted we come back here to get the map. The others were ready to call it quits, but *I* said—"

"The *others*—oh, my goodness," Ella said breathlessly. "Is *Frederic* really with you?"

"Yes, Frederic, that's right," Liam said. He lowered his voice, feeling somewhat ashamed for flirting with his friend's fiancée. But at the same time he thought, how could he help himself? Ella was just, like, you know, *wow*.

"Yes," Duncan butted in. He didn't like what he was seeing. Liam seemed to be smitten with Ella. "*Frederic* is actually the reason we're all here. *He* found us all and got us together to come after you in the first place. It was *his* idea." He shot a disapproving look at Liam, who gave a sheepish shrug in return.

"So who are you people?" Ella asked.

"We are the League of Princes Charming," Duncan offered eagerly.

"No, League of *Princes*," Liam cut in. "Just League of Princes."

"Fine," Duncan conceded. "But we *are* all Princes Charming."

"Is that how Frederic got hooked up with you? Because of him being called Prince Charming in that song about me?" Ella asked.

"Exactly!" Duncan beamed. "And I'm from the Snow White song."

Ella turned to Liam, who was looking a bit red-faced. "And what about you? Whose Prince Charming are you?" She nudged Liam playfully with her elbow.

"Sleeping Beauty's," Liam reluctantly admitted. "But don't believe everything you've heard about me."

"I haven't heard much of anything about anybody lately," Ella said. "I've been a bit preoccupied."

"Really?" Liam asked. "So there's nothing you think you know about me? Prince Liam from Erinthia? You haven't heard any rumors?"

"Nope," Ella said.

"So as far as you're concerned, I'm just a guy bravely risking his own life in order to save the lives of others."

"Oh, wait—Erinthia! Yes!"

"I knew it," he muttered glumly.

"Your sister is looking for you," Ella said.

"Lila?"

"Yeah, she's a great kid."

"How do you know—"

Duncan stomped his foot and said, "We should really go outside now and make sure FREDERIC is okay."

"You're right; let's go," Ella said. She found it touching that Frederic had gone through the trouble of getting these other princes to search for her, and she didn't want to see him get into any kind of real trouble on her behalf. "Where is Frederic, anyway? Keeping lookout in the trees or something?"

"No, he's out there distracting the giant," Duncan said.

"The giant?" Ella gasped, and gave Liam a shove. "You left Frederic with a giant? Are you trying to kill him?"

"He can handle it," Liam protested. "Trust me, he's changed."

"You're a lunatic," Ella cried. "Frederic's afraid of dust bunnies! We have to go help him, right now!" She shoved

Liam aside and ran toward the exit. But just as she reached the doors, she heard a sizzling sound and a cry of pain from behind her. She turned to see Liam on the ground, clutching his chest. Zaubera stood in an open doorway, smiling wickedly. She raised her hand and zapped Liam again with a crackling streak of blue energy.

"So nice that you came back to pay old Zaubera another visit," the witch said. Her red and black rags fluttered as an unnatural wind stirred up around her.

Ella shivered with the terrifying realization that the witch was even more powerful than she'd previously thought. She also realized that the witch was apparently not named Wendy. But that was less terrifying.

"Leave him alone!" Ella cried, running back to Liam's side. "Take me. I'm the one you want!"

"Oh, don't worry—you're not going anywhere either, my little starlet," Zaubera sneered. She nailed Ella with a blast of sorcerous lightning, sending her to the floor next to Liam.

"You despicable fiend," Liam hissed from his place on the ground.

"You didn't think I was going to let Prince Charming run in here and steal away my Cinderella, did you?" Zaubera said.

"How does she know who you are?" Duncan asked, flabbergasted.

Zaubera looked at Liam. "Aha," she said with a green-toothed smile. "*You're* the one. Frankly, I assumed it would be you. The other three are kind of . . . you know."

Liam reached up and thrust the map into Duncan's hands. "Remember the plan, Duncan," he sputtered. "Take it. Go!"

Without a word, Duncan sped off with the map. He ran, not toward the exit, but straight into a nearby wall. He bounced backward a few steps, spun around, and ran behind a large rack of magic wands, where he spilled over a table full of jarred frogs with a crash and a clatter.

"There's no way out over there," the witch called out helpfully.

A second later, Duncan burst back into view and dashed out through the main doors.

Zaubera rubbed her hands together and grinned devilishly. "I have Cinderella *and* Prince Charming!"

"Ha!" Liam shouted. He and Ella were both still on the floor, too sore and winded to attempt a getaway. "My friend just escaped with your map, *witch*. Your evil plot is foiled."

"Oh, really?" Zaubera said, sounding rather amused.

"Did you notice I made no attempt to stop him?"

"Face it, *witch*: You've lost," Liam said. "With that map, my friends will free the bards in no time."

"You mean *these* bards?" Zaubera asked. She snapped her bony fingers, and four dark-purple vines descended from the ceiling. At the end of each, wrapped up in coils of slithering ivy, was a kidnapped bard. Lyrical Leif, Tyrese the Tuneful, Wallace Fitzwallace, and Reynaldo, Duke of Rhyme, all gagged by curling ivy, stared plaintively at Liam and Ella.

"Crud," Liam muttered.

"Yes, crud indeed," Zaubera grinned. "I've had it up to here with the libelous, inaccurate story-songs of these mewling melody-makers. They ruined my reputation, and I'm finally going to get my payback."

"You're insane, *witch*," Ella said. "You're going to slaughter these men just because they told the world how Rapunzel escaped from you?"

"Rapunzel never escaped from me!" Zaubera shrieked. "I *let* that little hooligan go! No one escapes Zaubera!"

"Um," Liam interrupted. "Actually, we all have at least once."

"NO ONE ESCAPES ZAUBERA!" the witch yelled even louder. "And anyway, I'm not going to kill the bards.

I need them to witness my massacre and sing to the world about it. No, the bards are my publicity team. I'm going to kill everybody else. With the help of you two, of course." The moving vines whisked the bards out of sight.

"We'll never help you, *witch*!" Ella spat.

"You all say 'witch' like it's an insult," Zaubera said. "I *am* a witch. And anyway, yours is not exactly a voluntary position."

Zaubera snapped her fingers again. Purple vines snaked swiftly along the floor and wrapped themselves around Liam and Ella.

"Come," Zaubera said. "I'm taking you and your boyfriend upstairs now."

"He's not my boyfriend," Ella said.

"Yeah, I'm not her, uh, what you said . . . ," Liam mumbled.

"Boyfriend, fiancée . . . whatever," Zaubera sniffed. "You're Cinderella and Prince Charming—that's all the heroes are going to care about."

Liam and Ella cast each other confused glances, neither understanding what the witch meant. Zaubera started up the spiral staircase to her tower observatory. The wriggling vines followed, dragging her prisoners with them. "You should feel privileged, really," the witch said. "This is going to be the biggest massacre in recorded history, and you two get to be the headlining victims."

"You're forgetting one thing, witch," Liam said. "My friends."

Zaubera chuckled. "If the rest of your pals are anything like that little fellow who couldn't find the exit, I'm not too concerned."

27

PRINCE CHARMING GETS GOOD NEWS AND BAD NEWS

Duncan burst out into the fading sunlight and zipped straight around to the back of the fortress to find Gustav. He kept his eyes closed, hoping that would prevent the giant from seeing him as he dashed by.

"Finally!" Gustav said, standing up and sheathing his sword. "Do you know how bored I've been?"

"The witch got Liam and Ella!" Duncan cried.

"Criminy Pete!" Gustav cursed. "Can't that goody-goody do anything right? Wait, did you say Ella?"

"But look, I got the map!" Duncan added.

"Well, that's dandy," Gustav said. "But how do we beat the giant when the dragon is still asleep?"

Duncan looked over Gustav's shoulder. "Um," he said.

"The dragon's not asleep."

The freshly awakened dragon roared and whipped its tail into Gustav from behind. Gustav slammed into Duncan, and both men tumbled to the ground. The creature reared over them, about to let loose with a powerful gust of flame. *If I die like this,* Gustav thought, *I'll never live it down.*

But before the men could be flash-fried, they heard a gruff voice yell something in a language they didn't understand. The dragon backed away from them.

"Banchuk!"

"Grut!"

"Tchaka!" More strange commands rang out, each in a different grumbly voice. The dragon got down on all fours and swerved around. Gustav and Duncan scrambled to their feet.

Leaning against the tower wall, catching their breath, they were awestruck by what they saw. The dwarfs, Flik, Frak, and Frank, surrounded the dragon, barking bizarre foreign words and making mysterious hand gestures.

The dragon began to calm down.

"Frank?" Duncan called out.

Frank held a finger up to shush him, never taking his eyes off the dragon.

"Banchuk! Grut!" The dragon lowered its head. Flik

walked right up and pet its nose. The beast closed its reptilian eyes, and though Gustav wasn't quite sure, he thought he heard it purr.

Frank sauntered over to the princes.

"What are you two staring at?" he asked. "Dwarves are *expert* dragon tamers."

"Of course they are," Gustav said. He untied the drippy sack that hung from his belt and threw it to the ground. "And I carried around this stinking muskrat meat for nothing."

"Show me how! Show me how!" Duncan said, bouncing.

"No," Frank said.

"Come on, tell me some of those words," Duncan begged. "Just one or two. What was it: *chup-chup?*" The dragon thwacked its tail into the dirt.

"No," Frank repeated. "And stop trying to say dragon commands before you accidentally make it eat one of us."

Duncan grumbled. "Why are you here, anyway? I told you three to go to Snow."

"They did." Snow White climbed out of her wagon and ran to Duncan.

"Snow!" Duncan exclaimed. The two embraced.

"Yeah, that's right, don't trust the dwarves," Frank said

bitterly. "We're good for nothing."

"What are you doing here?" Duncan asked as Snow spun him around to do a 360-degree injury check.

"Frank and the dwarfs did just what you asked of them," she explained. "And when I heard about this crazy mission you were supposedly on, I demanded they take me right back to you. If even half of what they told me is true, you've gone completely insane. Why are you dressed like a ninja?"

"I assume you didn't get the note from the bird, then?" Duncan asked.

"Are you talking about Monday Bird? Because that little slacker never showed up last week," Snow said.

"That's so unlike her!" Duncan remarked. "But anyway, no, I was talking about the robin I sent."

"No, no robin," Snow said. "Duncan, we're getting off topic. Thank goodness the dwarfs and I showed up when we did. A few seconds later and . . . oh, I don't want to think about it."

"We could've handled it," Gustav interjected. Snow looked at him.

"Are you one of the, uh, other princes?" she asked.

Gustav walked over and shook her hand, chuckling as he did. "I'm Gustav. You're a very lucky woman." Snow eyed him with suspicion for a second—there was no way this man could have been a Prince Charming—then turned back to her husband.

"Anyway, I'm so glad you're okay," she said. "What were you thinking, running off like that? To battle witches and giants? You get winded chasing squirrels."

"Oh, it's been fun. But I'm still so surprised that you came after me," Duncan said, then added sheepishly, "I thought you were tired of me."

"Oh, Dunky," she said, caressing his wavy hair. "You drive me mad sometimes, but I still love you. I said I wanted a break; I didn't want you to run away."

Gustav groaned.

"Just promise me you'll never do anything crazy again," Snow said. "Oh, who am I kidding? Just don't do anything crazy for the rest of the day. How about that?"

Duncan was silent.

"Duncan, I'm taking you home now," she said.

"Uh . . . soon, okay?" he replied, and noticed the disappointment on Snow's face. "You see, I've got these friends—seriously, they're really my friends—and some of them are in big trouble. Liam's inside that big scary place, and he's been captured by a really nasty witch. And Cinderella's up there, too! You should meet her—she's very nice. And

Frederic got taken off by a giant somewhere. And—"

"I'm here! And I'm fine," Frederic said as he ran up to them.

"You're all right? What happened?" Gustav asked. "Where's the giant?"

"Okay, so it turned out that Reese—that's the giant—he made the dummy that's up in that cell in the tower. He didn't want the witch to find out Ella had escaped," Frederic explained. "Oh, new person! Frederic of Harmonia, at your service. And you are?"

"Snow White," she replied.

"Well, that's a pleasant surprise."

"Ooh! That reminds me . . . ," Duncan said.

"And, oh my goodness, is that the dragon?" Frederic asked with a start.

Frank shoved his way in between Duncan and Snow White. "Don't worry about her," Frank said with a satisfied grin. "That dragon is *ours* now."

"Oh, you fellows are here, too?" Frederic said. "I missed a lot, huh?"

"Yes, Frederic," Duncan said. "And most importantly—"

"Not now," Frederic interrupted. "I've got to tell you this story. So the giant is terrified of the witch. He's afraid she'd do something terrible to him if she found out Ella was gone, something involving bacon. I didn't quite follow that part. But anyway, when I explained to him that Liam had found the dummy and that he was in the tower right now, probably talking to the witch about it—"

"Frederic," Duncan interrupted urgently.

"Just a moment! So I convinced Reese that he should run away and go into hiding. But he was certain the witch would hunt him down if he did, so I told him he should try to fool her again with a dummy of himself. He fancies himself a fabulous sculptor. Soooooo . . ." He led them toward the front of the tower and motioned to a large *something* sitting out in the meadow. "*That's* the giant."

An enormous pine tree had been stripped of all but two large branches, which stuck out to either side like a pair of arms. There was a crude face carved into the trunk near the top—two dots for eyes and a crooked slash for a mouth. Several dead yaks were piled onto the treetop for hair. And the tree was wearing the giant's shirt.

"Does that mean the giant's running around half-naked?" Gustav asked with a shudder.

"Unfortunately, yes."

"Frederic!" Duncan shouted. Normally, his friend's story would have held him rapt with attention, but he could no longer wait to break his news. "Ella's inside!"

"Really? Ella's here?"

"She got captured again by the witch," Duncan said. "Liam did, too."

"Where are they?" Frederick asked.

"Based on the crazy lights I'm seeing up there," Gustav said, pointing to the tip of the observatory tower, "I'd say top floor."

"Well, what are we standing here for?" Frederic said. "Let's go."

"I'm right behind you," Gustav said. The two of them ran to the doors of the fortress. Frederic called back, "Duncan, are you coming?"

Duncan glanced from his friends to his wife, who was vigorously shaking her head. Those other princes were his first real friends. He'd imagined the four of them as old men, laughing together about their past escapades. It was one of the happiest daydreams he'd had in years. But Snow was his wife. And the first person to ever treat him with respect.

"I don't think I can," Duncan said sorrowfully.

"It's okay," Frederic said. "I understand. Really. You've been a good friend, Duncan."

Frederic and Gustav entered the tower, ready for anything. But perhaps they would have chosen to stay with Duncan if they'd known the title of the next chapter.

28

PRINCE CHARMING IS DOOMED

This is the second time in two days that I've been tied to something, and I'm getting a little sick of it," Liam complained. Magical purple vines bound both him and Ella to black marble pillars in Zaubera's sky-high observatory.

"Well, this is the third witch's tower I've been in this month," Ella commiserated from the pillar next to Liam.

"No talking, you two," Zaubera scolded. She was at her desk, hurriedly sketching final details onto a diagram she'd titled, "The Grand Demise of Cinderella and Prince Charming."

"What's the matter, witch? Can't concentrate?" Liam asked.

"Have no fear, Handsome. I'm fully capable of focusing

on more than one thing at a time," Zaubera replied without looking up. "Case in point: I'm carrying on a conversation with you, diagramming your doom, *and* using my unmatched mental strength to keep you two tied up nice and tight. Go ahead—try to wriggle free of my vines."

Liam and Ella both struggled against their bindings but were unable to budge them. "We've got to do something to rattle her or we'll never get out of here," Liam whispered to Ella.

"I've got excellent hearing, too," Zaubera singsonged.

"Why don't you just zap us and be done with it?" Ella asked.

"Who would that impress?" the witch responded. With a sprightly energy that belied her age, Zaubera popped up from her seat and ran over to show Liam and Ella the new drawing she'd just finished. "See this? *This* will be remembered."

Liam and Ella couldn't quite decipher the complicated diagram, but what they could glean from it terrified them. Apparently, the witch planned to tie the two of them to the top of her observatory's spire so they'd be in full view of— but utterly unreachable to—anybody who approached the fortress. According to the sketch, Zaubera was expecting huge amounts of people to charge the stronghold. She'd labeled them simply "heroes." And whichever side they approached from, they'd be met with a grisly and certain doom. Rockslides would crush anyone coming from the east; those to the north would be tossed about and dashed into pieces by spontaneous tornadoes; people on the southern side would be engulfed in a wall of flame; and intruders from the west would be fried by a seemingly endless chain of lightning.

"We're just the bait," Liam said, horrified.

'That's right, genius," Zaubera said. "It's going to be spectacular. Just to be clear, though, I *am* going to kill you two as well. At the end."

"Why are you doing this?" Ella asked.

"I hate heroes," the witch said. "You think you're better than everyone else. You think you can steal everybody else's thunder? I'm finally going to get the fame I deserve. And I'm going to do it by destroying as many obnoxious heroes as I can. And it will be laughably easy. Because I know heroes. Whenever there's a problem somewhere, you people think you're the only ones who can save the day. You can't help yourselves. You see a chance at glory and you rush headlong into it. Once I tell the world that I've kidnapped the most famous couple in the world, all I have to do is sit back and wait for the heroes to show up.

And when they do, I will destroy them all. Because they will underestimate me and overestimate themselves. I will sit up here and pick them off long before they ever touch my fortress's walls. And they'll keep coming."

Liam twisted and wiggled the fingers of his right hand until he was able to pull out one of the scrolls stuffed into his side pants pocket.

"One problem, witch: No one knows you've got us," he said triumphantly. "Because we intercepted your ransom notes."

Zaubera's thin lips curled into a cold grin. "Oh, those notes got delivered to precisely the right people," she said. "They were meant for you to read."

Liam was speechless.

"As soon as I found out you were Prince Charming, I knew I had to have you for my grand finale. That courier you thought you were so lucky to catch? I had him follow your tracks from here and told him to make sure you four got the notes. I figured you would behave like typically predictable heroes and run straight back. Thank you for proving me right. Now I've got you as my extra-special bonus prisoner, and your three friends are no doubt dying outside as we speak. They'll still be too stupid to run off for help. Am I wrong?"

Liam said nothing, his head hung low. How had he miscalculated so badly? Everything he'd done in the past two days played right into the witch's hands. He was a failure.

"Besides," said Zaubera. "Did you really think I'd announce my plot to the world with anything as mundane as handwritten notes? Watch this. The show's about to begin."

The witch made a few quick hand gestures and the observatory's conical roof opened up above them, revealing a cloudless sky. Then, pumping her arms in the air, she launched a series of intensely bright sparks upward through the hole in the ceiling. It seemed to go on for minutes. Liam and Ella shut their eyes tight to keep out the blinding light. When the crackling sound stopped, they opened their eyes again and looked upward. There was a message, written in fire across the sky: CINDERELLA AND PRINCE CHARMING ARE MINE.

Thanks to the central location of the Orphaned Wastes, the enormous fiery letters could be seen from nearly every part of the five kingdoms that surrounded it. Throughout Sturmhagen, Sylvaria, Avondell, Harmonia, and Erinthia, people were scrambling in a panic. No one knew who had sent the message, but they knew it was obviously a magic-user of incredible power—and they had no reason to doubt what she said. And just as Zaubera had hoped, heroes everywhere snapped into action. Knights donned their armor; rangers filled their quivers and tossed their bows over their shoulders. Soldier readied their lances, warriors sharpened their swords, swashbucklers buckled their swashes. In a matter of time, they would all converge on Mount Batwing.

"Her plan's going to work," Liam said in a resigned tone.

"Why do you say that?" Ella asked, frustrated.

"Because she's right," Liam said. "There are loads of people out there who consider themselves heroes, and they're going to come. I would."

"Well, snap out of your funk, hero," Ella said. "Because you and I need to get out of here and stop her before anybody else shows up."

"You're right," Liam said. "We should have several hours at least. Maybe even until morning. We need to get out of these vines before then."

"Ooh-hoo-hoo!" Zaubera howled gleefully. She was standing over by the observatory's big westward-facing window. "First guests have arrived! And it's an entire army. I have to say, that was even faster than I expected."

"Impossible," Liam muttered. He and Ella glanced out

the west window. Men on horses—hundreds of them—were rising up over a distant hill, riding fast toward the fortress. They couldn't be more than twenty minutes away.

"But how?" Liam asked.

"I'm sorry, Liam," Ella said. "I sort of sent your sister for help. That would be Erinthia's army."

"Is Lila with them?" Liam gasped.

Ella tried to shrug, but the vines had suddenly tightened to a point where they didn't even allow that much movement. Zaubera was dashing about in a wild fury, taking quick peeks through all of the observatory's other windows.

She scrambled to the east-facing window and, without really looking, called out, "Reese, we've got an early curtain! Ready the props!" The tree she was speaking to, of course, did nothing.

Zaubera then ran to the northern window and yelled, "Bards, take your places!" Liam and Ella heard the bards whimpering outside as the purple vines dragged the songwriters to perches along the fortress walls.

The witch zipped to the southward window and grumbled. "Where are those bandits? No-shows, eh? Oh well, I was just going to kill them when I was done anyway."

She turned back to the center of the room. "And now for the stars," Zaubera said.

The witch twirled her hands. Liam and Ella struggled fruitlessly against their bindings as the animated vines slithered around them both, peeling them from the black stone pillars and lifting them upward toward the opening in the ceiling. Zaubera checked on the approaching army again and saw that the soldiers were being led by a golden coach.

"Excellent," the witch purred. "We've got royalty in the house."

Lila! Liam thought. "You don't need to do this," he begged. "Kill me if you must, but leave the people out there alone."

"So chivalrous," Zaubera mocked. "Can't bear the thought of others being harmed, can you? That's why it will be so much fun to make you watch their deaths."

"No," Liam wheezed, as the vines squeezed the breath out of him.

That was when he heard the familiar sound of Gustav's growl. The bald and burly prince bounded up from the stairwell and rushed toward Zaubera with his sword drawn. The witch quickly worked up another ball of blue energy and hurled it at him.

"Gustav, this was all a trap!" Liam yelled. "She's going to kill that army out there! My sister's with them! Duck!" Gustav ducked. The glowing blue orb sailed over the prince's head and blasted a hole right through the northern wall of the tower. Orange sunlight poured into the observatory as bricks, debris, and hundreds of rejected doom-plan diagrams rained down onto the lawn below.

As dust and smoke filled the air, Frederic appeared at the top of the steps.

"Frederic!" Ella called. Frederic had imagined this moment—him running to Ella with open arms, calling her name—but being as winded as he was, doubled over with his hands on his knees, all he could do was nod in her general direction.

Gustav set upon the witch, repeatedly slashing at her with his sword. Zaubera dodged the blows but seemed to be struggling.

"Not so good fighting in close quarters, eh, old lady?" Gustav taunted as he kept on swinging.

"Ella, I can't believe you're here," Frederic called up as he attempted to cut the magical bindings that held her and Liam suspended halfway through the hole in the roof.

"My sword's doing nothing to these vines," he said.

"She controls them with her mind," Ella said.

"Frederic, we need to break her concentration," Liam said.

"She's in a wrestling match with Gustav—*that's* not breaking her concentration?"

"She's incredibly powerful," Liam stressed. "We need to *really* break her concentration. And fast." He looked westward. The army was getting closer. Ten minutes, tops.

"Gustav will do it," Frederic said. "Look, the witch is starting to flag. You know she'll tire out before Gustav. Nothing stops Gustav."

Frederic was right. Zaubera was slowing down. Gustav finally managed to land a blow against her. His sword sliced through the witch's gown of rags and into her left arm, drawing blood.

Liam tried the vines again, but they were still tight.

"Man, she's tough," he groused.

Gustav landed another slicing blow across Zaubera's shoulder. The witch stumbled backward and braced herself against the eastern windowsill.

"You're done, old lady!" Gustav roared as he advanced on her. But before he could strike a third time, he spied something outside that stopped him cold. "You're kidding me," he said. "My brothers?"

Zaubera grabbed Gustav with her uninjured right

hand, lifted him over her head, and threw him clear across the room. The brawny prince's body smashed into a marble column. Gustav slid to the floor with a thud.

"I miss my armor," he groaned.

Zaubera turned to look out the window behind her. Gustav's brothers were weaving their way around the base of Mount Batwing. They'd be at the fortress in six or seven minutes. "Well, well," the witch said as she wiped a trickle of blood from the corner of her mouth. "A whole gaggle of *princes*. That's priceless."

Frederic hacked wildly at the vines, but to no avail. "I'm so sorry," he panted. "There's nothing I can do."

Zaubera licked her colorless lips as she cracked her knuckles and formed a huge ball of sparking blue energy between her hands. It was triple the size of any of the magic bolts they'd yet seen her throw.

Suddenly a strangely melodious sound rose from the top of the stairwell, drawing everyone's attention.

"Wild card!" Duncan sang as he pranced into the center of the room. Zaubera's ball of energy fizzled out as she stared, agape, at the newcomer. "Check it out, witch! Meat!" Duncan exclaimed as he opened a damp burlap sack, whipped out a muskrat steak, and chucked it at Zaubera. The slab of stinky meat slapped into her forehead—*thwap!*—and slid to the floor, leaving a trail of viscous grease and greenish chunks of fat along the witch's puzzled face. It was an attack that was so unexpected, so . . . stupid, that it left Zaubera completely flummoxed.

"Ack!" she barked, as she tried to wipe the gooey muskrat fat from her eyes. In a panic, the witch shot fireballs and lightning bolts blindly around the room. One shattered a pair of magic mirrors on the wall. Another sizzled her black cat (What? You thought she didn't have one?). A third almost hit Gustav, but instead sent a series of cracks coursing through the pillar he was hiding behind.

The fourth blast smashed directly into Duncan. It lifted him off his feet and sent him careening backward. Daring Duncan, Prince of Sylvaria, sailed through the gaping hole in the tower's back wall, out into thin air, and plummeted out of sight.

Everybody stared in horror at the empty space where Duncan had just been—including Zaubera, who, with grease in her eyes, hadn't actually seen what happened to him. It was during that moment, when the only sound was that of brick and tile dropping to the floor, that Liam made a crucial discovery. He felt the ivy around his chest give.

"The vines!" he whispered. "They're loose! Duncan did it! He finally broke her focus!"

Frederic swung with all his might and chopped through Ella's vines at last. She tumbled to the floor and Frederic helped her untangle herself. Ella touched her palm to Frederic's cheek and whispered, "Thank you," before grabbing his sword and rushing to cut down Liam.

By that point, Zaubera had managed to gather herself. She noticed Frederic and Ella freeing Liam and raised her arm in their direction.

"Hey, Lady Lipless! Over here!" Gustav shouted.

Zaubera zinged a quick blue bolt at him. It hit him in the chest and slammed him into a cracked and chipping pillar. As Gustav hit the floor, the top of the pillar dislodged from the crumbling ceiling, and the enormous stone column began to topple—with dazed and wearied Gustav directly below it.

Frederic saw the huge hunk of gothic architecture about to crush his friend. With all the speed he could muster, he sprinted across the room. Only a few feet away, and with Gustav disappearing under the shadow of the falling pillar, Frederic dove. He slammed his outstretched palms into Gustav's side and shoved his friend to safety, just as the crumbling column crashed down.

Gustav rolled over and hoisted himself up onto his hands and knees. "Thank you," he panted. He grabbed

Frederic's hand and gave it a squeeze of gratitude. The hand felt lifeless and cold inside his. That was when he realized that Ella was screaming Frederic's name. His head still in a daze, Gustav looked over to his friend. Frederic's hand, which Gustav still held tightly, jutted awkwardly out from among the strewn chunks of fallen marble; his body was crushed beneath the pillar.

"No," Gustav whispered.

Ella joined Gustav, and the two hurriedly tossed aside heavy chunks of stone, clearing enough space to let Gustav peer under the fallen column. In the cramped darkness below the debris, he could see Frederic's gentle face. Frederic's eyes were closed. Gustav finally knew what real fear felt like.

"I'll get you out," Gustav said softly. He planted his shoulder against the pillar and started pushing.

On the other side of the disintegrating observatory chamber, Liam steeled himself for battle. He had no weapon, and the witch was obscenely powerful. His only hope was to take her out the same way she'd taken out Duncan—through the hole in the wall. By this time, the crumbling bricks had widened the opening into a gap that stretched several yards across. He just had to get the witch over to it. With that goal in mind, he tried an old Gustav move: the running tackle.

Liam lowered his head, released a wild scream, and charged directly at Zaubera. He pounded, shoulder-first, into Zaubera's gut, and the two hit the floor together in a flailing of limbs and flapping of rags. They rolled to within a few feet of the broken wall before coming to a stop. But the witch got to her feet first. She stood over Liam and laughed.

"You fools!" she cackled. "Why do you keep trying? Don't you see you can never—"

She didn't get to finish. Ella ran up and socked her in the jaw with a surprisingly powerful uppercut. The witch staggered backward to the edge of the crumbling hole in the wall. She waved her arms wildly, trying to right herself. One heel inched over the edge, then the other.

Then she regained her balance. And smiled with satisfaction.

"Aw, come *on*," Liam muttered.

"You people are not listening to me," Zaubera said, as she held out her arms once again to conjure up her diabolical bolts of magical energy. "Zaubera will not be ignored."

Suddenly a loud flapping sound filled the air, and the sky that could be seen through the ruined wall behind her was blotted out by the dragon rising up outside the tower. The enormous red creature beat its powerful leathery wings as it hovered directly outside the hole. Sitting astride the dragon's neck was Duncan.

"Hey, guys," he called. "Look what the dwarfs just showed me how to do! *Kwanchuk!*"

The dragon belched a huge plume of fire that Zaubera barely managed to duck. Ella and Liam dove to avoid the flames themselves. The witch shrieked, her gown of rags ablaze. Duncan shrieked, too. "Oh, no! That's the wrong one!" he shouted. "Um, *chik-chunk?*"

The dragon sailed forward, plunging its enormous head into the observatory through the hole in the tower wall. The beast opened its mouth and curled its anaconda-like tongue around Zaubera. Howling, the witch clawed at the giant tongue, but to no avail.

"*Kolchak?*" Duncan guessed.

"Heroes," Zaubera hissed as the dragon pulled her into its mouth and swallowed her whole. One small fiery hiccup later, the witch was gone.

"Well, that was far more gruesome than I'd hoped," Duncan said with a grimace. "But we beat the witch. Hooray for that, I suppose." He flashed an uncomfortable smile at Liam and Ella.

With every beat of the dragon's wings, more rafters tumbled down, and roofing tiles flew loose.

"Duncan, go!" Liam shouted over the din. "We'll meet you downstairs! The whole room's going to cave in!"

Duncan nodded. He and the dragon veered off and headed back down to the ground.

Liam and Ella dodged raining rubble as they ran over to Gustav. The big prince had strained every muscle in his body to roll the big stone pillar off of Frederic. He was kneeling over his friend's broken body when Liam and Ella approached. Liam went cold at the sight of his gravely injured friend.

"Let me help you carry him," Liam said. "We've got to get out of here fast."

Gustav waved him away. "I've got him," he said, without looking up. "Go." He picked Frederic up as carefully as possible and limped down twenty flights of stairs behind Liam and Ella. From several stories below, they could hear the remaining walls of the observatory crash down.

As they emerged from the fortress, Duncan and Snow ran to greet them.

"The dragon caught me!" Duncan called out excitedly. "I thought I was a goner, but then—ha!—suddenly I was on a big lizard. And then I finally convinced Frank to tell me . . . dragon . . . words . . ."

Duncan's voiced trailed off. Gustav laid Frederic's motionless body on the grass. "Oh, dear," he said.

"Is he alive?" Ella asked.

Gustav put his head to Frederic's chest. "He's breathing, but only barely. It doesn't look good."

Ella buried her face in her hands and wept. Duncan's legs went wobbly. He leaned against Snow White for support as he wiped the sloppy tears from his cheeks.

Liam knelt down beside Frederic. "He's too far gone," he said somberly. "We can't save him."

With sudden determination, Gustav scooped Frederic back up into his arms. "But I know someone who can," he said. "We need to travel fast. Duncan, go get your dragon."

29

PRINCE CHARMING DOES EXACTLY WHAT HE SAID HE'D NEVER DO

In a lush but secluded valley far to the south of Sturmhagen, Rapunzel returned to her rough-hewn wooden cottage after a long and tiring day of healing the sick and injured. She regretted the need to keep her location secret, but knew that if news of her special talents became common knowledge, every farmhand with chapped lips or gnome with a paper cut would show up on her doorstep, eager for a quick fix. She preferred to save her abilities to aid those truly in need. Rapunzel had a network of sprites and fairies that scoured the countryside, scouting out the sick and wounded for her. If there were a coach crash, wolf attack, or outbreak of slug pox, she'd hear about it and show up to fix things.

Earlier that day, she'd gone to a nearby village, where a batch of tainted gruel had given everyone a nasty stomach bug. After that she stopped in a forest vale to tend to a family of pixies that had been accidentally inhaled by a bear. Considering it a good day's work, she was now eager to head inside for a quiet evening with a book and a bowl of turnip soup. But alas, it was not to be. She knew she was in for some overtime when a tremendous winged dragon set down in her yard. She wiped her hands on the apron of her white dress and stepped outside to light the pair of lanterns that flanked her front door.

Two riders slid down off the neck of the dragon. The first landed flat on his face, but stood back up almost immediately. The second, a big bald man who walked with a limp, was carrying a large bundle in his arms.

The men wore the black trappings of thieves and assassins. As they approached, Rapunzel realized that the bundle the bald man carried was actually a third person. The injured man had probably been hurt in the process of a robbery or while the trio was escaping from a prison somewhere. She was distressed; she didn't like aiding criminals.

The bald man walked right up to her and laid his

companion down at her feet. The smaller man stood back, out of the way. Rapunzel glanced down at the man on the ground and gasped. He looked *that* bad.

"Can you fix him?" the big man asked. Rapunzel knew that voice.

"Gustav?" She was stunned. Between the black clothing, the bald scalp, and the fact that she'd never expected to see him again, she hadn't recognized the man who, just a few months earlier, the whole world expected her to marry.

"You cut your hair," Gustav said. Rapunzel's shimmery blond hair came down to her mid-thigh, but it was nowhere near the length it had been.

"So did you," Rapunzel responded. She spoke with a twinkly, almost musical voice, reminiscent of wind chimes.

"My friend—can you fix him?" Gustav repeated. Rapunzel's eyes widened at the sound of the word "friend." She'd never heard Gustav use that word to refer to anyone.

"What happened to him?" she asked. She kept her eyes locked on Gustav's. Their usual coldness seemed to fade away as he thought about the injured man.

"He saved my life," Gustav said. "Twice, really. Maybe more. I don't even know. Look, Frederic is a big goober, and he makes me feel like I'm going to sprain my eyeballs from rolling them so much, but he's a good guy. He doesn't deserve to die because of me."

Rapunzel was amazed. Gustav was expressing some honest feelings. This might have been a bigger miracle than when she cured his blindness. "It's okay, Gustav," she said with a soothing, angelic lilt. "You can let it out. Don't be afraid to cry."

Gustav scowled. "I'm not going to *cry*," he snapped. "*You* cry. You're the one with the magic tears."

He reached out and gave Rapunzel's hair a quick, hard yank.

"Ow!" she yipped, pulling back from him. "That hurt."

"I'm sorry," Gustav sighed. "But would you make with the tears already? Before he dies."

Rapunzel dropped to her knees beside Frederic. "To risk your life for a man as brutish and awful as Gustav, you must be a saint," she whispered. "Your sacrifice may be the most noble I've seen."

And tears fell from her eyes.

As the salty droplets hit Frederic's body, he seemed to vibrate, and a low hum could be heard. Then his eyes popped open.

"Huzzah!" Duncan cheered.

Frederic sat up. "Gustav? Where are we? What happened?"

Gustav closed his eyes and took a deep breath. "Thank you," he whispered to Rapunzel. It was the first "thank you" she'd ever gotten from him.

"Duncan!" Frederic shouted. "Duncan, you're alive!"

"I was never dead!" he responded gleefully.

Duncan hoisted Frederic to his feet. "How do you feel?" he asked with a big, eager smile.

"Um, fine, I guess," Frederic said, testing his legs and arms. "Great, actually. This is the best I've felt since I left Harmonia."

"Oh, thank you, Miss Rapunzel!" Duncan sang out loudly, surprising Rapunzel with a grateful embrace that involved his arms *and* legs. "Thank you, thank you, thank you!" He let go of her and hugged Frederic.

"Rapunzel?" Frederic was very confused. "You're Rapunzel?"

"Yes," she replied.

"Did you just, um, do some, you know . . . magic?" Frederic pointed to his eyes. "Did you make me better?"

She nodded and smiled at him. There was something warm and instantly likable about Frederic that made her feel very, very good about having helped save his life.

Frederic quietly took Rapunzel's hand in both of his and kissed it gently. He didn't know if it was part of her magic, or just the way he was feeling about her at that moment, but he would have sworn she was glowing. "You're amazing. You know, with what you do," he said. "Helping people the way you helped me—it's very admirable. If you ever need any assistance . . . if there's anything I could ever do . . ."

Rapunzel blushed. "I tend to do all right by myself," she said. "But if I ever need a hand, I'll know who to ask. If you see a sprite at your door someday, don't shoo her away. I may have sent her."

"Sprites, right," Frederic said. "They're the tiny bluish ones? With the antenna thingies?"

"They prefer to call them 'feelers,' but yes," Rapunzel said with a grin.

"I'll get an itty-bitty guest room set up. Just in case." Frederic realized he was still holding Rapunzel's hand. "Oh, my fiancée is going to be so excited to hear that I met you. Which reminds me: Where *is* Ella? And Liam? What about the witch?"

Duncan put his arm around Frederic. "Come," he said. "I'll fill you in."

"One second." Frederic turned to Gustav. "Thank *you*, Gustav. I know what it meant for you to bring me *here*, of all places."

"It didn't mean anything special," Gustav said. "We're supposed to be a team, right? I just did my part."

"Well, thanks all the same," Frederic said as Duncan led him away.

Frederic gave a startled little jump when he spotted the dragon, huffing small poofs of smoke from its nostrils as it napped on the grass.

"The dwarfs made the dragon all nice, right?" he asked.

"Yep, don't worry. I got to ride her!" Duncan beamed. "So did you, actually. Although you were almost dead, so you probably don't remember. And don't worry about my driving—I promised Frank I'd just stick to left, right, up, and down."

"You're welcome, by the way," Rapunzel said to Gustav.

"Huh? Oh. Yeah, whatever," Gustav mumbled. "I've got to go."

"Don't you want me to fix you, too? You're limping."

"It's fine. I don't need your help," Gustav said. It came out more bitterly than he'd intended.

"I'll never understand you, Gustav," she said.

"What's to understand?"

"Frederic's obviously a warm and kind human being. I could sense it in him immediately. And you and he care about each other."

"Bah."

"You still feel the need to be a gruff, emotionless, manly hero, as if that's what everyone expects you to be. There are obviously other parts of you that you don't feel comfortable admitting to. But they're the *good* parts."

"I'm *all* good parts, okay?" Gustav grumbled. "I don't need you to tell me about myself."

Rapunzel wanted to tell him that there was nothing wrong with letting people know you cared about them and that he didn't need to push friends away if he felt them getting too close, but she dropped the topic. She had no desire to provoke Gustav into one of his childish arguments. But she was right: There were parts of Gustav that he didn't want to admit to, especially the part that still sort of, kind of, liked Rapunzel.

Gustav and Rapunzel stood in silence for a few moments.

"So, why'd you cut the hair?" he finally asked.

"The only reason I ever kept it as long as I did was because Zaubera ordered me to," Rapunzel said. "It was a rather inconvenient length once I was no longer confined to a single room."

Gustav sniffed. "My haircut wasn't exactly by choice. That's my barber, back there." He pointed over his

411

shoulder to the dragon. Duncan had woken the creature, and he and Frederic were already mounted upon its neck.

"I need to go," Gustav said brusquely.

"Gustav, before you leave—I have one question," Rapunzel called. "How did you find me?"

"I've known you were here for months. I followed you when you first left, just to make sure you were safe. Then I went home."

He turned abruptly and joined his friends on the dragon. Rapunzel shook her head as she watched them soar skyward. "Like I said, I will never understand you."

30

PRINCE CHARMING ALMOST SAVES THE DAY

Do you think he'll be okay?" Ella asked as she, Liam, and Snow White stood on the meadow outside Zaubera's fortress and watched Gustav and Duncan fly off on the dragon with the injured Frederic.

"We can only hope," Liam said, raising a hand to shield his eyes from the setting sun. "I can't believe I'm saying this, but I think Gustav knows best right now."

All around them the lush green grass dried up suddenly, turning yellow and brittle. The wind blew up clouds of dirt at their feet. Ella turned to Liam, concerned.

"The witch is dead," he surmised.

"Excuse me! Sir? Misses?" The voice came from high above them. Liam and Ella looked up to see Lyrical Leif tangled in a web of purple vines. "Might you be able to assist us in finding our way to solid ground?"

"The bards!" Liam said. Leif and the three other songwriters were all strung along the upper edges of the fortress wall. "Just a moment, gentlemen!"

"Oh, look! There's Wallace Fitzwallace," Snow said, and offered the dangling bard a friendly wave. "Sing us a song, Fitzy!"

Liam ran to the dwarfs, who were waiting nearby.

"Flik, Frak, Frank!" Liam called. "Could you bring your wagon over here and lend a hand?"

"You don't think those are our real names, do you?" Frank grumbled. "That's just what Duncan calls us."

"Sorry, didn't realize. What are your real names?"

"Eh, doesn't matter," Frank said. "We're coming with the wagon."

With the wagon in place under Lyrical Leif, Liam and Ella climbed up on top of it.

"If I give you a boost, I think you'll be able to reach him," Liam said.

But Ella was staring off at the approaching army, particularly the golden coach at its lead, which was just now rolling into the field before Zaubera's fortress. "Doesn't Erinthia's flag have a gold star in the middle?" Ella asked.

"Yes, why?" Liam asked.

"Then whose banner is flying on that coach?"

Liam turned to look. His mouth went dry at the sight of the Avondellian flag. "Briar Rose," he said.

Inside the gilded carriage, Briar Rose, Lila, and Ruffian the Blue watched the huge tower crumble down into the black stone fortress before them. The three dropped their jaws in unison at the sight of the dragon soaring off into the violet sky.

"What in the world is going on over there?" Briar finally asked.

"I hope we're not too late," Lila gasped.

"Shut up," Briar snapped. "Did my fiancé just get squashed or eaten? Did he? Tell me something, bounty hunter."

With a deep sigh, the sullen bounty hunter lifted a spyglass to his right eye and peered ahead. "Hmmm. Hmm. Ehhh . . ."

"What is that supposed to mean?" Briar barked. "Tell us something!"

"Yeah, come on, Ruffian—use your words," Lila added.

"It's too bumpy," Ruffian whined.

Briar let out an annoyed grunt, then leaned out the

window and shouted to her army's commander. "Halt! Everybody halt right here!"

The coach jerked to a stop, and all five hundred cavalry horses stopped with it.

"We await your order, Your Highness," the army commander shouted.

Briar ducked back into the carriage. "Well?"

"Your prince is still alive," Ruffian droned. He turned away from the spyglass to cast an annoyed glare at the princesses.

"Let me see," Briar said. "Out of the way, girl." She shoved Lila backward, knocking her off the bench onto the floor of the coach. Briar grabbed the spyglass from the bounty hunter and used it to survey the scene ahead of them.

Thank you, Lila thought as she lay behind Briar and Ruffian. *Finally a chance to get rid of these cuffs.* She pulled out the hairpin that Ella had given her. It released her wayward ringlet, but more importantly, it gave her a lock-picking tool. While Briar and Ruffian argued ("Where is he? You said you saw him." "I did. He had his arm around a girl in strange blue shorts." "Girl? What girl? Who is she?" "How would I know who she is?"), Lila stuck the pin into the lock on her shackles, twisted it, and popped the cuffs open.

With Ruffian and Briar still going at it ("If you would just give me my spyglass back, I could take another look." "You think I can't use a stupid telescope?"), Lila took big tufts of the Avondellian princess's curly hair and tied them in knots through one of the handcuffs. As Ruffian reached to grab the spyglass back, Lila stood up and snapped the other cuff over the bounty hunter's wrist.

"Heyyyy," Ruffian said.

"What the—," Briar began to shout, but Lila quickly leapt past her captors. Ruffian and Briar both attempted to grab the girl, but thanks to the shackles, the two got tangled into a human knot. As Ruffian tumbled over Briar, he pulled the princess's ample hair across her face like a mask. As Briar tried to scream, her mouth was stuffed full of her own fluffy auburn curls.

"Bye, guys!" Lila said as she shimmied through the open window of the carriage and sprinted away.

Ruffian tried to get up to chase her, but as soon as he moved, he yanked Briar Rose down by the hair. Briar shrieked, then growled.

"I'm cuffed to your hair," Ruffian said in disbelief. For the first time in years, Ruffian the Blue's mouth curved into something resembling a smile.

He took another step toward the door but stopped

when Briar let out another muffled scream. She grabbed him by the hood and pulled him back to her.

"Zhah hurff!" Briar gurgled through a mouthful of hair. Translation: *That hurts!*

Ruffian tried to untie the knotted curls that were looped through the manacle. "It's too difficult. Your hair is so thick and full-bodied," he said. He pulled out a knife.

"Goo. Mah. Cuh. My. Hai-uh." (*Do. Not. Cut. My. Hair.*)

Ruffian tossed his hands up. "What do you want from me?" he moaned. He turned to the window and said in a soft, slow monotone, "Guard. A little assist in here." It was Ruffian's way of calling for help.

"Goo ooh ee-meh mo how ooh yeh-ooh?" (*Do you even know how to yell?*)

"Guard," Ruffian said again, slightly louder, but still in a tone that would be fully acceptable to most librarians.

Outside the coach, a soldier watched Lila running away. "Commander, should we be stopping her?" he asked.

"Have you seen the princess when she's angry?" the commander said. "We're not doing a thing unless she tells us to."

"They've stopped," Ella said, referring to the Avondellian army.

"I'm not sure what's going on down there," Liam said. "But now's our chance to free the bards." He bent down and cupped his hands for Ella to step into.

"Wait, look!" Ella shouted. She and Liam ran to the edge of the wagon top to see the girl who was speeding across the meadow toward them.

"Lila!" they shouted in unison.

Lila reached the wagon, scrambled up onto its roof, and threw her arms around Liam.

"I can't believe you're here," Liam said.

"Likewise," Lila said. She broke off the hug and turned to Ella. "And it is so awesome that you made it, too! But, come on. We've probably got about three seconds to get out of here." She grabbed both Liam and Ella by the hand and tried to lead them down off the wagon top.

"Okay," Liam said. "We just need to get the bards down first."

"Thank you," Lyrical Leif called down.

"You don't understand," Lila said. "The instant Briar Rose gets free, that entire army is going to come charging after you."

"Gets free?" Ella asked. "What did you do to her?"

"I'll tell you later. Come on!" Lila hopped down.

"But the bards!" Liam protested.

"I'm sure these strapping young men here can handle the bards," Lila said. She gestured to Gustav's brothers, who had just marched up to them.

"The princes of Sturmhagen are here," Henrik

Fig. 41 The Princes of
STURMHAGEN

announced. "Somebody point to the people who need saving."

Liam looked to Briar's gold carriage. It was rocking and bouncing as if a brawl was going on inside it. Some of the surrounding soldiers were approaching the coach suspiciously. "Okay, let's go," Liam said. "These men will help you out!" he yelled up to the bards as he jumped to the ground. Ella followed.

"Hello, Princess Snow, sorry for the lack of a formal introduction," Liam said. "But can you and the dwarfs get us out of here?"

"Of course," Snow replied. "Hop in."

Frank huffed but drove everybody away speedily nonetheless.

Henrik looked up. "Ah! Master Leif! Your heroes have arrived."

31

PRINCE CHARMING
GETS JUST WHAT HE
THINKS HE WANTED

Duncan, Gustav, and Frederic flew on dragonback to
Castle Sturmhagen, where they'd arranged to meet
Liam and Ella (Snow and the dwarfs gave Lila a ride
back home after the young princess explained that she
needed to pretend she'd been in her room this whole time).
After a heartfelt reunion (during which Gustav was so
overwhelmed by emotion that he actually gave Frederic
a pat on the back), the group met with King Olaf and
Queen Berthilda of Sturmhagen, who were clad head to
toe in thick furs. The princes reported everything to them:
the foiling of the Bandit King's army, the tricking of the
giant, the taming of the dragon, the witch's demise. The

generally hard-to-impress royal couple listened intently and began to regard their youngest son with something approaching admiration. (They seemed perturbed only once, when Frederic said to them, "Oh, by the way, you're going to have to turn over some of your land to the trolls.")

Pennyfeather the Mellifluous was on hand to hear the princes' tale. He tipped his floppy hat to Ella when he saw her and excitedly jotted down the details for what he was sure would become his greatest and most popular story-song yet.

"And now, Father, we're heading back out there to make sure those bards get home safely," Gustav said when they were done.

"You'll do no such thing," King Olaf decreed. "You people are a mess. Gustav, your scalp has been seared and you're favoring your left leg. Prince Liam is limping as well. The young woman looks like she's been run through a wheat thresher. And there's obviously *something* wrong with that small fellow." He pointed at Duncan.

"You men—and you as well, miss"—Queen Berthilda gestured to Ella—"need to relax and recuperate. You've done Sturmhagen and the world a great favor; let us take care of you in return."

"But the bards—," Gustav started.

"Your brothers, I'm sure, are taking care of them," Olaf insisted.

"But we've done *everything* so far," Gustav said. "*Us.* We should be the ones to—"

King Olaf raised his hand to hush his youngest son. "Gustav," he said, "I'm proud of you. You can relax now."

For the first time in his life, Gustav blushed.

After that, the red carpet (well, really it was a fur carpet—everything was made of fur in Sturmhagen) was rolled out for the former Princes Charming and their companions. Their injuries were tended to, their thirst and hunger sated, their unkemptness re-kempted. Everyone was supplied with a much-appreciated change of clothing. Frederic even refrained from complaining about the tacky badger-pelt trim on the jacket they gave him.

It took little more than a week for Pennyfeather's new song, "Cinderella and the League of Princes," to become a global sensation. People went gaga over the story of four princes who were recruited by their leader, Cinderella, to save the world from an all-powerful witch. Pennyfeather was a typical bard; he was bound to get some stuff wrong. But hey, he got all four of the princes' names right. He also failed to even mention Zaubera's name, ensuring once and for all that the witch would never achieve the fame she'd so desperately sought.

Soon afterward, a grand parade was held outside Castle Sturmhagen. Tremendous flower arrangements adorned every corner along the parade route, and a marching band raised their horns in a musical victory salute. Nearly the entire population of Sturmhagen—as well as hundreds of cheering admirers from neighboring kingdoms—turned out for the celebration. They all saw the banners that read HOORAY FOR CINDERELLA AND HER LEAGUE OF PRINCES!

"It figures. We're still second fiddle to the girl," Gustav said. "No offense."

"None taken," said Ella. "Sorry about this, guys. I had no idea. I don't even want to be famous."

"It's fine," Liam said. "These people are here today to celebrate all of us."

"And they finally know our names," Frederic said. "Gustav, I do believe you're now officially the biggest hero in your family."

That got a smile out of the big man.

The guests of honor rode in the back of an ornate, open-top coach pulled by a team of headdress-wearing show horses. Ella and the princes waved to their adoring public as they rolled by. Frederic was pleasantly surprised to see Reginald at the front of the crowd.

"Reginald, I'm so touched you came," Frederic called to him. The valet left the crowd and jogged up to the side of the coach.

"Wouldn't miss it for the world," Reginald replied, beaming proudly.

"I don't suppose Father is here, too," Frederic asked, with a tinge of hopefulness.

"No," Reginald said, bobbing along next to the moving coach. "He wanted me to tell you he forgives you and can't wait to see you home again. But don't trust him completely. He also asked me to deliver this note to the Flimsham brothers; he wants to borrow their tiger again."

"Thanks for the heads-up," Frederic said, as the parade moved on and Reginald dropped back into the crowd.

They rounded a busy corner to see even more fawning fans and giddy celebrants. Huge tapestries bearing the likeness of the princes were rolled down from the upper windows of the castle as they passed.

"Well, going home after this may not be as much fun as I'd hoped," Frederic said.

"At least you have a home to go to," Liam said. "Based on what Lila said, my people are going to force me to marry Briar Rose if I set foot anywhere near Erinthia." He sighed. "What am I going to do?"

"Why don't you come home and stay with me in Harmonia until things calm down in your kingdom?" Frederic said. "I can always use an ally against my father, anyway."

"Thank you, Frederic," Liam replied gratefully. "I think I will."

Ella leaned forward. "You know, Frederic," she said. "Maybe I was hasty in leaving. I think I'll return to the palace with you, too. If you'll have me back."

Considering all they'd been through, he wondered if maybe there was a chance for him and Ella to end up together after all. He would have to work extra hard to stand out next to Liam, he knew, but for the first time in his life, he felt up to the challenge.

"Two of my best friends living with me? I can't think of anything I'd like more," Frederic said. "Oh, but I should tell you both: If a sprite ever comes to the door, don't send her away. She'll be delivering a message for me."

"Hey! Someone in the crowd is carrying a 'Duncan the Daring' sign!" Duncan shouted. "Oh, it's Frank," he added, less enthusiastically. "Do you think he means it in the good way?"

"Hard to say with those guys," Liam said. "But *we*

all believe it, right?"

Gustav rolled his eyes.

The parade ended at a large stone platform, on top of which stood a life-size statue of Cinderella and the four princes standing in heroic poses. The sculpture had been somewhat hastily constructed the previous day. The coach came to a stop, and the heroes disembarked. They climbed the steps of the platform to get a closer look at the artwork.

"Hey, Statue Me is taller than *Me* Me," Duncan said. "I like that."

"Criminy Pete," Gustav cursed. "They couldn't have made me with hair? It's starting to grow back, you know."

"What in the world is this

Fig. 42
Honor STATUE

statue made of?" Liam asked as he poked at his alter ego and heard a hollow thunking sound.

"I believe that would be papier-mâché," Frederic said. "Considering how little time they had to prepare, I suppose this was the best we could get."

"Let's hope it doesn't rain," Liam said.

Ella quietly stepped down from the platform to give the guys their moment in the spotlight. The princes faced the enormous crowd. People were waving, cheering, and calling their names—their *real* names. Not one "Prince Charming" was heard.

At one point or another, each of the four princes had dreamed of a moment like this. But it was more than just the hordes of fans that made the moment so wonderful. Duncan expressed the sentiment perfectly:

"I'm with these guys!" he shouted, his arms raised high in the air.

Some people in the audience started chuckling. The princes assumed they were mocking Duncan.

"Yeah, the Flighty Flutist over here is a friend of mine," Gustav sniffed defensively. "So what?"

More crowd members began to laugh, and several started pointing.

Liam and Frederic looked at each other, confused.

The princes turned around in time to see two black-clad thieves pick up the lightweight statue and heave it into a wagon that was parked right behind the platform—a wagon that was already filled to the brim with oversize flower arrangements, "League of Princes" banners, dozens of trumpets, and four enormous personalized tapestries with the princes' faces on them. At the driver's seat of that wagon was Deeb Rauber.

"That's right, princes," the smirking boy yelled. "I just stole you! In fact, I stole your whole parade. While you losers were celebrating, I was riding behind you, snatching everything!" He guffawed and wiggled his backside at them, as his henchmen jumped onto waiting horses. Then Rauber and his bandits tore off with the goods.

"I knew you should have let me crush him," Gustav grumbled.

Ella dashed back onto the platform to join the men. "What the heck is my cousin doing here?"

"Your *what*?" Frederic gasped.

"I'm telling your mom, Deeb!" she called out, as Rauber's wagon disappeared down the road.

"What are we standing here for?" Liam shouted. "We can't let Rauber get away." He was about to run after the thieves when he heard jeers from the crowd.

"Ha-ha! A little kid just swiped their statue!"

"I thought they *stopped* the Bandit King!"

"These are supposed to be our heroes? What a joke!"

Before long, the entire crowd seemed to be laughing at them. Worst of all, Pennyfeather the Mellifluous was there, and he started feverishly scribbling down ideas for a new song.

"Oh, no," Liam groused when he saw Pennyfeather. "Not *this*! You're not going to write a song about *this* now, are you?"

"Here we go again," Gustav muttered.

"It wasn't a very good statue anyway," Frederic said.

"We should get that giant to make a new one," Duncan suggested, but the others could barely hear him over the roars of laughter.

Just then all sixteen of Gustav's brothers marched up onto the platform. For a brief, reality-twisting moment, Gustav thought they might actually be there to defend him. He was wrong, of course.

"Everybody, quiet," Henrik shouted. "We have something very special for you all."

Lyrical Leif, Tyrese the Tuneful, Wallace Fitzwallace, and Reynaldo, Duke of Rhyme all sashayed onto the now very crowded platform. Leif came to the forefront and addressed the crowd.

"Ladies and gentlemen," the bard said. "A little over a week ago, my fellow songsmiths and I suffered through an incredibly harrowing experience as we were all kidnapped by a devious witch. But our lives were saved, thanks to a group of brave and stalwart heroes. And to show our gratitude, my fellow bards and I teamed up to write the ultimate story-song. We present it to you now. Ladies and gentlemen: 'The Sixteen Hero Princes of Sturmhagen'!"

"Sixteen?" Gustav howled, as the four bards began singing together. "SIXTEEN?"

Gustav seemed as if he were about to tackle all the bards and snap their mandolins with his teeth, but Liam and Frederic held him back.

"Well, now what?" Frederic asked.

"Rauber's long gone, I'm sure," Liam said mournfully.

"And we're laughingstocks again," Gustav grumbled.

"It's a disaster," Liam said. "Where do we go from here?"

"Someplace where people like us?" Duncan suggested with a cautious grin.

Frederic's eyes brightened. "You're right," he said. "I know just where we should go."

PRINCE CHARMING GOES WHERE EVERYBODY KNOWS HIS NAME

Liam, Frederic, Gustav, and Duncan stepped across the threshold of the Stumpy Boarhound and were greeted by a raucous round of applause (cheering that got even louder when Ella entered as well).

"Oh, we were so hopin' you would come back," Ripsnard the bartender said jubilantly.

"I take it you've heard the new song about us?" Liam asked.

"I heard it? Business has been booming because of it," Ripsnard said. He pointed to a hand-painted sign that hung over the bar between a dented shield and a mounted yeti head. It read: THE STUMPY BOARHOUND — BIRTHPLACE OF THE LEAGUE OF PRINCES. "To be truthful, we sorta owe you guys."

"Yeah, I've gotten dozens of new recruits for me crew in the past week," the bearded pirate chimed in. "When gawkers pop in to check out the official League of Princes Founding Table back there in the corner, I flash 'em me gappy smile and say, 'Yep, that tooth got knocked out by Prince Gustav the Mighty.'"

Gustav grinned.

"Well, this is what we wanted, right?" Frederic said as dozens of the Boarhound's regulars swarmed them for autographs. "A hero's welcome?"

"Yeah, but what happens when they find out about what went down at the parade?" Liam asked as he signed the handle of a thief's dagger.

"Ya mean the Bandit King swipin' yer statue right out from under ya?" the pirate asked.

"You know about that already?" Ella asked. "That happened this morning."

"News travels fast," said Ripsnard.

"They know about it and they still like us," Duncan said, high-fiving the half-ogre thug.

"Oh, sure," Ripsnard said. "'Cause we know a bunch of guys as tough as yerselves ain't gonna let an insult like that go unanswered. We're all eager to see what happens next."

The princes exchanged glances.

"So are we," said Liam.

Duncan sat down at the Official League Founding Table, pulled out a sheaf of paper and a quill, and began writing.

Gustav goggled at him in exasperated disbelief. "Where in the world did you get all that—ah, never mind."

"What are you doing, Duncan?" Frederic asked.

"Writing a book," Duncan replied. "These good people have given me an idea. Now that I am officially a hero, I believe it's my responsibility to share my knowledge of heroics with the world—to offer some wisdom and advice to any other young men and women who might find themselves needing to save their kingdoms someday."

"Some sort of handbook for would-be adventurers?" Frederic asked with a raised eyebrow.

Duncan nodded.

"And you think *you're* the one to write it?" Gustav asked.

"Oh, I'd be very happy for any input you fellows are willing to give as well," Duncan replied.

"Duncan, I think all four—or five— of us have a whole lot left to learn when it comes to being a hero," Liam said.

"So it'll be a work in progress," Duncan responded, as he scribbled out the title of his book: PRINCE CHARMING'S

GUIDE TO SAVING YOUR KINGDOM.

"Hey, take it from me, you never know what direction life's going to take you in," Ella said. "I'd be happy to add my two bits. But call it 'The Hero's Guide.'"

"I suppose contributing to a work of literature is much more my speed than storming a witch's fortress anyway," Frederic added.

"I think you're wasting your time," Gustav said.

The bearded pirate stepped up and slapped a handful of gold pieces down on the table in front of Duncan. "I'll be wantin' ten copies as soon as the writin' of 'em's been done."

The princes looked at one another.

"Putting our names on something like that," Liam said, "it'll be a lot to live up to."

Frederic smiled. "So let's live up to it."

◀ ACKNOWLEDGMENTS ▶

Much like the princes, I couldn't have done it alone.

Endless thanks go to Noelle Howey, my secret weapon. I can't say how lucky I am to be married to one of the best writers and editors alive. I get love, support, and expert literary advice all in one place. I can't even count how many plot holes, inconsistencies, and awful jokes my readers were spared thanks to Noelle's keen insight and good taste. We all owe her, really.

I also need to thank my daughter, Bryn, who, in addition to being the inspiration for Lila, also functioned as my test audience and was never afraid to say, "This part could be better, Dad." Thanks also to her brother, Dashiell, for remaining a solid fan despite his unhappiness with the book's lack of ninjas.

Gratitude must be expressed to my agents, the always supportive Jill Grinberg, who urged me to go for it when I first mentioned this whole Prince Charming idea, and the incredible Cheryl Pientka, who worked enough magic in getting this book sold to make me feel like I was in a fairy tale myself.

And a heaping helping of encomiums to Walden Pond's Jordan Brown, who championed this book from the moment he read it and always pushed me to improve it. Working with Jordan has been a crash course in creating middle-grade fiction. And a whole lot of fun, to boot. To have an editor with such boundless enthusiasm and energy—not to mention one who knows his stuff so well—has been an amazing experience.

Last but not least, thanks to everyone who read *Hero's Guide* in its earlier incarnations and provided priceless feedback: Neil Sklar, Ivan Cohen, Christine Howey, Brad Barton, Evan Narcisse, and Katelyn Detweiler. Every note and comment made a difference.